HOT FUDGE

An Onalee O'Conner Mystery-Book Three

By Connie Doherty

Connie Doherty

Hot Fudge

Publisher: The Dancing Turtle Press

Cover Artist: Meredith Krell

All rights reserved. No part of this book may be used or reproduced electronically or in print without written permission, except in the case of brief quotations embodied in reviews. Due to copyright laws, no one may trade, sell or give e-books away.

This is a work of fiction. Names, characters, places and incidents are products of the author's imagination. Locales and public names are sometimes used for atmospheric purposes. Any resemblance to actual events, locales, organizations, or persons living or dead is entirely coincidental. All trademarks, service marks, registered trademarks and registered service marks are the property of their respective owners and are used herein for identification purposes only.

Published in the United States of America.

ISBN 978 0 9975251 -2-0

Hot Fudge

This book is dedicated to everyone everywhere who has ever helped any animal. Thank you!

Hot Fudge

Chapter One

Fat snowflakes dance in the breeze before falling silently to earth. Others cling to the outstretched arms of the evergreens. All the world is a study in white and black, its usual clamor, hushed. Along the shores of Little Traverse Bay, the pearl blue waves quietly meet the shore and recede, meet and recede, as the snow descends into their depths. *Winter is a time of grace and wonder*, I thought as I glided along.

On the other hand, it must be said that not everyone who lives above the forty-fifth parallel in this northwest corner of the Lower Peninsula of Michigan is similarly enthralled with our cold season. To some of its detractors it's known as the "dead season" and it did work out that way for one resident of the north.

Connie Doherty

We'd had a green Christmas so instead of Yule lights reflecting off drifts of snow, our town was cloaked in drab shades of brown and grey. "A green Christmas means a full cemetery," the old folks say.

Even New Years Eve was just foggy and drizzly rather than throwing down its usual howling blizzard. Finally by early January the snow had begun falling and I, Onalee O'Conner, jumped on my cross-country skis.

As I skied near the water's edge of Little Traverse Bay, my standard poodle Dashiell loped along, sometimes beside me, most often ahead. I watched him as he veered off, halted, buried his nose in the snow and snorted, spraying snow in a cloud around his head.

The water in the bay was cold, bitter cold, and ice would probably soon form around its edges. The lake never looks prettier than when its blue waves lap against a snowy shoreline. *It should freeze over in another five or six weeks*, I thought. But for now, Dash still cavorted in the frigid waves when another dog was around.

I skied as far as the main beach of the county park then climbed a small dune, followed a trail through the woods, and meandered back to the bike path. Dash was on a leash as I carried my lightweight cross-country skis and poles. We walked past the parking lot behind the grocery store and on to our house.

Dash was ready to be home and get some breakfast in his gullet. After readying his kibbles and fresh water, I changed from cross-country boots to street boots, jumped in the car, and drove downtown.

My good friend Marti Gonzalez had just moved to Petoskey and we were going to meet for breakfast. By gunning the car and taking two shortcuts, I managed to slide into a chair across from Marti, a mere twenty minutes late. She was just shucking off her coat. As usual our internal lateness-gauges were in sync. At the counter, we ordered muffins, coffees, and ice waters, and then made our way back to the table.

"I can't believe I'm up here for good now and can come loll around this coffee shop shooting the breeze with you anytime I feel like it," Marti said and took a sip of coffee.

"I know. How cool is that?" I pinched off a piece of muffin along its side, carefully saving its streusel top for last. When I'd swallowed it along with some coffee I asked, "So, you're not moving in with Frank?"

"Ha. Are you kidding me? Remember, I'm a good Mexican-American girl. If I did that, my mom would thrust aside her tombstone, leap out of her grave and drive up here. Or would she fly? Anyway, I would never have another moment of peace."

Hmmm. Fearless Gonzalez has an Achilles heal after all. "Okay. So have you two set a date yet?"

She scowled at me over the brim of her mug. "In the last two months, I've closed down my appraisal business, sold my house and moved to a different town. I've barely seen Frank, let alone started to plan our wedding. And now" she paused, "I've got a job!" With that, she got up for a refill of her coffee.

I called after her. "What? You're not going to open up a Petoskey branch of Gonzalez Appraising and Consulting?"

She sat back down. "I switched this time and got the Sumatra." She took a sip. "I like it better than the Lake Street Blend. What are you drinking?"

Hot Fudge

I sighed. "Sumatra. I know the system. Since you're one of us now, I'll fill you in. Their strongest blend is always in the middle. Now, your plan?"

"Good to know. Thanks." Infuriatingly, she took another sip before continuing. "I'm going to take a break from appraising and work for a while at Lupita's. Probably at least until after the wedding. Then, I'll figure out my next move."

"Ohhhh. Lupita's, huh? That might be fun. Do you get free samples? What experience do you have? When—"

"Whoa. Yes, it will be fun and also hard work. I do get free samples and maybe an occasional one for a family member or friend. I actually do have some experience making candy. I worked part-time for a chocolatier when I was in high school. If you were starting to ask me when I got the job, I found out yesterday. If you want to know when I start, the answer is Monday."

"Do you have to get up at four a.m. or some crazy hour like that?"

A horror stricken look crossed Marti's normally agreeable countenance. "No! It's a fudge shop and coffee house, not a bakery."

"Yeah, I guess you're right. So what are your hours? Are you full-time? Do you get benefits?"

"My hours will vary somewhat, especially in the summer when they will be much longer. They're not super busy in the winter, so it'll only be part-time. I actually like the idea of that, for now. My benefits package will continue to be provided by Gonzalez Appraising and Consulting."

"Gotcha. No benefits. Well, except of course the free fudge and that's huge."

"Sure is. How's your Hapkido class going?"

I'd started taking my self-defense class a few weeks ago. "Good. Great exercise and I'm learning a lot."

After another cup of coffee, we left and walked out into a snowy winter morning. "This is supposed to keep up for a couple of days. Want to go cross-country skiing tomorrow?"

The wind whooshed up the street splattering us both with snow. "Are you crazy? It's freezing out here," Marti said, shaking.

"You'll be warm when you ski. It's fun," I wheedled.

Hot Fudge

"I stay warm when I sip hot cocoa and read a book. You go ahead, and if I decide to go I'll call."

She left to continue settling into her small apartment above the tee-shirt shop. Yesterday, she'd declined my offer of help saying, "Thanks, but it's a one-person job, On."

Early Monday morning Dash and I went our usual route along the lakeshore and back through the woods I on my skis, he on four paws. Once again we didn't see any other humans or canines. We had fun and got good exercise, but it was a little disappointing. "Have our friends all gone into hibernation?" I asked Dash. With the typical glint in his eye, he looked at me for a couple of seconds *(Was he pondering my question?)* before whirling away and chasing a squirrel up a tree.

Back and ensconced in the World Headquarters of O'Conner Appraisal, I, president and sole employee, opened up the file on my problem du jour. It was a large tract of vacant land near the Pigeon River State Forest. The property I was appraising consisted of four hundred fifty-one acres of heavily forested land with two small streams crossing it. These large parcels of land don't change hands that often anymore, so there weren't many comparable sales to choose from. Before the snow fell, I had spent hours traipsing over my subject parcel, but sooner or later I was going to have to snowshoe down seasonal roads to find the highly inaccessible comparable sales and inspect them.

I spent most of the day making phone calls to brokers about the comps and consulting aerial photographs and soil maps. Soil maps can tell you a lot about a property including where the swampy areas, if any, are located. By the time I finished, I was beginning to get a pretty good picture of what the properties were like.

On and off during the day, my thoughts turned to Marti. I wondered how her first day of work was going. Appraising can be demanding and we often put in very long hours, but most of it is in a comfy chair in front of our computers. About four o'clock I glanced at my watch. Marti's feet must be killing her about now, I thought. Then again, I'm a big believer in breaks from routine and this would probably be a positive thing for her in the end.

A little before five, I turned my computer off and went into the kitchen where a pot of black bean chili had been bubbling all afternoon. I turned

Hot Fudge

the heat up a bit and checked the small loaves of bread that had been rising for the last hour. They were ready so I turned the oven to 450 degrees. Meanwhile, I washed some greens and other veggies for salads. The oven announced it was at temperature so I popped the loaves in, threw some cold water against the insides of the oven, and set the timer for ten minutes. Just then the doorbell rang and Marti opened the door. On top of the situation as always, Dash ran to greet her. He wove around her as she removed her boots and jacket.

"Hey Dash. It's good to see you sweetie," she said as she petted his head. "On, it smells wonderful in here."

Marti and Dash came out to the kitchen. "It'll be ready in a couple of minutes. Want a glass of wine?"

Without waiting for her answer, I poured us each a glass and set down Dash's dinner. The timer buzzed and I looked in the oven. The bread was golden brown and I pulled it out, then spooned helpings of the chili into bowls for Marti and me. As we ate, I asked about her day.

"It was interesting. Not real busy, and only one person bought fudge. But we did have quite a few coffee customers."

"Do you think you're going to like it?"

"Sure. I mean I wouldn't want to stay there long term, but for a while, it'll be perfect."

"How's your boss?"

"He seems very nice so far."

"Lupita is a 'he'?"

"My boss, the owner is Ed, short for Eduardo. He named the place after his mom, Lupita, who had taught him how to cook as a little boy."

"Oh. Are they from Mexico?"

"No, his mom and dad came from Puerto Rico, but Ed was born here."

"How'd they wind up in Petoskey?" *I always wonder how people find this small corner of the world from far away places.*

"It wasn't that slow at the shop. I don't know his entire life story yet. Write down your questions and I'll see if I can get you the answers," said Sacrastica Gonzalez. She took another spoonful and smiled. "This chili sure hits the spot on a frigid day. It's delicious."

Frigid? It was twenty-five degrees and partly sunny today. Wait until we hit twenty below.

Hot Fudge

Marti helped with the kitchen cleanup, then it was time for Poodle Boy's last walk of the night. "Dash, see if your Auntie Marti wants to come with us."

She smiled. "No, Dash. Tell your mom that it's Auntie's pajama time."

Throughout the next week, I tried to get Ms. G. out cross-country skiing, ice skating, or even just walking, but all to no avail. During this time she voiced many complaints about the snow and cold. Winter was fleeting by. I was afraid that spring would be here before we knew it and Marti would never get to enjoy the snow. I called her again on a Sunday, her day off. We chatted about her wedding plans for awhile before I moved into the solicitation portion of the call. "What are you up to today? Will you be seeing Frank?"

"No, he's in a crunch-time at work right now. I just started a great book so I'll probably curl up here and read."

"It's beautiful out. Why don't you try cross-country skiing?"

"It's cold—"

That did it, I lost all restraint. "Are you a hothouse flower, Ms. Gonzalez?" I demanded.

"No, but—"

"You have to at least be willing to try it."

"I will, but I'm waiting until it's warmer."

"Say, June?"

There was a pause. I've never been sure when they're considered pregnant but this one might have been. She finally spoke, "Oh, all right, but I'm only going so you'll quit nagging me."

For the record, I don't nag . . . at least not as much as some. I drove into town and picked up Marti at one-fifteen. It was twenty degrees out, calm, and a light snow was falling. In short it was perfect for someone's first foray into the magical realm of the north woods on a winter's day. Marti was over-dressed in snow pants and a warm down jacket. She looked bunchy and I suspected the presence of long underwear. I had gone over the importance of not bundling up for this aerobic exercise and how she would stay warm even as the mercury plunged. Alas, my words had been in vain.

I tsk tsked to myself, but adhering to my "live and let live" philosophy of life, revealed nothing of my disapproving thoughts to Miss Stubborn-as-a-Mule Gonzalez. I had borrowed some gear for Marti and that, along with my equipment was stowed in the back of the car. We drove a little ways out of Petoskey to the seasonal town of Bay View. I pulled up in front of a cottage and parked the car.

Marti peered out the passenger window at the boarded up cottages. "Wow, it looks totally deserted."

Marti had visited Northern Michigan many times, but she still had a lot to learn about the area. This was a fun place to start her education, I thought, along with offering unplowed level streets, great for beginner skiers. "Bay View is an association. The homeowners don't own the land under their houses, they lease it from Bay View. Because of that there are rules such as the fact that they can't open up their cottages until the last weekend of April and they have to be out of them by November first each year."

"They look more like beautiful homes than cottages. All of these places can only be used for half the year?"

"Yup. If the owners come up to ski, they have to stay somewhere else."

"Amazing. Look at that one over there, On. I love all the gingerbread on these places."

"I know. Getting to see these cottages up close as we leisurely ski by is half of the enjoyment."

I showed her how to step into her ski bindings and then gave a demonstration of the kick and glide technique of classic skiing. She tried it and toppled over. Uh oh, I thought, but *she* giggled. *Good sign.*

"This isn't as easy as I thought it would be," she said, struggling to stand back up.

"Actually, getting up after you fall is the hardest part of the whole thing." I showed her my limited bag of tricks and with a few more pushes on her poles, she eventually righted herself. Many more falls later, she began to stay on her feet. She wasn't exactly gliding but her shuffle moved her forward. After we'd gone about a half-mile she stopped, ripped off her hat, stuffed it in her pocket and tore open her jacket.

"I'm roasting. How can it be this hot out here in the snow and cold?"

Hot Fudge

Rising above any petty urge to utter an, "I told you so," or even a knowing nod of the head, I said, "Remember, we're burning up a lot of calories."

"I sure didn't need this long underwear," she muttered under her breath.

We skied around the streets for about an hour. Marti kept up a running commentary about the houses we passed. I couldn't always hear them because of the sound of our skis swishing through the snow, but I knew she was expressing her appreciation of the color-combinations, inviting front porches, and clever cottage names. She was steadier but I'd still hear an occasional, "Whoa," and over she'd go again. I was proud of myself. I never laughed once although I did have to turn away and hide a smile when with one unfortunate mishap, she plunged her stocking foot into the cold snow.

By this time, we were near the far end of town from where we'd started, and there was a path I wanted to take. "Think you're ready for the woods?"

She stopped and looked at me, sweat glistening on her forehead. "How hard is it? I'm getting better, but boy these skis are skinny! Can you buy wider ones? Say, about a foot?"

"Maybe not that wide but you can go broader. They're more for back country, though. Anyway, where we're going is pretty flat. We'll save hills for another day."

We turned into a gate and onto a path through the trees behind the cottages. After we'd gone a few hundred feet, we came to one of my favorite spots in Northern Michigan. The snow had been falling in a desultory way, but it now came down heavier, large butterflies filling the air. We were beneath towering hemlock trees in the midst of a cedar swamp, moving in single file along the narrow trail. I heard Ms. Gonzalez gasp.

"On, it's beautiful."

I stopped and turned around. Marti, leaning on her ski poles, gazed at the gnarled old trees, their branches laden with snow. I smiled. "I just love it in here, and I wanted to show it to you."

In a hushed voice she said, "People told me I was nuts to move up here in January and I have to admit, I wasn't wild about the timing, myself. But, this . . . this isn't like winters in other places."

"No, you're right. As my mother used to say, 'Summer is wonderful and lots of fun, but there's no season as lovely as winter.'"

We skied on through the silent forest, not seeing any other skiers, and eventually came back out to the street by the car. As we were removing our skis, Marti said, "Well, I can add yet another athletic pursuit onto my list that I'm not a natural at."

"But, did you like it?"

She grinned, "I loved it. Although, I still think that when I buy my own pair, I'll get the really, really wide ones." She spread her hands about two feet apart.

I took Marti home to nurse her bruises and went on a walk around the neighborhood with Dash. I pondered life as I followed behind my favorite dog. It always seemed to me that the people who were happiest living in Northern Michigan were the ones who enjoyed each of the four seasons. Since Marti was casting her lot with Frank and becoming a permanent resident of the north, I hoped that she too, would become a winter-embracer.

Chapter Two

Over a week had gone by since Marti's first cross-country ski adventure, and she'd been out numerous times since then. After her second time, she'd purchased skis, (regular not wide-body), boots, and poles. On this day, Marti and I sat in the airport in St. Ignace waiting to board a plane that would take us to Mackinac Island. I was appraising a storefront in the downtown.

After the Straits of Mackinac fill with ice, the ferries stop running and visitors can fly over to the island. Alternatively, there is an ice "bridge" which is actually just a path over ice that's deemed safe for crossing. Christmas trees outline the safe passageway, and people snowmobile and cross-country ski over it. I hadn't heard if the ice bridge had formed yet. Besides, we were going to stay overnight and were too laden down with gear to ski across.

Hot Fudge

The plane was ready and we, the only two passengers, climbed aboard. As the little aircraft climbed into the sky, I looked around. It was a clear, cold morning. To our right, the majestic Mackinac Bridge arched between the two shores of the Upper and Lower Peninsulas of Michigan. Mackinac Island and Bois Blanc Island were on our left.

"Is this your first plane trip to the island?" our pilot, Mark asked.

Marti grinned at him. "Yup, in fact, I've never even been to Mackinac Island, before."

He smiled back, "Would you like to fly closer to the bridge so you can get some pictures?"

"That would be great," I said.

He changed course and we flew along the huge cables that swooped up to the top of the towers.

"Did you get enough photos?"

Marti and I nodded. "Yes. Thanks."

We banked and minutes later soared down and onto the airport runway. Only a few businesses of any kind are open in the winter and we'd called and made a reservation to stay at a bed and breakfast. Cars have been banned from the island since 1898 according to our visitors' guide, so the people at the airport called for a dray to pick us up and take us to our lodging. Soon Marti and I were sitting under heavy blankets behind Bonnie our driver, a pleasant lady originally from Dayton, Ohio, and two horses named Champ and Donavon.

"This is so cool," Marti said as we plodded along through snowy woods. We were the only ones on the road until we reached town. There, a couple of people zipped by on snowmobiles. Along the main street, we saw the two restaurants that were open and a grocery store. Everything else was closed up.

"Either Frank or I will have to bring you up here in the summer. It's really something to see. People visit this island from all over the world. Ferry boats are coming and going all day from both Mackinaw City and St. Ignace. There's lots to do and it's so beautiful."

We pulled up in front of a quaint old two-story house, got our luggage and ski equipment out of the dray, paid and tipped Bonnie, and walked in to what would be our home for the night. The owner, Marie was waiting for us and showed us to our room upstairs.

Hot Fudge

***

I needed to meet the building owner for my inspection and left for the half-mile walk back to the downtown. As soon as I reached Chevalier Street, I saw the subject property, a small house converted for retail use. It was painted turquoise with pink shutters. There were lights on inside and when I pushed the door, it opened.

"Hello. Mr. Arnault?"

"In here. The back office."

I walked through the displays of clothes and into an open door behind the counter. A very short, balding, middle-aged man got up from behind his desk and extended his hand, grinning. "I'm Rene Arnault and you must be Onalee O'Conner. Welcome to my store and also to Mackinac Island."

What a gracious fellow. "Thank you." We walked around the interior of the building as I took pictures and notes. Then Mr. Arnault waded through snow as I circled the exterior. All the while we talked.

"Are you familiar with the island?"

"Yes, I was born and raised in Petoskey."

The crinkly lines around his eyes curved up as he smiled. "How wonderful. I, too was born in the north, but in St. Ignace."

"Oh. Your teams always beat ours in high school."

He laughed. "Yes, St Ignace kids are tough. Tell me, have you appraised other properties on the island?"

"A couple."

"Then you know that it's a very special place. There is nothing else like it."

"It is unique." *He's afraid I might not realize how much his building is worth.* "I'll take that into consideration in my appraisal." I jotted down some measurements and walked to the next section of the building. "How was business for you last summer?"

"Excellent. I believe everyone had a good season. In fact, maybe too good."

"Too good?"

"More than ever, there are outsiders trying to buy up our real estate and edge us out." He studied me. "You haven't heard of the Stone group?"

"No. What's happening?"

Hot Fudge

"They've bought up four buildings, including the businesses in some cases. They're also buying up houses and we know they've gotten their hands on four or maybe five, so far." He spread his arms wide. "We don't know why they're doing this. All they'll tell us is that they're investing. This is a small community and we who are part of it, love it the way it is."

"Are they doing anything illegal?"

He shook his head. "No, or we'd stop them in a heart beat."

"Do you think they're hurting property values?"

"It seems to be quite the opposite. At least, so far. Because of the added demand from them, prices have gone up and up, and as I'm sure you know, they were already high to begin with."

"How do they find properties for sale? Is there a broker they're working with?"

"They've sent letters, I believe, to every property owner on the island. I've gotten three since I own this store, another commercial property, and my house. I'll email you a copy. They don't work with a broker, per se, but with a lawyer who has a broker's license."

"What is your concern with them?"

"As I said, all of us who live or work here love the island. It's very different from any other place on earth. We don't want someone coming in and putting in some huge development."

"And you think that could happen?"

"Yes. As you well know, since you've done some appraisals here, this place can be a goldmine."

"Can you form a group to buy some of the properties out from under the Stones?"

"Four of us, who are very concerned, have talked about something along those lines, but we can't compete with their mega-billions. Don't get me wrong, I have a very good life and am comfortable financially, but I can't throw millions of dollars at every property that someone wants to sell. And it's an upward spiral. The more the prices go up, the more islanders there are who feel this is an opportunity they would be fools to pass up. A lot of us are getting close to retirement age and sometimes there are no family members who can or who wish to take over."

"How long has this been going on?"

"I'd say, about three years."

Hot Fudge

"Do the Stones live here?"

"They have a house here and use it occasionally. They're out of New York City, but the wife has a connection to Northern Michigan." He raised his finger. "In fact, come to think of it, I believe she was a Petoskey girl."

I finished my inspection and said goodbye to Mr. Arnault. I took notes about the neighborhood and headed back to the bed and breakfast. As I passed the post-office, I noticed the flag was flying at half-staff. *Hmmm, I didn't know anyone important who died in the last day or so.* By the time I got back, I'd been gone about two hours, and Marti was deep into a discussion with Marie. They seemed to be really hitting it off. The three of us talked for a few minutes and then I remembered the flag. "Hey Marie, I noticed that the flag was at half-staff, what happened, do you know?

"Bob Solbert died." When both Marti and I looked puzzled she added, "When someone on the island dies, the flag is flown at half-staff and everyone flocks to the post-office to find out who it was."

I went upstairs to change out of my business clothes and then Ms. Gonzalez and I walked into town for lunch. We had a leisurely meal and then hotfooted it back to Trish's place, added a few more layers of clothes (it was eight degrees and falling), and clamped on our skis.

We had a map showing the streets and groomed trails, all forty miles of them. We skied along snow-packed roads and up a long elevation in order to get to the trails. Some of the going was icy and a little rough, but both Marti and I were used to non-groomed surfaces. Marti was skiing like a champ these days although she still didn't have any experience with big hills. Until today.

We finally got to the first trail and it was perfectly groomed. What a treat. It led us through a pretty grove of hardwoods as we crossed the island. We branched off onto a trail that took us to a towering natural formation called Arch Rock. On this day, snow clung to outcroppings on the stone curving high across the pure blue northern sky. We snapped a few pictures but didn't tarry too long. Trust me, at eight degrees, it's best to keep moving.

We moved away from the water and found ourselves at the top of a steep slope. As Marti watched, I went first to scout out treacherous areas of the descent. There were a few bumps along the way, but I rode my skis to the bottom. Marti wasn't as lucky. Black curly hair streaming out behind her, she soared down the hill, made it over a couple of the small jumps, but the biggest one did her in. She went down in an explosion of powder.

"Did you see how fast I was going? Whoowee! That was fun."

Yes, my friend Marti was now a bona fide winter-embracer.

We skied various trails for the next several hours before wending back towards the village. We made our way down to Lake Shore Boulevard, the road that circles the island's perimeter. As we skied, the sun set over the Straits. A little later we got to a vantage point where we could see the Mackinac Bridge amidst a sea of red ice and crimson sky. We risked frozen fingers for a few more photos. It was dusk by the time we returned to the B and B.

The following day we had a lovely breakfast of hot coffee, freshly baked popovers with pots of homemade raspberry and strawberry jams, and large bowls of oatmeal. Over breakfast we studied the map. We planned to take a late afternoon plane back to St. Ignace, so we had to choose our route carefully to be able to see as many of the interesting sights as possible. It was four degrees, but was expected to climb to the teens by midday.

We skied down Main Street past closed up restaurants and stores.

"I've never seen so many fudge shops in my life," Marti said.

"I know. In the summer, this street is redolent of fudge and horse manure."

"Euwww!"

"You get used to it. That's just Mackinac Island for you."

We started a long climb up Cadotte Avenue towards the Grand Hotel. Near the top of the hill, the imposing white structure rose up on our left. We stopped to gaze at it.

"This is where they filmed that movie, *Somewhere in Time.*"

"Really? That was so romantic." Marti stopped to admire the building, a dreamy look on her face. "Frank and I should rent that movie some night."

"Yeah, guys love those kinds of films."

Hot Fudge

Marti turned to me. "Frank would be willing to watch it with me." She paused. "I guess this is as good a time as any to tell you . . . our wedding is in about four weeks. Will you be my maid of honor?"

"Of course. But four weeks? That's not much time. Do you have your dress? How did you get a venue that fast? Wow."

"I told Frank about that beautiful place you took me to the first time I cross-country skied. Remember?"

"Sure. But—"

"He knew of another one like it but on state land near his house. We went there last weekend, and . . . it's perfect. So . . . we're going to get married in a cedar swamp."

"Whoa!"

Marti's eyes were shining. "It's about a quarter of a mile off a county road and there's a two-track that goes almost to it. We figure most people will ski or snowshoe in, but we'll have snowmobiles available for anyone who can't. It's not going to be a very big ceremony, but we'll invite a few more to a party at Frank's house." She paused, then asked. "What do you think, will you do it?"

"I'd love to." I skied over and hugged her. "So what do we wear?"

She grinned, "A clean parka, your best blue jeans, and warmest socks."

"Will there be music?"

"I don't think so, but we haven't worked out all of the details yet."

We skied further up Cadotte and turned off onto Hoban Road to see the year-round town of Harrisonville. We snapped pictures of the quaint police station and also saw the general store. As the day wore on, we also came across several cemeteries, Fort Mackinac, and a huge rock called Sugar Loaf. Midafternoon we returned to Marie's place, packed, and waited for the dray.

As forecasted, the day had warmed up to sixteen degrees and snow was falling softly. We had the same driver and two horses. I wondered if they were the only ones on the island for the winter. The horses' hooves clop-clopped softly on the snow-covered road as we made our way through the woods. *This is truly a Currier and Ives moment.*

The plane was circling as we pulled our luggage off the dray and said our goodbyes to Bonnie, Champ and Donavon. We hurried into the small terminal.

Hot Fudge

The airport manager greeted us. "Hi ladies. I'm glad you're a few minutes early. Heavier snow is moving in and the window for flying is going to close very soon." He hustled us out to the plane, stowed our luggage, and off we flew.

Chapter Three

The storm held off long enough for us to touch down in St. Ignace, and drive back to Petoskey. As we neared town, I got excited to see Dash. My friend Gwen was staying with him. Since he was a rescue and had some separation anxiety, I didn't have the heart to put him in a kennel, even for just one night.

After dropping Marti off at her apartment, I sped back to my place. Soon my arms were circling the most gorgeous dog in town. Gwen and I talked for a bit and she took off. I heated up some leftover soup for me and filled Poodle Boy's bowl full of kibbles. Just before bedtime, we walked out into a thick snowstorm. Judging from our footsteps, we'd already gotten about four inches. Dash threw himself into the soft snow and wriggled around in it, loving it as much as I did.

Hot Fudge

Several days later, I was in downtown Petoskey to pick up a book I'd ordered from our local bookstore, so I stopped into Lupita's to see if Ms. Gonzalez was working. She was and served me up a free sample of peanut butter fudge.

"It's delicious. Did you make it?"

"I did, and it's not as easy as you'd think."

"I know. None of mine has ever turned out."

She grinned. "That's what you have Lupita's for."

"Got any Frank-free nights that you can come for dinner, Missy?" It seemed to me that the twosome was practically inseparable these days, and I had never seen my friend so happy. Next time I saw Frank I was going to hug the daylights out of him.

"How about Friday?"

"That's perfect."

"What are we having?"

"I was thinking we'd have white bean wedding bell soup."

She eyed me. "That's not really the name of it."

"It is now."

I heard the door open behind me and a blast of wintry air whistled in.

"Uh oh," Marti said quietly, then forced a smile. Looking past me she said, "Hi. He's not here right now. In fact, you just missed him."

Heaving a sigh, the man glared at Marti. "Again? He knew I was coming to see him." He strode the rest of the way to the counter and stood directly in front of Marti, looming over her. "When will he be back?"

"I don't know."

"You do work here, don't you?" He looked over at me and shook his head.

I glared back. I wouldn't be an accomplice to his bad behavior toward my friend.

He checked his watch. "I've got a couple of other stops to make. Tell Ed that I'll be back in thirty minutes." He turned and marched to the door.

After he'd left I asked, "Who was that jerk?"

"Robin Stone."

"Really? What does he want?"

She cocked her head. "You've heard of him?"

"I have, as of a few days ago when I inspected that property on the island."

"Huh. Anyway, I'm not sure what he wants. I just know that things get really tense when he walks through the door. I'm pretty sure that Ed can't stand him."

***

Friday afternoon I was finishing up my appraisal of the large tract of vacant land and ready to start research for the Mackinac Island property. Most of our reports are completely electronic now, saving us time and printing expenses. So, at 3:20, I hit send and my report zipped off to my client.

I got up, stretched, and sped to the kitchen to begin preparations for the bean soup. In about thirty minutes, the pot was simmering on the stove. I had shoveled once already today, but that had been early this morning. Several hours later, the county snowplow deposited heavy snow about ten inches deep across the bottom of my drive, so it was shoveling time again. I dressed in a lightweight winter jacket. Just like cross-country skiing, snow removal is hot work unless the temperature is in single digits or below zero. The sky was a vivid blue now that the snow clouds had moved on to the eastern half of the state.

Like most days, I used my beloved snow scoop instead of a shovel. The scoop is much larger and helps me take care of the snow in about one-third to one-half the time a shovel requires. This afternoon, Miss Scoop and I cleaned out the drive in about thirty minutes.

Marti showed up about 5:30. We each had two bowls of the soup, a tried and true recipe. Between mouthfuls, I tried to pump her for information about Robin Stone, but she couldn't tell me any more than she had the other day. She had done her own squeezing of Ed, her boss, but he wasn't talking.

After dinner it was time to take my faithful companion Mr. Dash for a walk, and Marti opted to join us. We put on our boots, hats, mittens, neck gaiters, and coats. Once again, the temperature was falling and snow crunched under foot. It was a clear night and millions of stars studded the sky.

We stopped as Dash examined a bush and lifted his leg.

Hot Fudge

Marti looked up at the splendor above us. "I love the night sky here. There are so many stars. Can you see them better in the winter?"

"It seems like it."

"Do you ever see the northern lights?"

"I have but not very often. Usually I hear about them the next day," I heard the frustration in my voice.

"That's too bad. What do I have to do to see them?"

Dash was finished so we moved on. "Be at the right place at the right time, which is usually about four a.m."

"Oh no."

"Although, once you're out at Frank's house in the boonies, you'll have a better chance of seeing them. You'll be a little further north and more importantly, away from city lights."

Marti smiled.

"In just a few weeks, right?"

"Yup." She smiled again. "Say On, who are you bringing to the wedding?"

"Ha! I'm still between dating opportunities, as you well know."

"You've got time. Get busy."

Hot Fudge

Chapter Four

Tuesday afternoon, I was at my usual outpost in front of the computer. I had taken Dash cross-country skiing that morning for our three-mile jaunt, and had been working on the Mackinac Island job ever since. I researched sales going back five years. The economy had been improving during that time, but I was pretty sure that it couldn't account for the dramatic increases in price levels I was seeing. I wondered if, as Rene Arnault had said, it was the "Stone effect." I would definitely need to talk with lots of property owners and real estate brokers to hear more viewpoints.

My Hapkido class was at one o'clock and Dash and I went out for our afternoon walk about two-thirty. Afterwards as we were walking through the front door, I heard my phone ringing. I ran over and got it just before the caller, Marti, was sent to voice mail. "Good afternoon, Miss G. How—"

"On! Something terrible has happened! It's . . . It's—" she was crying.

"Marti. Where are you? I'm coming."

There was a pause. I was just about to break in again. "I'm at Lupita's. That man. . . That man Robin Stone just keeled over dead here."

"What?" It was starting to sink in. "Marti, I'm on my way. Bye." I hadn't taken my jacket and boots off and my keys were still in my hand. Clicking Dash's leash off his collar, I ran out the door and hopped into my car.

I sped into town, but had to park about a block away. Part of the street was closed off and there were police cars, an ambulance, and a fire truck. Bystanders had gathered outside the shop and police were moving in and out of it. I wove my way through the crowd in hopes of seeing Marti. Finally, I caught sight of her through the front window. She was sitting on a barstool at the counter and I thought I could see Ed sitting at a table at the far end of the restaurant. Policemen seemed to be questioning them. I could also see a body sprawled out on the floor and other police were photographing the scene.

Hot Fudge

An officer I didn't recognize, stopped me from entering the building, so I tried to get Marti's attention through the window. She finally caught sight of me and gave me a small wave.

"Onalee."

I turned around and saw Frank jogging down the street. Reaching me he said, "I got a call from Marti just a few minutes ago and came as fast as I could. What's going on?"

"She told you that a man died in there?"

"Yeah, but that's all she said."

"I don't know any more than that either."

He stared at me for a moment, then left and tried to get through the door. He had a longer conversation with the cop guarding the door than I'd had, but it was to no avail.

He returned to where I stood waiting. It was another cold day and we stomped our feet trying to keep warm. Finally, the examination of the body seemed to be finished. They hoisted it onto a gurney, covered it with a blanket, and as the crowd parted, wheeled it out to a waiting ambulance. No lights or siren would be needed for this run. A short time after that,

Marti got up, disappeared for a minute into the back and then came out in her coat and boots. Frank quickly went over and held her. A few minutes later, with Frank's arm still around her, Marti walked towards me. She left Frank and came over and hugged me. "On, Frank and I are going out to his house. We'll talk later, okay?"

I was hugging her back and felt her trembling. "Of course. Do whatever you need to. Just take care of yourself."

"Thanks. And thank you for coming." She rejoined Frank and walked away, his arm once again around her protectively.

As I turned to go back to my car, I looked again at Lupita's. Standing in the doorway, staring at me was Police Detective Costas. He raised his hand and I waved back. *Oh no. Just what I need, good ole' Costas spotting me at the scene of yet another death.*

Hot Fudge

Chapter Five

Marti had lots of time off now. Lupita's was closed indefinitely. I didn't hear from her until she called in the late afternoon on the day after the incident. She didn't want to talk much, but we made a plan to go cross-country skiing the following morning.

Frank dropped her off at her apartment where she gathered her cross-country gear and drove to my place. When she came in the house, she looked like her old self, but seemed subdued. Dash and I were ready and the three of us took off for the county park.

The wind-driven snow stung our faces as we skied near the shore. Ice now covered much of this portion of the bay stilling the waters, and I missed my old friends, the waves. Talking was difficult because of the blizzard, so we mostly slipped along in silence. We headed inland, skiing through the forest and made it to the far end of my route. We turned around and as we traversed the path through the woods, we followed the tracks we'd made earlier. As soon as we left the shelter of the trees and faced the wind off the lake again, all traces of our tracks had been swept away. I broke a new trail for us and Dash trotted along right behind with Marti behind him. It was arduous slogging through the deep snow but exhilarating.

Back at the house, we changed into dry clothes, I fed the Mighty Poodle, and put a pot of coffee on. I'd baked a batch of giant blueberry ricotta muffins the night before and put two in the microwave to warm.

Marti and I poured ourselves mugs of coffee, plated up the gooey muffins, and sat down at the table. Finished with his meal, Dash ambled over and laid down by my feet, head resting on his paws, and eyes pinned on mine. As I sipped my coffee, Marti began her tale.

"Here's how it happened. That man Robin Stone you saw when you were at Lupita's, came back a couple of more times that day but never met with Ed. The weird thing is, the second time he came, Ed was there, hiding out in the back. He'd seen him coming down the street and told me to say he hadn't returned. I asked Ed what was going on, but he pretended not to hear me."

"Hmmm. That's strange."

"Yeah. It was like he was scared of him. The next few days, Stone didn't show up at the shop, at least not that I'm aware of. I tried a couple of more times to get Ed to talk about it. He finally got really ticked off and told me to drop it and never bring it up again. I actually felt a little threatened by him, like he might hit me or something." She shook her head, remembering.

"Ed? He seems like such a nice guy."

"I know. That's what I'd always thought, but Stone was really eating at him, I guess."

Neither of us had touched our muffins as the story unfolded. Eventually, I had to succumb to the temptation. It was a new recipe, after all. I pulled a chunk off, one large enough to include part of the still-warm ribbon of ricotta. "Ohhh." *Oops. I don't like to comment on my own cooking.* I looked over at Marti. Her eyes were closed as she munched.

"On, these are the best yet."

Dash raised his head and stared hard at the rest of the muffin. "Sweetie, it's entirely possible that a few wayward crumbs might fall to the floor, but I can't in good conscience give you more than that."

We each had a few more bites between sips of hot coffee. Eventually Marti began again. "So, we hadn't seen the guy until Tuesday when he walked in and right up to the counter. Ed was helping a regular customer of ours, Mrs. Darnley, so he couldn't just walk away.

"As Stone waited he studied the fudge in the case. He kept drumming his fingers and it was really annoying, like he wanted us all to look at him. I figured I'd try to defuse the tension a bit and started to cut off a piece of chocolate fudge for him. Glancing over, Ed said, 'Peanut butter's his favorite.' Really? I thought. He knows that? Anyway, I chopped off some of the peanut butter for him. As he was eating it, he said something like, 'Just let me have the whole slice.' I did, and started boxing it up for him. 'Forget all that nonsense. Just give me the fudge,' he told me. I handed him the candy in a piece of wax paper."

Marti took another sip of coffee. "Ed finished with Mrs. Darnley and motioned for Stone to follow him to the back room. They closed the door

Hot Fudge

and even standing close to it as I straightened boxes on the shelves, I couldn't make out much of what they said. Then, I heard a sound like someone getting sick, then a chair scraping the floor, and footsteps so I moved away from the door. Stone burst through it, almost made it across the restaurant, then got sick again. Really sick. He collapsed and thrashed around clutching his stomach, moaning.

"I remember rushing over to where he lay. He was breathing fast and sweating. I knew I couldn't do anything for him, so I called 9-1-1. It seemed like it took forever to answer all their questions. Part way through I noticed his breathing had slowed way down. I thought that might be a good sign, but it wasn't. The 9-1-1 lady asked me to feel his pulse. I did, but it seemed really weak. Time was slipping away. I remember telling her something like, 'Please! Just send someone. He's still alive, but it looks really bad.' The woman told me they were already on their way. After I hung up the phone, I saw Ed. He was standing by the counter staring at Stone. I looked down at him again, but by then I thought he was dead. As I was trying to think of something else to do, the EMS people came, a man and a woman. Right after that the police and a fire truck showed up." She paused and looked over at me. "On, I sold him that fudge."

"Did you make that batch or did Ed?"

"Ed did. But it couldn't have been what killed him, could it?"

"I don't know. Did you ever find out what was going on between Ed and Stone?"

"No. Ed told me diddly-squat. And now, we're closed for who knows how long."

"You didn't mention anyone else being there. Was there?"

"No. Mrs. Darnley left and no one else had come in."

"Did you find out anything from the police?"

She snorted. "Zilch. Your Detective Costas told us nothing but was downright pushy with his questions. And to think, I'd always liked the guy."

I'm not an "I-told-you-so" sort of person. "There's definitely a dark side there," I said, mildly.

"Do you think he had a heart attack or was it something else?" I asked.

"I'm not a doctor, but it didn't look like a heart attack to me. He didn't clutch his chest."

We ate the rest of our muffins and I poured us more coffee. "There was an article about it in the newspaper."

"I figured there would be, but Frank doesn't get the paper. I suppose I could've gone online, but honestly, yesterday I didn't want to hear anything more about it."

I went over to the coffee table and retrieved the paper. I laid it down between us and we read the article, although it was my third time. It gave some basic facts about Robin Stone, such as that he was 54, had one son 18 years old and a wife. He lived in Petoskey part-time and New York City. There was also a discussion of his connection to Mackinac Island. The article went on to summarize the events surrounding the bizarre death inside Lupita's, "a local establishment."

Marti finished and looked up, "It doesn't mention that there was still some fudge in his fist when he died."

"There was? It's a really good thing they didn't say anything about that. Otherwise, you'd never get any more business."

She sighed. "I suppose you're right. Is there an obituary?"

"No. Maybe in tonight's paper. I imagine the family is still in a state of shock and hasn't had time to put one together yet."

Marti was staring off into space. I felt bad for her and was just about to bestow a few consoling words when she said, "I wonder what the funeral arrangements are?"

Oh no. I gave her a narrow look, but she didn't notice. *Ole Bounce-Back Gonzalez is ready to jump in with both gum shoes and look for a murder.* "Why do you want to know?" I asked.

"We've been over this before, On. If at all possible, we need to attend."

"Does Frank know about your continuing predilection for crime solving?"

"Not crime solving. It's justice I seek."

"You didn't even like the guy. Besides, don't you think he died of natural causes?"

"You're right. I didn't like him. No, by justice I mean I want the restoration of the good reputation of Lupita's. This could ruin Ed and I'm willing to bet he didn't die of natural causes."

"If Stone was murdered, don't you think it's entirely possible that Ed is the perp?"

"See? I'm sure that's exactly what lots of people are thinking. I'll bet other folks knew that something was going on between Ed and Stone."

"How long have you known Ed?"

Marti sighed. "Four weeks, but during that time we've been together a lot, and I've come to know him as a warm human being and straight shooter."

"And one who you were afraid was going to hit you last week."

Chapter Six

Marti left and I settled down to work. I made some progress on my report, took Dash out for his afternoon sojourn and waited for the newspaper. It finally came and I tore it open looking for the Stone obituary. It was there. I scanned through it and called Marti. "Okay, Ms. G, it's in there tonight. I'll read it to you."

"Thanks, On, but I bought it already. I was going to call you. So, what do you think?"

"Hmmm, that he was a really high-powered guy, a Wall Street investment banker. There's going to be a memorial for him tomorrow. Want to go?"

"Of course," she said.

The following morning was clear and a frosty fourteen degrees. After the service, Marti and I hurried out of the funeral home under the watchful eyes of Detective Costas. We hadn't learned much for our efforts, although we did get to see his business partner, Charlie Kemp. He gave a eulogy on behalf of Mr. Stone. We also noted a woman and young man seated in the front row that I assumed were the current Mrs. Stone and Robin Junior. They were not seated together. Some of the attendees, including Mr. Kemp, were elegantly attired and probably represented the New York City contingent.

"I didn't see your boss," I said as we walked along, snow crunching under our feet.

"Me neither, but I didn't think we would."

"And I didn't expect to see you two there, although I suppose I should have," came a familiar voice.

Over my shoulder, I saw Mr. Costas coming up on our heels. "Good morning, Camille," I said giving my voice a cheery ring. "Any progress on the case?"

"Yes. Our main suspect at this point is an employee of the fudge shop. We are monitoring the actions of her and her abettor closely."

I saw Marti flinch. *The big bully.* "My friend Marti, here, has been through a very trying ordeal, so back off. If as usual you need a target, use me, I have thick skin." I noticed I'd balled up my fists inside my down mittens as I'd drawn myself up to my full five feet four inches.

Costas studied me for a moment. "I'll pretend I didn't just hear you threaten an officer of the law, Ms. O'Conner, but only if you agree not to interfere in my investigation."

I smiled at him. "Of course I agree. That's a very reasonable request, Officer."

As Costas walked away, Marti turned on me. "You didn't have to stick up for me. I'm not guilty."

"I know, but I didn't like his nasty insinuation."

"So, you're agreeing—"

"Not to interfere, but nothing was mentioned about aiding the investigation."

***

Marti and Frank were spending the day together so Dash and I were on our own that afternoon. Since it was a Saturday, I thought it prudent to stay away from more populated areas with the Dash Dog off leash. We drove north to a segment of the North Country Trail. This path running through Michigan, starts in North Dakota and ends up in New York state. It's the longest scenic trail in the United States. Due to the extreme hills in this section of the trail, I snowshoed while Dash followed along behind me. Even with his avoidance of the deep drifts, we still had to stop periodically and dig snow out of his pads. It wasn't much fun for either one of us, and we cut our outing short. On the way back to town, I made a quick stop at a local pet supply store and bought my boy a pair of boots. They were a bit pricey, but he was worth it.

When we returned to the house, I started a fire in the woodstove. It was only eleven degrees out and forecasted to go well below zero during the night. The phone rang as I was busy chopping vegetables for soup. It was my neighbor, Mrs. Stirnaman, calling to let me know she'd be out of town for two months, and to ask a favor. She took her friend, Mrs. Willowby shopping every week and wondered if I could fill in for her. I said I'd be happy to.

Connie Doherty

I had met Mrs. W. on several occasions as she and my neighbor enjoyed a cup of coffee on Mrs. Stirnaman's deck. She was a lively octogenarian and I was looking forward to spending time with her. I phoned her to find out when she wanted to go and heard she'd been expecting my call.

"What's a good day for you?" I asked.

"Whatever is best for you, dear. I'm very flexible."

"How about Monday?"

"Wonderful."

"What time would you like to go?"

"Anytime. I know you're a working lady."

Great. The earlier in the day, the better. "How about nine a.m.?"

"Is a.m. in the morning? I always forget."

"Yup."

"I suppose I could be up that early—"

Oops, she's not a morning person. "Would the afternoon be better?"

"I think afternoons are a lovely time to shop, don't you, dear?"

Hot Fudge

Next best is as late in the day as possible. "Sure. What about three o'clock?"

"Don't you need to be home to start dinner, by then, dear? But if that is good for you it's fine with me."

Okay, so we've narrowed it down to afternoons before three. "Is two o'clock good or would earlier be better?"

"Two is fine and one o'clock would be marvelous."

I think we've zeroed in on it. "Okay, I'll pick you up at one. Say Mrs. Willowby, I'm making a pot of vegetable soup, can I bring you some?"

"Glory be, Onalee, that's kind of you, but I just cooked up a big batch of carcass soup myself, from leftover turkey. In the winter it seems like we go from one kettle of soup to the next, doesn't it?"

I laughed, picturing her, industriously stirring up tasty broths in her kitchen. "It sure does. Nothing beats it on a cold day."

We hung up and I got back to my chopping. Soon the soup was simmering and my kitchen smelled like garlic and onions. I put another log on the fire and cracked open a new book. Dash, stretched out in front of the fire, cocked open one eye, sighed and dropped back off to sleep.

Connie Doherty

I read for a while, but then my mind meandered back to Robin Stone. I wondered if the cause of death had been determined yet. If it was murder, who were the suspects? It certainly seemed as though Marti's boss, Ed could be on that list. Actually, I suppose Marti might be as well, but with no motive or mean bone in her body, she wouldn't be for long. If Mr. Costas were at all a reasonable person, I might consider asking him to a dinner of homemade soup. I'd loosen his tongue with a glass or two of wine and then gradually commence a friendly grilling session. But knowing the detective, liquor would probably make him even more uncooperative and cantankerous than usual. Instead I ate my soup in the company of a first rate detective novel and a good-as-gold poodle.

The following morning, the mercury slunk down to negative nine, a perfect time to try out Dash's new footwear. I picked up one of his paws, stuffed his foot in, and fastened the Velcro. Dash was not happy and was wriggling to escape my grasp. I held on, talking to him in soothing tones. Slowly, one after another of his feet were ensconced in the bright blue boots. It only took us about fifteen minutes and we were out the door. Dash and I drove over to the bike path.

Hot Fudge

I opened the car door for him, he leaped out, and suddenly the sky filled with flying blue doggie boots. He must have been working on the Velcro on our drive over. I scurried around and gathered up the useless galoshes and tossed them in the car for another day. With no protective padding on Dash's feet, I only allowed him to stay outside for ten minutes. We'd both have to wait until warmer temperatures to partake in any meaningful exercise.

Later in the day, it was still only three above zero, and too cold for an extended walk. The blue boots were in the closet and neither of us had the heart to try them again. As Dashiell and I walked quickly along the beach, I heard someone call us. Turning around, I saw our good friends Susan the person and Riley the dog. We let the two canines off their leashes and they galloped towards each other, tongues hanging out and ears flapping.

"Onalee. It's been a long time since we've run into you. How have you two been?"

"Great. Did you know that my friend Marti has moved up here?"

"No, I didn't, but that's wonderful."

"Anything new with you and Riley?"

She curled her lip up. "No. He's unfortunately still addicted to watching television. At this point, I think I've tried everything. He's even happy watching reruns," she said shaking her head.

I laughed. "Good old Riley. He is one crazy guy."

We watched as the two dogs chased each other down the beach. They turned around, came back, and started dog-wrestling accompanied by lots of fake growling. Dash, the standard poodle had thirty pounds on Riley the Tibetan terrier, but he rolled around, letting Riley get the best of him. After a few minutes of their roughhousing, we stepped in and attached their leashes. They'd had enough exposure to the cold. We said our goodbyes with promises of getting together again soon.

The following day's newspaper mentioned that authorities now suspected foul play in the death of Robin Stone and police were pursuing leads in the case. There were several persons of interest, but they remained unnamed.

My doorbell rang. Marti was standing on the porch. I opened the door, and she barged in. "Did your paper come yet?" She asked.

"Yes, I was just reading it."

"Did you get to the part yet about 'foul play'?"

"Yes."

"What do you think?"

"I think you're looking for trouble again."

"Are you going to stand there and tell me that you're not even a teensy bit interested in solving this case?"

"Well, maybe I'm slightly interested. But you, on the other hand are all revved up. I can tell just by looking at you."

"This does affect Lupita's you know and my livelihood, so of course I'm interested. The first thing we need to do is to write down our list of suspects." She leaned down and started to untie her boots.

"Hang on there, Inspector Gonzalez. I'm taking a friend of Mrs. Stirnaman's grocery shopping and I have to leave here in a couple of minutes."

"Oh." Still hanging on to her boot laces, she grinned. "Why don't I stay here with Dash and work on the list while you're gone on your mission of mercy?"

I sighed but went to my office and got a legal pad and pen for Marti. "I'm not sure when we'll get back. I think she may want to go to the bank or elsewhere."

"That's okay, Take your time," Marti said, shooing me out of my own front door.

I pulled up in from of a small house painted with creamy yellow and pale purple stripes. *Oh goody.* I'd noticed this place before, but I didn't realize Mrs. Stirnaman's friend was the person behind the creative exterior. A curtain twitched in the front window and I was opening my door when she appeared on her porch. "I'm coming, dear. Don't bother to get out of your car," she called.

The front steps looked icy so I sprinted over to give her my arm.

"You act like I'm an old lady, Onalee. Don't spoil me." She grinned, looking up at me, and taking my arm. She stopped and gazed at her yard. "Just look at that. I have a garden full of diamonds."

"You sure do." All around us, the sun sparked off the crystals of snow. As soon as she was settled in the car, I took off. "Do you need to go anywhere besides the grocery store?"

Hot Fudge

"No, not today, but thank you."

"Which store do you like to shop at?"

"Anywhere is fine, but Maybelle and I usually go to Foodrights."

"Yup, I shop there, too." I turned the corner in order to go back towards Foodrights. At the store, we went our separate ways. I gathered the few items I needed for my next soup and nightly salads, then turned back to look for Mrs. W. She had only covered a couple of isles, so I went back to help her. "Since you're here, I'll just run down this aisle and pick up two cans of beans. Stay with the cart, won't you dear?"

I stood there as she made her way slowly down the aisle and back. "You know if you tell me the items you want, I could go find them for you," I said.

"I only have a few more things, and I like to look them over, but thank you for offering."

Down the next aisle she needed a sack of brown sugar.

"I could grab that for you," I tried again.

"I won't know what size I need until I see it, but please stay with the cart."

Has there been a recent spate of shopping cart thefts I wasn't aware of? I thought as I stood by her cart until she returned bearing a standard one pound bag of brown sugar. In this fashion, we worked our way along. When we got to the front of the store she steered away from the self-checkout lanes to one of the long lines waiting for a cashier. "Have you ever tried the self-checkout stations? I can show you how to do it, if you want to."

She beamed at me. "You young people are amazing. You can do everything, but I'm scared of them. And when it comes right down to it, I don't think they're any faster. Brenda is a marvel. You'll see."

Eventually, it was our turn to be checked out, and I helped Mrs. W. load her groceries onto the belt, with mine behind hers. When Brenda saw who it was, a smile broke out, "Hello, Mrs. Willowby. How are you today?"

"Just fine, thank you. And how are you and your lovely Tina?"

They talked a bit more and I was introduced as "the wonderful young lady" who was helping Mrs. W. that day. All of the years I'd been going to this store and I had never met any of the people who worked there. Mrs.

Hot Fudge

Willowby chatted like an old friend with Brenda, several employees in the produce department, her bagger, and the store manager.

At Mrs. Willowby's house and over her objections, I carried her groceries in. "Can I make you a cup of tea or coffee, dear?" She asked fastening her dark button eyes on me.

I set the bags on her kitchen counter. "I probably should get back to work. Can I have a rain check?"

"Of course."

Returning to my house, I saw Marti and Dash walking down the street towards me.

"Hi, On. He seemed to want to go out and I figured you wouldn't mind."

"Not at all. Thanks." We went inside. "How'd you do on your list?" I asked as we removed our boots.

Marti retrieved the pad of paper and held it out to me. She had numbers written from one to ten but with only one name written down—Ed. She was staring at me. "Uh oh."

Chapter Seven

"I know. It looks bad, doesn't it? But, we've just started, and there have got to be plenty of perps. We just have to uncover them."

"Righto. A high flyer like Mr. Stone probably had lots of enemies. I'm going to need to go back to Mackinac Island to look at comps. I could do some checking around while I'm there. In fact, if you could take care of Dash, and I can get hold of a few people, I'll go tomorrow, as long as the weather looks good."

At 9:00, the following morning I was driving over the Mackinac Bridge. Everything is pronounced Mack-in-naw, but the bridge, the island and the county in the Upper Peninsula are spelled Mackinac, while the city is spelled Mackinaw. As someone explained to me long ago, everything in the Lower Peninsula, is spelled Mackinaw, everything north of that is Mackinac.

Hot Fudge

The sky was a watery blue and clear. It should be a good day for flying. At the airport I boarded the plane, carrying only my purse, phone and briefcase.

On the island, I again met Mr. Arnault, the owner of the property I was appraising. He was waiting for me outside the terminal and with a roar we were off, riding his snowmobile into town. He parked the machine outside his store and we walked from there to one of the two year-round restaurants. Sitting down in the empty cafe, we both ordered coffee. When I had been on the island before, he had given me the names and telephone numbers of other real estate owners on the island and said that from them I should be able to get details on leases that I could use for rent comparables.

Several of the people had been very helpful, but I still needed a couple of more properties. Also, I had unearthed some sales, but needed to get the inside story on them. *This man needs to learn he can never tell an appraiser that he'll be willing to help in every possible way. It was like giving me a license to kill. Speaking of which . . .* "You heard, of course, that Mr. Stone was murdered in Petoskey?"

"Oh my, yes. What a shocker, eh? And poisoned in a fudge shop, to boot." A small smile played around his lips. "It's been a sizzling hot topic of conversation here ever since."

"What are people saying about it?"

A server arrived at our table with a coffee pot and bowl of creamers. "I made you a fresh pot, Mr. Arnault."

He gave me a meaningful look, and smiled at the woman. "Thank you, Anne."

"Of course, Darlin'."

I also chimed in with a thank you. After she poured our coffee and left, Arnault leaned in across the table, and resumed, "Anne's a great gal, but like all of us on this island, she lives for a tidbit of gossip. Now, where were we? Oh yes, the unfortunate Mr. Robin Stone. It has certainly caused turmoil here. Of course none of the businesses or buildings he owns are open now, but everyone wonders what will happen to them. His employees don't know if they'll have jobs come May. Thank heavens this isn't the middle of summer."

"What about his partner?"

Hot Fudge

"Charlie Kemp?"

"I think that's the name. Do you think he'll keep things going?"

"He's a complete unknown. Usually he doesn't even seem to be around, but when he is, he just sits," Arnault pushed out his lip, frowned and crossed his arms, "like this. I don't think I've ever heard him talk. He wouldn't even say hello when I met with them."

"Huh. Strange. Do you know what he did for the partnership?"

"We all called him, 'The Muscle.' He acted like a body guard."

"I read in the paper that Stone was an investment banker, and I assume that's how he made his money."

"You're close. He owned and managed a hedge fund. He made billions, or so I've heard."

"Which he then parlayed into Mackinac Island real estate and businesses."

Arnault's eyes twinkled. "Parlay. Now that's a word I have not heard for some time. I believe it originally came from the Italian language. Thank you for using it, my dear."

I laughed. "You're welcome."

We each sipped our coffee. "Did Stone lease any commercial space in any of his buildings?" *Hmm. This one question might open up information channels for both my appraisal and our investigation.*

"Yes. His building near the corner of Main and Charboneau was rented last summer by the, Your Name Is News, shop."

I was scribbling down the details as he talked. Hopefully, later on, I'd be able to read most of it. "Do you know what rate he got?"

"I heard he got a big number, even for the Island, but I don't know the particulars. Call Amanda Randall. She's the tenant. Tell her I sent you."

"Is she on the island now?"

Arnault nodded. "She should be. I think if you call the number for the business, you'll get her, or you can leave a message."

"Thanks. I asked him what he knew of sales on the island. I had found a few through the Multiple Listing System and from the assessor. Most of them had sold to and from LLC's, Limited Liability Companies, and the people weren't named. I'd gotten some names and phone numbers from brokers and the assessor, but Arnault helped me with a few as well. I took notes as he spoke. He told me if the buyers and sellers were likely to be on the island, spending the winter on the mainland, or even in the southern sunshine. What a wealth of information he was.

We were finishing up and I wanted to circle back to the "Stone Affair." "Do you think that Stone Enterprises will keep their island buildings and businesses?"

"That's what all of the speculation is about. If they decide to sell, we have to assume they won't try to sell them all at once and flood the market. You can see why this concentration of ownership worries us."

"I sure can. Do you think that's why somebody murdered him?"

Arnault lifted his eyebrows. "I guess that's a possibility, but he drove at least one man out of business, that I know of."

"Really? How did he do that?"

"He undercut him as well as out-marketed him. Stone was a smart cookie."

"Yeah, he must've been to make his billions. What was the business?"

"It was Mac's Taco Shack, and it had been around for, oh, probably thirty years. But then along came Mr. Stone with Paco's Tacos, humongous helpings, delicious combinations, and cheaper prices. Bill just couldn't compete, though he tried for most of two summers."

"Bill?"

Arnault smiled. "Bill Reneveere." He spelled it for me. "If you don't mind me asking, what's your interest in all of this?"

"Um, actually the fudge shop where Stone died is where my good friend works. She was there when it happened. In fact she was the one who sold him the fudge."

He lowered his voice and leaned closer again, "Was he really clutching fudge when he died or is that just a tasteless rumor?"

"Well—" *I don't know what to say. Arnault has given me so much information, but validating that rumor would not be good for Lupita's.*

Seeing my hesitation, he said, "You don't have to answer that. It would be very bad for the fudge shop. I understand." He smiled. "Actually, there is another transaction that you may not be aware of. I don't think it's closed yet, but what I heard was that it was going to be another fudge shop," he paused and looked straight at me, "named Lupita's."

"Really?" *Holy jaw-dropper!*

"Yes. The building is right next door to Paco's Tacos on Main Street."

I felt my eyes narrow. "That's Stone's restaurant, right?"

"Yes. Our Mr. Stone was very upset to find that a building right between two that he owned was being bought out underneath him, or so I heard."

"And you have a person I can contact about this?"

"Of course, and yes, he is on the island for the winter."

We finally wrapped it up and I paid for Arnault's coffee. He left a ten dollar tip.

"They don't make much money, this time of the year," he explained.

We opened the door of the snug restaurant and stepped out into a heavy curtain of snow. *Uh oh!*

"Are you spending the night on the island again?"

"I wasn't planning on it. The radar showed clear skies for the next several days."

"The weather is notoriously hard to predict up here, but I hope it clears for you. Goodbye Miss Onalee O'Conner," he said as he shook my hand.

I put a call in to the airport. They told me they'd let me know when it looked like the clouds would lift. There wasn't much else I could do, it was up to Mother Nature. I'd planned on spending most of the afternoon looking at properties and talking with people so I called the lady who owned, Your Name is News. I figured I'd get her voicemail but she picked up.

I introduced myself and explained what I needed. An older appraiser once told me, "We're information beggars." That's what I felt like as I gave my spiel, but surprisingly, instead of blowing me off, she gave me her address and told me to come to her house. It was only a couple of blocks away.

Arriving at her address, I saw a cute house painted white with light blue shutters and a matching front door. Knocking, I stamped my feet to knock off some of the snow gathered on my boots. A tall woman answered the door. She looked to be about fifty and wore her hair long and pulled back in a single braid. She was dressed in jeans and a comfy looking rose-colored knit sweater.

"You must be the appraiser," she said with a grin. "Come on in."

Hot Fudge

I stepped into a summery room with a wide window overlooking a partially wooded backyard. She took my coat and asked if she could get me tea or coffee. "My brother is an appraiser down in Ohio, so I know a little about what you do and will help you as much as I can."

We sat in chairs that afforded us views of the outside as I wrote down the details of her lease. "Did a broker handle the transaction?" Lots of times the real estate brokers can give appraisers valuable insight into deals. In fact, I'd go so far as to say they are the unsung heroes in the world of appraising.

"No, like much of what happens on the island, it was word of mouth."

We thoroughly discussed the lease, before I segued into a discussion about Robin Stone.

"Before I entered into negotiations to lease the store, I knew him by reputation, only."

"Reputation?" I asked, mildly.

"He's been the talk of the town ever since he landed here, a couple of years ago."

"What do you think of him?"

Her bright blue eyes gazed at me intently." *Did I just stray into "over the line" territory?*

"I'm not sure what this has to do with your appraisal, but I would just say that like most residents of this historically significant, one-of-a kind gem, I find it very disconcerting to have someone like him come to town."

As she continued to study me, I explained to her about my friend being present when Stone died and how that had propelled us into searching for his killer.

She giggled. "My brother always says that he reminds himself of that television detective, Colombo, shuffling around, looking for clues about a property. I can't wait to tell him I've met an appraiser who's working to solve a murder mystery while she comes up with a value for a property. You'll be his hero." She started laughing again. After she got control of herself, she added, "So what do you want to know about the tale of Mr. Stone Conquers Mackinac Island?"

"I heard he was buying up buildings and it was making a lot of people mad."

"Exactly."

"Why were people so upset about it?"

"Rumors were flying about a future huge development of some kind."

"That would bring a lot of change, wouldn't it?"

"You're not kidding, and change isn't necessarily welcomed here."

"Is there anyone who was especially upset about it?"

She gave me a devilish grin. "In other words, who do I think done him in?"

"Um, yes, I guess that's what I do mean."

"It's a long list, but I suppose at the top of the list would be Bill Reneveere. He owned a taco shop until Stone put him out of business."

I'm not going to mention that I've heard that before. I want her take on it untainted. She recounted the story I'd heard from Rene Arnault.

"I guess he was ruthless."

"Yes he was. He was selling family sized tacos for about a dollar. It was nuts. And Bill didn't have the bucks to compete with him. Bill had started his business on a shoestring when he was, I don't know, probably 23 or 24 years old. He'd put his whole life into it. But Stone didn't care. To him all that mattered was that he wanted Bill's location. To my way of thinking, he used his money like a weapon. "

"And he had lots of it at his disposal. What is Reneveere doing now?"

"He's working up at the Grand. Cooking, I think."

"So, he's at the top of your list, who's next?"

"Hmmm. I suppose it could be Ed Soarez."

"The owner of Lupita"s?" I asked.

"Yes." Her eyes danced. "Where Mr. Stone went to his eternal rest."

"What was their connection?"

"They were fighting tooth and nail over a building that was located between two stores owned by Stone. Do you see what I mean? He's trying, or I guess I should say, was trying, to buy up buildings next to each other. He seemed to be planning to knock a bunch of those historical treasures down to put up some twenty-first century concrete and glass monolith."

"That would sure wreck the character of the island, wouldn't it?"

"Yup. Most of us who live here or own businesses here, love it just the way it is."

"What was going on with the building that Stone and Ed were fighting over? Was it listed for sale?"

"No, but the owner does want to sell. I heard that Ed put an offer in on it before Stone knew that it was on the market. The island scuttlebutt is that when Stone finally did hear about it, he went berserk and either tried to kill the deal or possibly did kill it."

"But, even if he stopped the sale somehow, it's not worth murdering someone over, is it? I mean there are other buildings."

"Yeah, but there are never many sales of commercial properties on Mackinac and for the last few years, anytime a place did come on the market, Stone snatched it up before anyone else got a chance to buy it."

"Okay, so, Bill Reneveere and Ed probably have motives. Who else?"

"On the island, he had just about everybody up in arms, but most of them probably weren't mad enough to bump him off. It seems to me that a guy like that probably collected enemies wherever he went. There might be disgruntled investors from his hedge fund, he was on his second or third wife, and there was also talk about girlfriends. I think the biggest job you'll have is narrowing down the field."

"Wow. I was only around him once, briefly, but he didn't seem like a very nice guy."

"He wasn't. Most of us up here are friendly competitors, but Stone was like your worst stereotype of a ruthless businessman."

We chatted a bit more, I thanked Amanda and hurried on my way. If anything, the snow was falling faster than before, but it was still only 1:30 and hopefully it would clear up. I walked around and found some of the buildings that I needed to take pictures of including the one that both Stone and Ed had been trying to buy.

It was a rather small structure housing a restaurant and situated on Main Street, between a tee-shirt shop and Paco's Tacos. There were no "For Sale" signs either by owner or by a realtor. It was rather nondescript but had a strong location, not far from one of the ferry docks. No one seemed to be around, but I'd gotten the phone number of the owner, Rod McCormick, from Mr. Arnault. I called, got voicemail, and left a message before thrusting half-frozen fingers back in my glove to warm up. As soon as feeling came back into my hand, I pawed through my notes and found

Hot Fudge

the phone number for Reneveere. Again, I got voicemail and left a message.

Chapter Eight

It was almost 2:30, and I'd taken the pictures I needed. There were still people to talk with but the snow was really closing in. It looked like we'd gotten about five inches and I'd received no calls from the airport. I decided it was time to turn the full power of the resources of O'Conner Appraisal towards Plan B, and hopefully there would be no need for a Plan C, because there wasn't one.

I began walking towards the Bed and Breakfast I'd stayed at several weeks ago to reserve a room for the night. It was a pleasant ten minute walk from the downtown. As I made my way, several snowmobiles zipped by through the mostly deserted street. A few minutes later, I turned up the familiar side-street and climbed the front porch stairs. After I'd rung the doorbell several times, Marie answered.

Hot Fudge

After we'd said our hellos and she invited me in, I explained that I would very likely need a room for the night because of no flights off the island. As I spoke, I saw a worried look cloud her eyes.

"Onalee, I'm so sorry, but we don't have any rooms. Other people have also gotten stranded today, and you're right, I don't think this storm is going to lift any time soon."

"That's okay, there is the other motel that is open year-round, I'll just go there."

Marie shook her head. "No, I've spoken with them. They're booked solid as well."

"Are there any alternatives?"

"I can't think of any."

The door behind me opened with a jingle of bells along with a cold gust of wind. Marie and I both turned to look. She smiled as I gasped.

Much later, I chuckled as I replayed the double-take I'd witnessed Mr. Costas perform, but at the time I was a bit on the nonplused side of the ledger myself. I quickly gathered my wits about me before speaking. "Hello, Detective. I hope you're not looking for a room for the night, because there are none available." As I was saying this to Mr. Far-Too-Smug, I caught movement out of the corner of my eye. Marie handed a key to Mr. C. "Hey, I thought there were no vacancies," I said, with possibly an edge of whininess in my delivery.

"Again I apologize, Onalee, but Camille stayed here last night and has the room reserved for tonight as well."

"Oh," was the short reply, issued from my usual glib self. "Okay then. Thanks, anyway." I forced my lips up into a smile. Then, inspiration struck. "Wait a minute. The ice bridge. Do you know anyone I can hire to take me across on a snowmobile?"

"It isn't formed yet. We still have open water to the east."

"Curses." With no Plan C in sight I shouldered past the detective and out the door, saying my goodbyes to Marie and a possibly smirking Costas as I left.

Hot Fudge

Chapter Nine

If worse came to worst, and it looked like it had, I could stay in one of the restaurants until it closed, then walk the streets until dawn. It was a safe town and I'd be fine if a trifle cold. Meanwhile, I needed to call Marti and beg her to stay the night with Dash. I was walking in the direction of the downtown when someone grabbed my shoulder. I spun around, ready to wield my dukes if necessary.

"Onalee, stop. Marie and I have an idea."

"What is it? She's completely full and so is the other motel." An eddy of snow picked up by a gust of wind whipped into our faces. *Maybe Plan C could be that the wind would blow the snow clouds out of here?*

He still held my shoulder. "I know. This isn't a great plan, but it will work. My room has two beds in it." He gave me a meaningful look.

"No. Oh, no." I pulled away from him.

He let me go, and I started to walk away. "Come on Onalee. It makes the most sense. It's no big deal, really. I promise I won't a-Costas you," he said and grinned.

I stopped. "Is that one of your standard lines?"

He cocked his head. "Nope, I reckon I never have used it afore, little lady, but it seemed right for this here occasion."

"Are you channeling John Wayne, or something?"

He ignored that remark. "Onalee. There aren't a lot of options. It's really no big deal. That is . . . unless you snore. Do you?"

"No. Do you?"

"Not as far as I know." He was smiling.

It was beginning to look like I had my Plan C. C for Camille. C for Costas. C for catastrophe. I sighed. "Okay."

Back at the B and B, Marie welcomed us warmly. "I'm so glad Camille suggested that solution. Since you guys are old friends, it just makes sense." Marie handed me a second key.

Old friends? Where did she get that idea? Since I now had a warm, dry area in which to cool my heels, I thought I'd make use of it. I removed my jacket and boots, and went into the living room. Seated in an armchair in front of a blazing fire, I called Marti. She said it was snowing hard in Petoskey, too, and that she'd be glad to stay the night with Dash. Mercifully, we ended the call without any questions about B and B logistics. If my luck held out, I might just be able keep this whole ugly incident on the down-low. I made four other calls, and was able to speak to one person. I got good information for my appraisal, but gathered nothing about Mr. Stone.

The next time I looked out the window, darkness was falling as the snow continued its onslaught. I heard the clamor of someone galloping down the stairs. Looking up, I saw Mr. Costas. *My roommate. Arghghghghrgh.*

"Hello there. I'm about to head into town for some dinner. You interested?"

I was feeling peckish and had been for some time. I'd had a dinner several months before with the Detective and it hadn't been too objectionable. There had been other people present, however. He waited as I dithered.

"Sure, that would be nice." I got up, "I just need to put my briefcase up in my, um. I mean the room." I scampered upstairs, unlocked the door and looked in. There were, indeed, two beds, and they were across the room from each other, as far apart as they could possibly be given the contours of the space. It looked like Costas had already staked out a bed so I used the other.

On went all of our outerwear and we were off. The snow had obliterated all of our tracks. We must have logged another three or four inches. *Where are my cross-country skis when I need them?* Making companionable small talk, we waded through the snowy streets. We stopped at a grocery store because I needed to buy a tooth brush and tooth paste. Costas disappeared as I wandered the aisles in my quest. As I was paying for my purchases, he plunked a bottle of wine on the counter. *Hmmm.*

The restaurant was more crowded than when Marti and I had been here. It must have been because of all of us strandedees. Our dinner conversation was light-hearted, masking the unanswered questions lurking beneath our superficial cordiality. We split the bill, not quibbling over the difference (his was fifty eight cents more), and left a good tip.

The wind had picked up while we were at dinner and we found ourselves in the midst of a good old fashioned blizzard. Once again, our footsteps had disappeared. Walking with our heads bent into the wind, we pushed our way up the street. Visibility was near zero as the driving snow partially obscured the buildings on either side of the road. It was exhilarating. I heard laughter.

"This is the best storm we've had in years," Costas said and skipped away. He reached down, scooped up some snow and threw it at me. Stunned by this surprising glimpse of Costas the boy, his shot hit my arm. I bent down and grabbed some snow of my own. It was too cold for good packing snow, but I molded it as well as I could and lobbed it at the Detective. As soon as the projectile left my hand, I snagged another fistful of snow. This time I ran straight at him as his snow bombs ricocheted around me. At short range I feinted to the left then tossed one at his head. Bull's eye!

"Uncle." Costas cried.

What sweet music to my ears. Maybe Marti will hear the tale of this adventure after all.

"Must I remind you that I'm packing heat?"

"Oh. I forgot about that."

"Hey, it's so beautiful out, do you want to keep walking for a while?"

I looked at him. His eyes were shining. *Holy metamorphoses.* "Sounds good to me."

We tromped through drifts of snow for about an hour and finally made our way back to thaw our frigid fingers and toes. Inside the B and B, was a small fire not much more than coals. But Marie had laid in a supply of firewood. Placing a log on the embers and using the bellows, I brought the flames back to life. Now, all I needed was my book. Costas had gone upstairs. More than likely, he was in the same room as my book. *What to do.* The desperate reader lurking inside me won out. I scampered up the stairs and tapped lightly on the bedroom door. Costas opened it. "Hi. What's up?"

"I just need to get my book, then I'll be out of your hair."

"You brought a book up here when you weren't planning to stay all night?"

"I always have one on me. You never know when you might have a few free minutes here and there," I said. I slid past him and dug a book out of my briefcase.

He'd walked over to his bed. "Actually, I was just about to do the same thing." He held a book up. "What are you reading?"

"It's a mystery."

A feral grin split his face. "Of course it is. Does it have an amateur sleuth by any chance who comes to the aid of a local force of bumbling policemen?"

"Sounds like you've read a few of that genre."

"My sister introduced me to them after you and your fellow conspirator meddled in two of my cases."

Ooh boy. It is definitely tread lightly time if I am going to keep myself from getting kicked out and spending the night in a snowbank. "They are silly and not at all realistic, but also lighthearted and fun to read. What are you reading?"

He looked a little sheepish. "Wild."

"By Cheryl Strayed?"

"That's the one. Have you read it?"

Mr. Macho Costas is reading about a woman's adventures? "Yup. It's a great book. Almost every woman I know has read it, or at least seen the movie."

Costas crossed his arms. "Meaning it's not suitable reading material for a guy? I love reading stories of personal courage. Women possess it just as much as men do, probably more."

"You're right. Anyway, I'm going downstairs. The fire is going pretty good now."

I went to the most comfortable easy chair and positioned it even closer to the fire. Then I added an ottoman in front of it. Now all that was missing was my favorite dog and my pajamas. Instead, a few minutes later, the detective came down.

"May I join you?"

"Of course. Pull up a chair. I'm sorry if I sounded snarky earlier."

He smiled. "That's okay. Truce?"

Hot Fudge

"Sounds good."

"And I've got a bottle of wine and two glasses. You in?"

We sat in front of the fire with our feet up reading and sipping the cabernet. It was surprisingly pleasant. I was starting to get a little drowsy when all of a sudden the front door burst open, and two couples came in laughing and stomping snow off their feet. After taking their coats off they swarmed to the living room, drawn to the fire. They were talking about playing cards until they saw us.

"Hello. We didn't see you," one of the ladies said. She looked back at her companions. "We don't want to disturb these two love birds, do we?"

Costas and I looked at each other. "No, no. We're just reading. There's room for everybody. You can play games or whatever you want," Costas said.

They exchanged more glances.

"Actually, I'm fighting to stay awake and losing. I think I'll mosey on up to bed," I said, picking up my book.

Upstairs I brushed my teeth and washed up with the bottle of hand soap I'd found on the counter. I got into bed and was drifting off to sleep when

Costas stole in. He rustled around in his bag, left for a few minutes, came back and climbed into his bed. That was the last thing I remembered.

Hot Fudge

Chapter Ten

The sound of a door softly opening, awakened me. *Who was in my room?* Then I remembered where I was. Apparently, what I'd heard was Costas going out, I was alone, and it was already nearly eight o'clock. Way past time to get up. I rolled out of bed, fully dressed. *What a time saver.* Then again, my slacks and sweater might not have looked slept in, but I sure felt rumpled. After rudimentary ablutions, I clambered down the stairs. Costas was at the dining room table, drinking coffee.

"Good morning," he said, smiling. "I figured you'd already be up and about by now. Doesn't that handsome dog of yours wake you up?"

"Actually, he's kind of a slugabed, but we usually are up before this."

Maria walked in just then with a steaming mug of coffee and jug of half and half. "I heard you pound down the stairs. How about oatmeal and honeyed blackberry scones for breakfast?"

I felt saliva form. "I think I need to move in here permanently."

She grinned, set my coffee down and hustled back to the kitchen.

"You know, that's not a half bad idea. This would be a great place to practice law enforcement. Besides, have you looked outside, yet? We may be up here 'til spring."

I savored the coffee a minute before answering. "You've got to be kidding me."

He shook his head. "In some ways I wish I were." He picked up his mug and looked directly at me. "But in other ways, this has been an unexpected pleasure."

My face heated up and I was at a loss for words. Just then, we both looked towards the stairs as the group from last night came bouncing down. They circled the table finding open chairs and issuing cheery good mornings. A round of first name introductions was made.

"Have you seen it outside? I think we're snowed in again," the dark-haired lady Cheryl said, laughing.

"We're up here celebrating their twenty-fifth wedding anniversary," Sandra added. "How long have you two been married?"

Hot Fudge

"Us? Um, no. We're not an us." I could hear the squeakiness of my normally dulcet voice. Panic will do that to you.

Sandra's cheeks were as red as mine must have been. "Oh, sorry. I thought—"

Costas laughed. "We're friends from the same town and both happened to get stranded here yesterday."

"I sure hope we didn't keep you up last night with our carousing," John said, shifting the subject to safer ground.

"As soon as I hit my pillow, I was out," Costas said.

Other than the fact that there were only two scones apiece, the rest of the breakfast went smoothly. Marie told us she wasn't expecting any new guests that night so we could leave our belongings in our rooms until we were able to get a flight out. I for one, hoped it would be sooner rather than later. I found a quiet spot and called Marti. She and Dash were in mid walk on the beach. She assured me she could stay the night again if I couldn't get back. *What a great friend.*

I went upstairs. The door was open and our room was empty. I searched through my briefcase and pulled out my legal pad. The two people I'd left messages for hadn't called back, but I had another source of local knowledge. I scampered back down the stairs. Marie was banging pots and pans in the kitchen. I knocked on the door and heard, "Come in."

Looking up from the kitchen sink she called over to me. "What can I do for you?"

"I've got a couple of questions. Do you know Bill Reneveere?"

"Sure do. Why?"

"I wanted to talk with him if he's still on the island and available."

She looked at me quizzically. "He is. Just a sec."

She opened the door to the private area of the house. A minute or so later she returned, holding a rolodex. She looked sheepish. "I know this is dating me, but I still have one of these things." She smiled. "Okay, actually, I have two of them. One for friends and family, one for business contacts. Please don't let this get out."

"They don't call me Low Tech O'Conner for nothing. I have three of them."

Marie's eyebrows arched in appreciation. "Wow." She flipped through until she found the right page. "So, what do you need?"

"I have a phone number for him, but I think it's a landline."

She disengaged the page and handed it to me. "Go ahead and take down any of this information you need."

I jotted down a second phone number and an address. "Do you think he's home now?"

She nodded. "With this snow, there's a pretty good chance he is."

"As long as you've gone to all the trouble of getting that out, is Rod McCormick in there?"

"He should be," she said cranking the file around to the "M" entries. "Yup. Here."

"Thanks." I quickly copied down his phone numbers and addresses. "How about him? Would he also be home?"

"Probably, but he might be at his store. Sometimes he paints and does other work there in the off season. Can I ask what all this is about?"

I told her I was appraising a property on the island.

She grinned. "Everybody knows that, but why would you want to talk with those two?"

"Then you probably also know that McCormick wants to sell his building."

"Yup and Eduardo Soarez and Robin Stone are both, or I guess were both, hot to buy it. So I can see why you might want to talk with him, but why Bill?"

I told her about Marti being at Ed's fudge shop when Stone died.

"How awful for her."

"It was. And hard on Ed and his business."

"I guess."

"The upshot is that we're looking into the murder a bit."

Marie chuckled. "Amateur sleuths. I love it. I read about people like you all the time. But isn't it scary?"

I nodded. "It can be. What do you know about those two men?"

"Bill is a good friend, and what Stone did to him was unconscionable." She shook her head. "That restaurant was his life. He ran a good, clean operation. He treated his customers and his employees well. He paid good wages, and gave back to the community. I could go on and on. We all just stood by basically powerless and watched him get driven out of business by Mr. Moneybags, Heart of Stone Stone. Actually, several of us talked to Stone about it, but we didn't get anywhere."

"That's terrible." I paused. "I hate to ask this, but do you think Bill could have been upset enough to kill Stone because of it?"

"Bill? No. He is the nicest guy you'll ever meet." She thought for a minute. "I have to say though, he does have a strong motive." She smiled, "I guess you'll have to check his alibi, eh? You can tell him you're a friend of mine."

"Thanks. How about Rod McCormick?"

"I can't imagine he'd want to knock off one of his buyers in a bidding war."

"No, I mainly wanted to talk with him about the offers and if his building actually sold."

"For your appraisal."

"Mostly, though I might stray into other topics as well, should they come up. And I guarantee you they will." I paused. "Marie, remember when we were here before you told us that the flag flies at half staff when someone from the island dies?" She nodded. "Stone had property here, did the flag fly at half mast for him?"

She smiled. "That's a good question. When we heard he'd died, Ron the postmaster called a few island movers and shakers to discuss what we should do. One opinion was that the flag was kind of a way to get news out to people and it should be done for Stone. Other people thought that since he wasn't well liked here, it would be hypocritical to honor him. The flag wasn't lowered."

"Wow, that's telling." Marie nodded again. I thanked her for her information, tried to talk her into letting me help with the kitchen clean up and got nowhere, but did get her marvelous recipe for scones. I went back up to the room for my briefcase, put on my boots, hat, and gloves, and went out into the snowy world. I was relieved that no one was around to ask questions about my destination, but I did wonder about the whereabouts of Mr. C.

Rod McCormick's house was closest to the B and B, and since my main purpose for coming to the island was allegedly for the appraisal, I went there first. By the time I knocked on his door it was almost ten o'clock,

Hot Fudge

late enough to be socially acceptable for house calls at least in most circles. A minute or so later the door was opened by a man who looked to be in his mid to late sixties. I introduced myself.

He nodded. "The gal who phoned yesterday. I was just about to call you back. Come in, it's snowing to beat the band out there."

"Thanks."

After removing my boots, he ushered me into his living room. We both chose chairs near his fireplace.

"It's a good day to sit by the fire, but not good for much else," he said.

I smiled. "It's quite the storm. I couldn't get a flight out yesterday."

"You're not the only one. My wife went to Petoskey for a doctor's appointment yesterday and is stranded in Mackinaw City. She couldn't even get back across the bridge yesterday. Now, in your message you said you're an appraiser?"

"Yes." I handed him my card. "People have mentioned that you were trying to sell your building on Main Street."

"That's right, and I have an offer on it, but it hasn't closed yet." He looked at me. "Are you appraising my building?"

I shook my head. "No. Is your buyer getting bank financing?"

"Yes, that's the main thing, I suppose, that we're waiting for." Again, he looked directly at me. "Do you know the story?"

"I've heard things, but I'd love to hear what you have to say about it."

"Sharon my wife, and I decided to sell the building. Our kids have good careers on the mainland and didn't want any part of coming back here to live. Sharon told her friend Angie who happened to mention it when she was having coffee at a little shop in Petoskey. The owner, Ed overheard them and the very next day he came to my restaurant to see me. He and I talked and I liked the young fellow. We both keep up on real estate values and we came to an agreement pretty quickly. So I never listed it. A real estate lawyer friend of mine wrote up a purchase agreement and by the close of business the next day, Ed had applied for a loan.

"Everything was fine and dandy until word got out," he smiled, "as it always does on this island. Up popped Robin Stone with a much higher offer.

"I didn't know what to do. I had an agreement with Ed and I like to think I'm a man of my word. But my wife and I are not wealthy people, and the additional money sure would have come in handy in our retirement. I talked it over with our lawyer and he told me Ed could sue me if I backed out of our contract." He shook his head. "I wouldn't have left him high and dry anyways. But there are other buildings and I knew that Stone really wanted this one because it sits right between two he already owns.

"So, I called Ed. I thought if I gave him some money he'd be willing to let me out of our deal. Unfortunately, he wouldn't do it. Although he did say he'd look around and if anything else was available and it worked for him, he would. I heard he did ask around, but I guess either the prices were too high," he tilted his head towards me. "Stone's buying spree has driven prices up, as you've probably heard. Or the location, or the building wasn't right. I also think the size and layout of my building appealed to Ed."

"Was Mr. Stone willing to let it go?"

McCormick laughed. "You obviously didn't know Robin Stone."

I shook my head. "No. I was around him once, but that was it."

"I've known a lot of very rich people in my time, and a lot of them were nice, genuine folks. But I've never known a billionaire and maybe that's the difference. The guy thought his money entitled him to anything he wanted in life. He didn't care who he had to walk over to get it."

"I haven't talked to anyone yet who had anything good to say about him. So, did he retaliate?"

He nodded. "He tried to talk me into backing out of the sale, and I'd heard he was leaning on Ed, too."

"Was that it?"

"He told me if I sold to him, he'd pay any legal fees and settlement if Ed sued me. I also believe he was behind a smear campaign against Ed." He glowered "You know Ed, short for Eduardo, is Hispanic, right?"

"I do."

"Out of nowhere I began to hear rumors that he was involved in a human trafficking ring. As you probably know some of that goes on in Michigan because of our proximity to Canada and the fact that there are just lakes and rivers for the border between our two countries. What with

Ed being a Hispanic as well as an outsider to the island, people were more than willing to believe it. I can't prove that Stone was behind that rumor, but I'm willing to bet that he was. The next thing I knew, other islanders were trying to talk me out of selling to Ed."

"What did you do?"

"Talked it over with the wife." He smiled. "She was mad as a hornet. She thinks Ed is a really nice guy, and said that Stone was being a bully and a racist. She said we'd sell to him over her dead body." He gave me a wry grin. "Kind of unfortunate turn of phrase as it turned out."

"Are you still under contract with Ed then?"

"Yup. For the originally agreed upon price and that's fine. We didn't need to make a boatload on the jacked up price Stone would've given us."

"When do you expect to close on the sale?"

"I don't know. I guess one of the big question marks is whether Ed goes to prison for Stone's death."

"Is that who you think did it?"

"As I said, both the wife and I like Ed. But I don't know. It seems like Stone really gave him a rough time." He chuckled. "I sure hope I didn't lose two bona fide buyers in one fell swoop."

"Yeah, I hope you didn't. What about other people Stone might have riled up?"

"Have you heard about Ed Reneveere? He owned a taco restaurant for many years until Stone ran him out of business."

"I'd heard about that. It sure seems like he has a motive."

"It does, but I just can't imagine him doing something like that."

"Anybody else?"

"He was murdered in Petoskey not on the island. Maybe you should be looking for suspects down there. Why are you so interested in this?"

I told him about my friend Marti working for Ed and being present at Stone's death.

He reached for my card where he'd laid it on the table and studied it. "You're from Petoskey?"

"Yes."

"Was Stone making trouble down there as well?"

"Other than upsetting Ed, I don't think so. I haven't heard of his buying up buildings around town like he was doing here."

There was a knock on the door. McCormick had a puzzled look on his face. "I never get visitors this time of year. Who in the blazes could that be?" He got up and went to the door. I heard muffled conversation then a cold breeze. I looked up as my roomy strode in.

Chapter Eleven

"It's funny. The young lady here and I were just discussing Mr. Stone. Have a seat, Detective and I'll answer any questions I can for you."

Mr. Costas was giving me a pointed look, but then again it probably matched my own glare. *What was he doing here? Had he followed me? Anyway, message received Mr. Costas. I'll give you some privacy.* After glancing at my card again, McCormick was starting introductions. "We're acquainted," I said, "and I've taken up enough of your time. Thank you so much." I scrambled to my feet. Mr. McCormick rose and walked me to the door.

"Can you tell me what the two offers were for your building?" I asked him on the way.

He smiled. "You've got more questions than Hog Island has snakes. I'm sorry, but I think I'm going to have to keep that under my hat until it closes. But I will tell you then, if you want to call me."

Hot Fudge

It was still storming too much for any flights out so I decided to pay a visit to Bill Reneveere. He lived on the outskirts of Harrisonville so I walked through downtown and up the long hill toward the Grand Hotel and beyond to the small town where many of the year-round islanders live. As I got closer, I could hear the steady sound of someone shoveling snow. It was a man clearing the walkway of a house next to Reneveere's. I walked up on Bill's porch and twisted the knob of an old fashioned doorbell. The wooden front door had a curtained window. Peering in, I didn't see any lights on and didn't hear eager feet pounding to answer my summons.

"Hello. What can I do for you?" I jumped. The shovelist had come up behind me. "Sorry ma'am. Didn't mean to scare you," he said smiling.

I struggled to regain my lost aplomb. "Hi, I was looking for Mr. Reneveere."

"You've found him. Bill's the name." He stuck out his hand.

I introduced myself as we shook hands. I told him I was doing an appraisal and was looking for leasing information.

"I did rent a building on Main Street for many years but I don't anymore."

"Oh. You don't? I guess I have old information," I said, being slightly less than completely honest, but all in the name of good amateur sleuthmanship. "I might still be able to use some of the facts, though." I wanted to get him talking about his shop and Stone.

"I guess I could use a break. Want to come in?"

Nice guy but also a man with a motive. And a heavy duty shovel. "I won't keep you too long and I don't want to tromp into your house with all this snow on my boots. Can you just tell me a little about the lease? I don't know much about it."

"I had a taco restaurant and I was renting about a thousand square feet. It was a great location and I'd been there for almost twenty years."

"Did you retire?"

He gave a short bark of laughter. "No, I kind of got forced out of business."

I put a puzzled look on my face. "How'd that happen?"

Hot Fudge

He leaned against the porch railing. "Someone with way more money that I had, was willing to practically give tacos away until my business dried up to nothing."

"That's terrible."

Shrugging his shoulders he said, "Oh, I don't know. What the guy did was legal and maybe it was the best thing that ever happened to me."

"Really? You're not mad?"

"I was, but there was nothing I could do. After it was all over and he bought some of my equipment, actually offered me a fair price for it, I got a nine to five job. I've got way less hours and no more stress."

"It's great that you have such a good attitude."

"It's a lot healthier. In fact, I'm a lot healthier than the poor guy who did it. He's dead as a doornail now and it seems he was killed. You probably heard about it if you're from around here."

"I might have. What was the man's name?"

"Robin Stone. It happened in a fudge shop in Petoskey."

"I did read about it. That was the guy?"

"Unfortunately it was. He set up his taco place just down the street from mine. He sold his product well below cost and undercut me. None of us could figure out why. If he'd competed fairly, there would've been enough business for everybody," he said heaving a sigh.

"That's a shame. Is his restaurant still open?"

"Of course, but it'll cost you a whole lot more now to buy a taco from him."

"I guess that's why he did it, eh? Get rid of the competition?"

"Seems that was a small part of it."

"Just a small part?"

"Yup. Before he'd opened his restaurant, he approached me and asked me to move my operation further down the street. I told him no, I needed to be close to the ferry docks. Jerry, my landlord and long-time friend, told me that Stone also tried to get him to either sell him the building or evict me so he could have the space. Jerry wouldn't do either one, though maybe if he had I'd still be in business." He shrugged his shoulders. "Oh well."

"Since you wouldn't move, Stone drove you out?"

"That's about the size of it."

"After you left, did he move in?"

"Oh yeah. He had a kind of one stop food shop. There was a deli, ice cream, frozen yogurt. It was designed to fill the bellies of the never-ending stream of hungry visitors just disembarking from the ferries. And fill the bank account of Mr. Stone. Ya gotta kind of admire his vision, I guess."

"But now he's dead. Got any idea who did it?"

"I'm sure I'm a suspect. A cop was up here again yesterday asking questions."

"But you're innocent?"

He grinned. "Absolutely."

"Even though the cops think otherwise?"

"Well," he looked up, scratching his chin, "there are a couple of . . . shall we say, thorny issues."

Thorny issues? We were out in the open but there was absolutely no one on the streets. And there was that shovel. I have nothing but my wits, which I don't care to see splattered all over this beautiful white snow. I edged further away from him. "Like what?" He noticed my subtle shift out of harm's way and caught my eye.

"Like the fact that I don't have an alibi. As a matter of fact I was in Petoskey when it happened. Also, around the time my business closed, I was pretty hot under the collar. I might have said some things I shouldn't have."

"Really? What did you say?"

He smiled again. "I'd rather not tell you. It doesn't reflect very well on me. Anyway, you came here for leasing information, not all this soap opera stuff." He told me what he'd paid for rent and also gave me the leasing terms. *Someone who treats appraisers this well couldn't be a murderer.* I thanked him and made my way past him, off the porch. At the road I turned back to wave, but he was on his phone.

The sky was brightening and a patch of blue shown through the trees. I called the airport and was told that it looked good for a flight in about thirty minutes. After that, I called Maria. I'd already paid for my half of the room for last night, but I wanted her to know I probably wouldn't be back. I was only about three-quarters of a mile from the airport and could walk. Throwing in a bit of esprit de corps, I asked her if she would tell Costas that a flight out looked likely. She told me he was already on his way. We ended the call and I power-slogged along the snowy roads. As I neared the airport, I heard the whine of the plane flying in. *Uh oh.* I muscled through the drifts even faster. After a few minutes, I pushed through the terminal door.

Chapter Twelve

"We knew you were coming and were going to wait as long as we could," the airport manager said, smiling as he watched me gasping for air. Costas, leaning against the counter, also took in the show.

Moments later, we walked back out on the runway and climbed up into the plane. It was just the pilot, Costas, and me. The detective turned to me. "Did you get all of your 'work' done?" He asked in a voice tinged with nastiness. Gone was last evening's thin veneer of bonhomie.

"Yes. Thank you for asking. However, I found it odd that you showed up at the McCormick house right after I did. Is it police procedure to follow law-abiding citizens around?"

"Only when said citizen is sticking his or her nose into an ongoing investigation."

"For your information, I'm appraising a property on the island and I was up here gathering comparables."

"Huh. That's funny, because I got a call from a Mr. Bill Reneveere. Do you know him?"

"Yes. We're acquainted."

Costas nodded. "He mentioned a certain woman who knocked on his door today to grill him for information regarding Robin Stone."

"In the course of my obtaining leasing data, Mr. Stone's name did come up. In fact, I'd like to make you aware of some facts I learned in our discussion. Stone drove Reneveere's taco restaurant out of business. Also, he told me he was in Petoskey at the time Stone died. Oh, one other thing. He mentioned he'd said some things he shouldn't have when his business went under. He wouldn't tell me what he'd said."

Costas stared at me as I jabbered. "You don't think—"

The pilot turned to us. "We're ready for takeoff." The plane taxied down the runway, gathering speed. As I watched out the window, we left earth. *What a miracle airplanes are. . . especially when they're cleared to fly.*

Costas turned from the window. "Thank you for sharing. Is there anything else you'd like to mention?"

"Yes. I'd like to know if Stone was poisoned and if so, with what?"

"Yes, but what the poison was, I'm not at liberty to say."

"So you do know?"

"We got the toxicology report back, yes."

"Was it the fudge that did him in?"

"Sugar is very bad for you, you know and artificial sweeteners aren't the answer either. Willpower is the best way."

I sighed. "In other words, you're not going to divulge anything."

"I wouldn't say that, but you go first. Tell me all you know."

"I just did." The plane was already descending.

"You told me nothing new."

"Oh. Since you tailed me to McCormick's, I imagine you know all about the fight between Stone and Ed Soarez over his building."

"I've known about it for some time."

"That's about it for me. Wait." I snapped my fingers. "The fudge Stone was eating was peanut butter."

"It's my favorite flavor."

We touched down. "Mine, too."

Hot Fudge

After we'd climbed out of the plane, the pilot turned to us. "Looks like we just made it. Snow's closing in again."

Looking up I saw fast-moving grey clouds overtaking us.

We thanked him and walked together to the parking lot. "Thanks for letting me stay in your room last night."

"Anytime. Now, drive safely."

We both started our cars, turned on the defrosters, and spent the next ten minutes pushing snow off our vehicles and then scraping the ice caked windshields. Despite my best efforts, Costas finished his ice and snow removal first. He came over with his scraper and started on my side windows. With the two of us working, the job was soon completed.

"Thanks, but you never did tell me anything about the murder."

"There's no time for idle chitchat. If we don't get a move on we won't get across the bridge before they close it again."

The wind swirled around us, but I didn't think it was strong enough to warrant a bridge closure. On the other hand, the detective was nothing if he wasn't one quick bunny. He was already halfway to his car. I got in mine and rolled slowly out of the parking lot, making sure Costas was also on his way. It wasn't that I was particularly concerned about him, but in our cold northern winters it is always a good idea to watch out for whomever you're with.

We drove through town and up to the bridge tollbooth. A few minutes later, I could feel the car rock a bit as I maneuvered over the pavement hanging high over the frozen Straits of Mackinac. Before we got to the south side the snow was falling again, and the drive home was slow going. An hour later, as I turned off the highway to go home, I saw the Costas-mobile in my rearview mirror driving on by.

As soon as my car pulled into the driveway I heard riotous barking from inside the house. This was only the second time Dash and I had been separated since we'd become a team. I ran up the porch stairs, threw open the door and almost got bowled over by sixty-five pounds of black fur and big heart. *How did I ever get along before Dash?* Marti was standing a few steps back, enjoying the scene. "Marti, thanks so much for staying with my boy."

"It was fun. We got a lot of walks and playtime in. I took the liberty of ordering pizza. It should be here any minute."

"Great. I'm starved."

"Did you get any intel on our case?"

I looked up from unlacing my boots. "I was on the island because of my appraisal."

"Yeah, right. Even if you didn't, I did," she said looking smug. Just then the doorbell rang setting off another round of poodle-speak. Marti reached for her purse. I argued, but as she pointed out, she's eaten many a meal under the roof of chez-O'Conner. She asked the pizza man in and paid him. After he left she said, "It wasn't snowing so hard when I placed the order, or I wouldn't have done it. I don't like asking the delivery people to come out on the road on nights like this."

"But you gave him a big tip?"

"Absolutely. Now let's eat."

Dash bolted down his kibbles and then polished off a couple bites of pizza for dessert. Meanwhile Marti told me about her sleuthing efforts. She'd been able to track down the ex-Mrs. Stone and Junior Stone who were both living in Petoskey. She'd tried to talk with them but they hadn't been home when she'd visited.

"Why is the ex living here?" I asked and then bit into a gooey morsel of the pie.

"Because their son loves the north. He graduated from high school last year and is going to the local college according to my sources. Also the first Mrs. Stone is from here."

"Who are your sources?"

Marti eyed me. "Frank."

"Fiancé Frank?"

"None other. It turns out that Mrs. Ex-Stone grew up down the street from Frank. She's older but she used to hang out with Frank's brother."

"So that's the Petoskey tie. Somehow I just assumed it was the current Mrs. Stone. How'd you find this out?"

Marti was pulling another slice from the box. "Frank and I were discussing the case. I showed him my list of suspects, of which there are a few more now, not just Ed. That's when he told me about Maureen."

"Is he in contact with her?"

"I don't think so, but his brother has been."

"What does Frank say about her?" I ate the last delicious bite of pizza.

"He likes her. Said that even though she was quite a bit older, she was always very nice to him and the other younger kids. He admitted he used to have a crush on her."

"It's too bad it's so stormy. Otherwise we could go over there tonight and try to catch her home. Does their son live with her?"

"I don't know, but I think so. On, I hate to run, but I need to get some things done at my place."

After Marti left, I cleaned up the kitchen and took Dashiell out. It was still blowing and snowing. According to the second law of Dashology: the farther down the mercury plummeteth, the longer it shall taketh for a leg lift. He is such a nice dog in numerous ways, but he, like so many of us, apparently harbors a small mean streak. I was chilled to the bone by the time we reached home. Marti had called to tell me she'd gotten through the blizzard to her apartment in one piece. I built a lovely fire and Dash and I stretched out in front of it for a couple of hours before turning in.

The following day, Saturday, was cloudy with no snow and calm winds. I clamped on my cross-country skis and Dash and I entered the county park. According to Marti, it had rained briefly before changing to snow and in the woods, everything was white. The trees were bowed over into fantastic shapes, arches of white lace in every size. Branches and some small trees had fallen under the weight of the ice and snow. The trail which is basically level nine months of the year, was now a series of hills and valleys of snow. It was our own personal snowly-coaster. Dash and I made our way to the end and circled back around. All of a sudden, I saw an animal dart out from the underbrush and heard, "Riley. Riley. Come."

"It's okay Susan, Riley's with us," I yelled as Dash ran to meet his friend. Susan skied around a clump of trees and into sight. After greetings, she turned around and skied back with me. As the two dogs played we caught up on each others' lives. We'd been friends almost since I'd adopted Dash, but we didn't really know much about each other. I was aware that she was single and seemed to have flexible hours since I'd run into her during the day when we were both taking our dogs on their outings. She lived in a cute house about a mile away from me. But I knew nothing else. I set out to expand my knowledge.

"I haven't seen you and Riley much lately. Have you been busy?"

"No more than usual, but we don't come here on the days I work."

"That explains it. Where do you work?"

"I'm a nurse at the hospital."

"So you work twelve-hour shifts?"

"You've got it. My neighbor walks the Wiley One around the block, so the poor guy doesn't have to wait hours and hours for me to get home." She stopped and scooped up after her dog. "Hey, I've got a question for you, now. Wasn't Marti working at Lupita's?"

"She was."

"That's where the man was poisoned on fudge, wasn't it?"

"He died, but I don't think it's been established that the fudge did him in."

"That's what everyone is saying at work."

"What about the HIPAA laws?"

She smiled. "No, that's just gossip, not hospital intel. So what does Marti know about it? Are you two hot on the trail of the killer?"

Hmmm. How much was I at liberty to say? "She was working the day he died, but she doesn't know how it happened. I don't believe the police do either."

"So . . . are you two in sleuth-mode now?"

"We have nosed around a bit." I changed the subject before she could ask further questions.

Later at home, I talked with Marti before she drove down to Detroit for a family shower and a combination wedding shower and bachelorette party. I was still trying to talk her into a similar party up here, but we only had a week left.

Marti had made me promise not to contact the Stones until she got back, even though I was itching to do so. Instead I worked on the appraisal for awhile, then nosed around the internet to find out what I could about Mr. Robin Stone. He wasn't the richest hedge fund manager, but according to one website he had been worth $3.4 billion, that's "B" as in bodacious, as of 2017. His group was named AmeriRock Funds. I assumed it was a takeoff on his name Stone. It had been founded in the mid 1990's by Stone and his partner, Charlie Kemp. Kemp was the man whom Rene Arnault had thought of as Stone's muscle, but from what I could gather, he was every bit as instrumental as Stone in forming and running AmeriRock Funds. Many hedge fund investors lost boatloads of money in the financial institutions collapse of 2008. If Stone also lost money at that time, he had kept his head above water, in fact, $3.4 billion above water as of 2017.

It seemed that it ran in the family. Stone's great-grandfather had become wealthy during the Florida real estate boom of the 1920s and had managed to get out before the bust. His grandfather and dad were both real estate lawyers who lived in luxury in Denver. Stone was born and raised in The Mile High City but had gone to Harvard. There he'd met Kemp, who came from old east coast money. The two became friends and both moved to New York City and eventually accepted jobs in one of the early hedge funds.

Many, but not all of the articles I read, blamed hedge funds for being one of the primary causes of the financial collapse of 2008. As far as I could tell, Kemp and Stone's fund was never investigated for financial fraud. But even if everything had been well-managed, some of the investors in his fund had most likely lost money and maybe lots of it, during that time.

So, it's a pretty sure bet that Robin Stone and Charlie Kemp had a number of disgruntled investors on their hands. But the worst of the crisis was in 2008 and 2009. The economy began rebounding in 2010 and had been strong now for at least six years. It would seem that anyone who lost big bucks and was enraged enough to kill Stone, would have done so years ago. I didn't think I would find his killer in the midst of his investors.

Although I failed to find any major scandal attached to Stone's personal life, I did read that he was divorced about four years ago and re-married within the year to a much younger woman. There might be some lingering hard feelings there. Maybe we could add the first Mrs. Stone's name as a suspect. I had also added the taco stand owner, Bill Reneveere's name.

I worked on my appraisal for a couple of hours and then called Mrs. Willowby.

I asked her when she'd like to shop during the coming week.

"You're the working lady. I can go anytime, dear."

"How about Tuesday?"

"Absolutely. I'll make a note to myself. What time will you be picking me up, dear?"

"How would two o'clock work for you?"

"Two o'clock would be fine. I'll just fix myself a late supper that night."

This was sounding familiar. "Would one o'clock be better?"

"Oh, Onalee, that would be superb, but will that be satisfactory for you?"

"I would love to go at one," I said. I was getting a chuckle out of this backing and forthing.

On Monday, I spoke with two more property owners from Mackinac Island. I was able to confirm their purchase information and get more scuttlebutt on Stone. Maybe more than I wanted to know from one Mr. Les Richards.

"All summer long I watched that guy sitting in my bar, picking up young hotties. He'd buy them expensive drinks and dinners and when he eventually left, they'd be draped all over him. I tell you, it was night in and night out. Whenever he was on the island. Some of my bartenders got a big laugh over it but I kept thinking, 'so where's this guy's wife?'"

"Was Mrs. Stone ever around?"

"I never saw her. Of course he probably wasn't stupid enough to bring her to his personal meat market."

"Was Stone's partner, Charlie Kemp usually with him?"

"Once in awhile, but Kemp didn't play the same games. Seemed like he'd leave once the action got too hot for him."

"Wow, Stone sounds like a real piece of work."

"I know. I've seen pictures of his wife. Second wife, that is. She's a real stunner, but those rich guys, you know? They have everything, but it's never enough. Like what he was trying to do to the island, and driving poor Bill Reneveere out of business. Did you know about that?"

"Yeah, I had heard about it. Sounds like there might have been a few people who wanted him dead."

Les laughed. "Probably more than a few. You're from Petoskey. What are the cops down there saying about it?"

"They're keeping pretty close-mouthed about it, although they finally admitted they suspected foul play. Have you heard who might have done it?"

"Nah. There's been talk of course, but sadly it always gets back to Reneveere having the best motive unless it was a jealous girlfriend or husband no one knows about. But, I just can't for the life of me believe Bill capable of such a thing."

"That's what I keep hearing. Everybody seems to really like the guy."

"Oh yeah. Now, there is one other guy. That Mexican from your town. I heard he was a real shady fella."

"Actually, he is as American as you or I. He was born here, and his parents came from Puerto Rico. A friend of mine worked for him and really likes him."

Les lowered his voice. "What I heard isn't so nice. You'd better tell your friend, if it's a girl, to be careful. There's something about sex trafficking and that Mexican or Puerto Rican or whatever, is smack dab in the middle of it."

"I heard that same rumor and also that Robin Stone may have started it."

Les didn't seem to hear me. "I just hope she's careful. People come up to Northern Michigan to get away from all those gangs and violence. Anyway, I've got to run. Good luck."

It sounded like Stone's stories about Ed had found at least some believers. That was a shame, but maybe by the time he opened his shop on the island, people would know the truth. That is, of course, assuming he didn't kill Robin Stone.

Marti got back in the early afternoon. I thought she'd drop over right after my Hapkido class so we could go to the House of Stone. Any self-respecting amateur sleuth would have. But no, she was all a-flutter over her recent bachelorette party and showers and had to go directly to Frank's house to show him their gifts and tell him all about it.

The upshot was that, other than going out with Dash, I worked all day and just about finished the report.

Chapter Thirteen

I sent the appraisal out by eleven a.m. and planned to take the rest of the day off. At 11:05, Marti called. I swear that woman has psychic powers sometimes.

"Hi On. Get your report finished?"

"Just."

"Yeah, I figured without me around to lead you astray, you'd get a lot of work done. So, you're probably in desperate need of fun and relaxation, right?"

"What did you have in mind?" My voice might have sounded a tinge wary.

"We need to pay a little visit to the Stones."

"I'm taking Mrs. Willowby shopping and have to pick her up at one o'clock, and I'll need to walk Dash when I get back. We could go after that. What do you think?"

"Perfect. When should I be at your house?"

"I can pick you up on the way to the Stones'. Now tell me about the bachelorette party."

I got to Mrs. Willowby's house just before 1:00. I'm not a prompt person by nature but was making a concerted effort to curb my dallying tendency. The older people I've known tend to really dislike having to wait for anyone not on time. Just like last time, Mrs. Willowby had been watching for me and was making her way out the door. I jumped out of my car to help her down the porch steps. "Hi Mrs. Willowby."

"Hello dear. This is so nice of you. I wonder. . . you mentioned that we could do a few errands?"

"Sure can. Where would you like to go?" I asked as we walked carefully along the icy path.

"I'd like to just pop into the bank for a minute if I could. Actually, I go to the credit union."

"It's right on the way," I said. We had made it to the car and I opened the door for her. We motored across town to the credit union and Mrs. W. spent about fifteen minutes inside.

Back in the Honda she asked, "If it's not too much of an inconvenience, dear, I'd love to dart into the pharmacy now. You know, the one close to Foodrights."

"Do you mean Tennyson's?" I asked as we came upon it and I began to slow for a left-hand turn.

"Yes. This is it. I'll just scurry in here and won't be but a minute," she said, her grin rounding up her pink apple cheeks.

After Mrs. W. had popped, darted, and scurried, we proceeded directly to Foodrights and wound through each of the aisles. We learned from Fred in produce that the parsnips were a little past prime, and from Leona in baked goods that the store-made snicker doodles would melt on our tongues today. We both bought some. Brenda in checkout greeted Mrs. W. warmly just like she had last week. But then she made eye contact with me, smiled and said, "It's Onalee, right?"

I grinned back at her. "How did you remember?"

"You're bringing our star customer in and we all appreciate that."

"It's my pleasure, Brenda." When Mrs. Stirnaman returned and I was no longer ferrying Mrs. Willowby, I knew that I'd still enjoy shopping more now that I, too, was on a first name basis with the people who work there.

It was four o'clock by the time I picked Marti up. "So where to?" I asked. Marti knew the address of the Stones but had somehow never gotten around to telling me where they lived.

"Oh, that's right." She giggled. A hollow sound to these ears. "I guess I must've forgotten to tell you before I went downstate."

I eyed her narrowly. "Apparently. But you're here now, and I'm not going there without you. Also, as you know, I could've found out their address online, but I didn't even try since I'd promised you I wouldn't."

"Whatever. Anyway, they live on West Lake Street."

We pulled up in front of a two-story house situated between the street and Little Traverse Bay. The house was modest, at least by billionaire standards. After ringing the doorbell, we could hear footsteps coming towards us inside the house. The door swung open, and a teenage boy stood staring at us. He was sandy-haired and had large dark brown eyes.

Marti shot him her most fetching grin. "Hi. My name is Marti and this is my friend Onalee. You must be Robin."

"Um, yup, Rob."

Marti gave him a closer look. "Wait. Haven't I seen you before? I work at Lupita's."

Something sparked in Rob's eyes and he looked away from us. "Yeah, I go in there between classes sometimes."

"You're usually with that cute girl, Miss Double Peppermint Non-Fat Latte. But you get just a straight coffee."

He smiled. "That's us. But why—"

"We're not making a delivery, if that's what you're wondering. Actually, I was there when . . . when—"

Rob looked stricken and watching him, tears welled up in Marti's eyes. Somebody quicker on their feet would have come up with the perfect words of comfort. Instead, I said, "We just wanted to stop by and see if there was anything you and your Mom needed." It wasn't original, but the best I could do.

"Nah. We're okay." He pursed his lips. "It's not like he was father of the year or anything."

"Who's at the door, Robbie? Invite them in. It's freezing cold out there."

Robbie, who had looked over his shoulder, turned back to us. "Wanna come in?" He stepped aside as we entered, and sauntered out of the room.

The first Mrs. Stone was walking towards us, with a questioning look on her face.

Again Marti made the introductions and then added, "Frank Korstering sends his regards."

"How do you know Frank? And by the way, I'm Maureen Stone."

"I'm engaged to him."

Maureen nodded her head. "I heard he was finally tying the knot. That's great. He's a really good man."

Marti smiled. "Thanks. I sure think so. He has nice things to say about you, too. You were a friend of his older brother Mike, right?"

"Yes." She gave us a rueful smile. "The one who got away I guess." She looked hard at me. "You look familiar."

"I grew up here, too. I graduated from Petoskey High a couple of years before Frank."

Hot Fudge

"Then you were two years behind me. My maiden name was Bennet. So, what can I do for you ladies?"

Marti jumped in. "I just moved up here in January and got a temporary job at Lupita's."

"Oh. Were you—"

"I was there when it happened. I'm so sorry."

Maureen huffed some air. "No, no. That's okay. It's just that it was such a shock." She looked directly in Marti's eyes, "We've been divorced for some time and should have been divorced for many more years than that."

"Onalee and I are trying to find out who did it, so we thought—"

"Thought I or my son might be able to tell you something? We've both already talked with the police." She frowned. "Are you working with them, now?"

"No, though we have helped them out on occasion," I chimed in.

"Then why are you doing this?"

"As you know, it happened at Lupita's. The owner, Ed is a super nice guy and a prime suspect. Also, there are all kinds of rumors now about his store. We're just hoping to clear things up quickly so Ed can get his store back open and bringing in some money," Marti said.

We were still standing in the entryway, and it didn't look promising for an invitation to pull up a chair beside the hearth and rest our weary bones.

Maureen sighed and shook her head. "Everybody thinks I have it so good. I got millions of dollars in our divorce settlement and I get a very comfortable alimony. Not bad for a small town girl, eh?" She paused and seemed to be studying the hardwood floor. "But after our first few years of marriage, it was really bad. I think all the money Robin was making went to his head. I cannot begin to tell you how many times he cheated on me. He was a horrible husband and a much worse father. Robbie never measured up. He was never good enough to be the son of the 'great' Robin Stone. Then after the divorce, it was as if Robbie was all of a sudden my son not our son. Robin hardly ever took time to be with him. What is it with men? I don't understand how they can turn their backs on their own flesh and blood."

"No, it doesn't seem possible that a dad could abandon his children or not pay child support, but we all know that some of them do."

"But the man you're getting, Frank never would," she said to Marti.

"Thanks, though we're probably too old to have kids."

"Is Rob doing okay?" I asked.

"He says he is, but I don't really think so. He's always craved Robin's approval, but like I said, he wasn't worthy, according to his dad. I've always thought he was a wonderful boy. Kind. Thoughtful. Anyway, now no matter what he does or how far he goes in life he'll never get his father's 'atta boy' that should be his just for being who he is." She swiped her eyes with the back of her hand. "It breaks my heart. Anyway, I shouldn't be unloading on you two."

Marti stepped forward and gave her a hug. "We understand. You've been through a lot. Do you have a close friend or a minister you can talk things out with?"

"Remember I told you everyone thinks I have it so good? We moved back here two years ago. At first my old friends called me all the time, but I don't know. Their lives and mine are so different. They all work full time and have kids and husbands. I got the feeling that they resented the fact that I have a beautiful house on the bay and 'more money than God' as I was told my best friend from high school, Cathy, said. I haven't seen any of them for months. Actually Cathy is the only one of them who called when Rob was killed, but I think it was only to satisfy her own morbid curiosity. I haven't heard anything from her, or any of the rest of them, since."

"Does Rob have anyone he can talk with?"

"No. Not that I know of."

"He has a sweet girlfriend."

Maureen looked perplexed. "He does? How would you know that?"

"They've been in Lupita's together."

"Really," she said frowning.

"I liked seeing them coming through the door. They're both polite, friendly kids. You did a good job with him, Maureen."

She smiled slightly, then shook her head. "I do wish I could help you two in your quest, but I don't think I know anything. Obviously. I didn't even know my own son has a girlfriend."

"Kids that age. You remember. We told our parents as little as possible," Marti said.

Maureen nodded. "I guess you're right."

"We were wondering, was there anybody who had it in for him?" I asked.

"Besides me, you mean?" She laughed. "It was not a so-called 'friendly' divorce. If it had been up to him and his merry band of purloining lawyers, Robbie and I would've been left penniless. Unfortunately for him, my lawyer was equally tenacious when she could see that someone was going to get a raw deal. It also didn't hurt that the judge was a woman."

"Divorces ought to be fair to both parties," I said.

"That's the way I feel. I didn't want to take him for all he was worth, but the marriage was a partnership and I felt entitled to my and Robbie's fair share." She swallowed. "Anyway, you wondered who I thought might want him dead? He's ticked off a lot of people through the years."

"Anyone in particular?" Marti asked.

"Not that I know of, but we didn't discuss his business very much."

What about his partner, Charlie Kemp?" I asked.

"I wouldn't think so. They were always really close."

"Some of the people on Mackinac Island called him 'The Muscle,'" I said.

She nodded. "I could see that. He's big and burly and hardly ever talks, but Robin used to say that he was incredibly smart."

"Do you know him very well?" I asked.

"Um, yeah. Pretty well. I think he's a decent guy, on the whole."

"So you don't think he's a good suspect?"

She shook her head. "No. I can't imagine him hurting his best friend."

Interesting. But, they say that usually the person who murders you is a close family member or friend. Not getting anywhere with the Kemp line of inquiry, I changed the subject. "Did you know about Robin's ventures on Mackinac Island?"

"We were divorced by the time he started stirring up trouble there, but I'm afraid I was the one who introduced him to the place."

"Oh?"

"We were in Petoskey visiting my family one July Fourth. It was early in our marriage, but I recognize now that even then I was always on pins and needles, afraid that he'd be dissatisfied with anything related to me.

Hot Fudge

Anyway, on our second day here, I could tell he was getting bored with small town life and my parents, so I suggested we go to the island. Have you ever seen that place in July?"

I nodded, while Mart said, "No, I've only been there in the winter."

"All I can tell you is that it's insane. The streets are absolutely clogged with people and horses and bikes. Visions of perpetually ringing cash registers mesmerized Robin. He wandered around like he was in a daze and didn't want to leave. I finally talked him into taking the last ferry. Ever since then, every time we visited Petoskey, we had to go to the island."

"You don't know about his real estate dealings and businesses, there?" I asked.

"Of course I heard about that poor man he drove out of business, and I know that the islanders were up in arms about some of his ideas, but that's about it."

"What ideas didn't they like?" Marti asked.

"He was trying to buy up buildings to get large blocks of real estate. Then, I guess, he planned to demo them and put up fancy big multi-story developments."

"I can't imagine such a thing on the island," I said.

"No, neither could I or most of the islanders. But as you know, money talks and Robin had it by the steam shovel full."

"Would you think anyone on the island would kill him?"

"I assume a lot of the people up there are pretty happy he's dead, but I don't know that anyone, other than the taco guy he bankrupted would actually go so far as to kill him. Then again I'm not the best person to ask about that. I haven't spent much energy keeping up on his activities since we parted ways."

"You said you stayed in your marriage longer than you should have. I imagine it was because of Robbie?" Marti asked.

Watch your step Miss Intrusive Gonzalez. A good appraiser as well as an amateur sleuth must be inquisitive, but it can also land you in hot water, as I've found out in the past. But Maureen seemed glad to have someone to talk with, even a couple of Nosy Parkers like us.

"Yup. I wanted so much for him to have a stable home and a loving family, but I seemed to be the only one with that vision."

"What made you finally decide to give up?"

Hot Fudge

Maureen gazed at me a moment before speaking. "We were arguing a lot and our disagreements were becoming more and more heated. His constant cheating was eating at me, but it wasn't just that. He had turned into an overbearing, self-centered, egotistical, selfish bully. Besides, he was just plain mean."

"One night, he had been saying unkind things to Robbie as usual. Rob was thirteen at the time. I couldn't take it anymore and I just lit into him. He fired back. We'd both had a couple of glasses of wine and that didn't help. All of a sudden he hauled off and smacked me. Hard. I fell back and he was on me, hitting. Robbie had left the room but was watching and ran back to help me. Robin turned on him. I scrambled for the phone and called 9-1-1. When it was all said and done, Robbie had a broken arm and a bloody nose. I was battered and bruised, but that meant nothing to me. That jerk had hurt my baby. I filed for a divorce the next day."

"Of course because there was a child involved and so many assets, the legal battle took months and months."

"Did either one of you have second thoughts?"

"No."

I studied her, thinking she'd add to her abrupt answer.

Finally, she did. "During that time even more 'other women' came to light. One day Robin came to the door and asked if we could talk. Wow, I thought, he actually wants to apologize and get back together. But no. He was outraged at the sum of money my lawyer was asking for and was hoping to strike a better deal with his naive little wife. We got into another shouting match and I wound up calling the police on him again.

"Before I filed I'd always thought that Robbie would have a really hard time with a divorce. He's such a sensitive kid. But since we'd been separated, Robbie seemed more relaxed and happy. I guess he'd been on his own set of pins and needles. So, to answer your question, I never wanted to resurrect my sham of a marriage and I know Robin didn't either. He loved his freedom."

"Were you surprised when he got remarried?" I asked.

She thought for a minute. "Maybe a little bit, but remember, she's fifteen to twenty years younger than him and gorgeous. It has also occurred to me that he might want another shot at fatherhood, since he'd made his fortune and would be able to be with his family more. My guess is that he thought this time around maybe he'd get the aggressive, football playing, money hungry son he'd been denied with Robbie."

I shifted my weight.

Maureen noticed it. "I'm so sorry. Would you two like to come in and have a cup of coffee or something?"

Marti and I looked at each other. *So often at times like this I'm reminded of that song, "Too much, too little, too late."*

"Thank you so much, but we need to be on our way and let you get back to what you were doing." I said as Marti turned and opened the door.

Back in the car, she said, "That went a lot better than I thought it would."

I nodded. "It did, but she didn't really give us any leads."

"No, but we now know that he was physically abusive besides being a ruthless businessperson."

"What do you think about adding her and her son's names to our list of suspects?" I said and fired up the car.

"I'd hate to think that either one of them was guilty . . . but I guess you never know."

Connie Doherty

"I think that's the one thing we've learned in our escapades."

Hot Fudge

Chapter Fourteen

Before I dropped Marti off at her apartment, I tried once again to talk her into a shower and bachelorette party.

"On, we're not in our twenties, you know. Between all that Frank has and my stuff we don't need anything. On top of that I had those two showers downstate last weekend. A bachelorette party seems kind of silly up here because I really don't know anybody."

"What are Susan, Lacey, and I, chopped lettuce?"

She grinned. "I haven't seen those two since I moved up here. If you want to have some low-key get together, I think it would be fun."

"Your wedding is next Sunday. Are you going to have a rehearsal dinner?"

"I guess we would if there were anything to rehearse, but no. This is a no-frills event."

"How about Saturday, then? We'll have a small dinner at my place. Oh, and Saturday is the second day of the Petoskey Winter Sports Carnival. We could all go to that in the afternoon. By the way, can you take Mrs. W. shopping next week? I signed up for a continuing education class and will be in Gaylord on that day."

"Sure. I'd love to meet her after all you've said about her."

"If you want, I can invite her to your bachelorette party. I think she's kind of lonely, especially with her bosom buddy Mrs. Stirnamen being out of town."

"Do it."

***

I had decided to sleep in a little this morning since I'd finished my appraisal. When I finally opened my eyes, Dash's face was right next to my head, his eyes burning into mine. *Did he will me awake?*

When he saw me lift my head his stub of a tail quivered. I looked at my watch. "It's eight o'clock. It's not that late, Dash." I rolled over, away from him. He yelped. "All right," I grumbled and got up.

Hot Fudge

Once again, I skied and Dash ran through several inches of clean fresh snow, although at twenty degrees, it was warmer than most of our mornings had been lately. After our exercise and healthy breakfasts, Dash staked out an area in front of the woodstove and I set about calling people for the Marti Party. I left messages for Susan and Lacey. Marti and I had gotten to know Lacey as a fellow dog owner and walker last fall. She'd also been somewhat involved in the case we were sleuthing at the time. *Can you use the word sleuthing as a verb I wondered?*

On my third phone call, Mrs. Willowby said she'd be happy to attend, except she didn't know Marti.

"I know, but she's heard a lot about you and wants to meet you."

She giggled. "I've never been to a bachelorette party, Onalee. We didn't have such things when I was a girl. Hells bells, it was the depression."

"So you'll come?"

"I'd treasure the chance to come."

With Mrs. Willowby, there would be at least three of us, four if you counted Dash. Then again, he couldn't be counted since he was a male. But by the end of the day I'd gotten confirmations from Susan and Lacey.

Connie Doherty

I'd also started working on my next appraisal. It was a partial interest in an old cottage in the Cincinnati Club, another one of our tony lakefront associations. Most of the properties in this community were built around 1900 or earlier and were usually only occupied in the summer. They were often passed down through families, but children or later generations often each received instead of 100% ownership, only a partial interest of 50% or even much less with additional interests going to other family members.

I'd contacted the association's office and arranged to pick up a key for the day after tomorrow. I'd promised Marti that we would hunt down her old boss Ed tomorrow and find out what we could from him. She'd also gotten wind that Charlie Kemp was still in town, and hoped to talk with him.

"Shouldn't you be focusing on your wedding and future husband rather than murder and mayhem?" I'd asked her.

"My new parka and azure silk long underwear are on order and should be here any day now. As you know, I'm a perfect size six and my outfit should not need any altering."

Hot Fudge

"You're just repeating something we both heard in a movie, Ms. Six Plus."

"So what? I'll never get another chance to use it and it is a great line. On another note, who are you bringing to my wedding?"

"I'd like to save you and Frank the expense of one extra mouth to feed so I'm planning to make a solo excursion."

"Isn't it against the law to attend a wedding by yourself?" She snapped her fingers. "By golly, speaking of the law. I know one handsome available someone who is just waiting to be asked."

I emitted a heavy sigh. "Haven't you gotten your belly full of Mr. Law and Order Costas by now? He hasn't been at all nice to you, lately."

"I'm not the one he's got the huge crush on. Really, Onalee. Don't be obtuse. It's not attractive."

"I wouldn't have thought you, of all people, would turn into a Bride-zilla, but I guess no one is immune."

We cut the call short, but in retrospect, not as short as we should have, and Dash and I went out for our afternoon sojourn. Snow was falling softly. We were really having a lovely winter. A flicker of color caught my eye. I quickly turned just in time to watch a crimson cardinal flit into the shelter of a cedar tree. His red against the white snow and green boughs was stunning.

I thought about my conversation with Marti. *Why was she forever trying to foist the detective on me? Even when I had been quite smitten by an out of town real estate broker named Rick, Marti was pushing Costas. I have so much admiration for Marti. She's intelligent, but even better, she's smart, and she's as honorable as anybody I've ever known. There's just that one fatal flaw.*

Dash had accomplished his goal and it was time for me to use one of our biodegradable poop bags, turn back, and leave the Marti-Costas conundrum for another day.

That night I leafed through recipe files and cookbooks as I half-watched a few shows on television. Around 7:30, Marti called to say she couldn't take Mrs. W. shopping because she'd be on her honeymoon. How in the world had that slipped her mind? Perhaps at forty-three she was still too young to commit to marriage? All I could do was hope for the best and believe in a happily ever after for Frank and my bestie.

Hot Fudge

Marti also mentioned that Lupita's was going to be open next week. She'd told Ed she would work there again after her honeymoon

Chapter Fifteen

By ten o'clock the following morning, I was knocking on Marti's door. Inside, as I waited for her to get ready, I marveled again at human adaptability. For even the briefest of forays in winter, we took time for hats, boots, neck gaiters and coats, with added minutes spent on donning long underwear and snow pants for extra frigid days. And yet? We never gave it a thought or cursed this imposition on our valuable time. Then, in summer when we often sallied forth in little more than a tee shirt, shorts and flip flops, we didn't pause to consider how fortunate we were to be able to leave the house so quickly and easily. Marti laced up and tied her boots, shucked on her coat, and we were off.

Marti thought Ed would be at Lupita's so we walked over there. The door was locked, but we could see a light on. After banging on the door, Ed came and opened it. Stepping inside we could see that he had been busy. The walls were now a creamy yellow and there were framed scenes of colorful birds, palm trees and beaches. Ed stood before us in a tee shirt and jeans stained with yellow paint and a big grin on his face.

"Martina. What a wonderful surprise. Have you and your amiga, Onalee come by to help me paint?" He and Marti hugged.

"Hi Ed. It's so good to see you again."

"There is no fresh fudge or other sweets but I have just brewed coffee. Would you like some?"

"Absolutely," Marti said, smiling.

Ed had also rearranged the tables and chairs and there were now booths along one wall. We got our coffee and sat in one of the new seats. "I really like these booths, Ed. Who did you get to build them so quickly?" Marti asked.

Ed pointed to himself. "Me. I found it to be good therapy." A sad look clouded his face. "Are you doing okay, Martina, really?"

She nodded. "Yeah, but it seems strange being back in here."

"Exactly. I . . . I could have opened back up much earlier. And I should have, you know, for the money, but I just couldn't do it. When finally I got the idea to paint and to change the place I could make myself spend time here again. What do you think of it?"

We both said we loved what he'd done.

"And I'm not finished. I'm going to introduce many more colors. It will be wild."

We chatted for a while before bringing up our real reason for visiting. "Ed, I was appraising a building on Mackinac Island. I'm done with it now, but there will probably be another one around the corner. Can I get the details of your purchase?"

Ed's smile faded, "I'm still waiting for the closing. Actually, I think we are waiting because of the appraiser."

"Everybody is busy these days." I paused. "I heard there were problems?"

Ed turned to Marti. "That building is the reason why Mr. Stone darkened our door. You see, he wanted to buy it and as a billionaire, he felt entitled to it. Except, that I had a valid offer on it. I did not know he wanted it. I'd never heard of Mr. Stone and his plans to remake Mackinac

Island into something, I guess, like Manhattan with big, tall modern buildings."

"Is that why he came in here all the time?" Marti asked, priming the pump. We assumed that Ed didn't know that we had at least some background information through our nosing around.

Ed nodded. "It was horrible. America is a free country. I had every right to buy that building."

"But Mr. Stone didn't see it that way?" I asked.

"No."

"Did he try to talk you out of it?"

"Yes. He offered me money if I'd step aside and let him buy the building."

I took a sip of the coffee. It was strong and delicious. "Did you think about doing that? Just pocketing the profit and buying something else at another time?"

"No. It was wonderful. The location was excellent. I had been watching for just such a property to become available for some time. Actually, I wanted to have a Lupita's on Mackinac Island before this one in Petoskey, but I couldn't find the right place."

"After you told Mr. Stone that you didn't want to take his money and you still planned to go ahead with your purchase, that was the end of it, right?"

Ed smiled. "Did you know Mr. Stone?"

"I was at the shop one time when he came in wondering where you were."

"Yes. Unfortunately, he stopped by often."

"Did he make other offers to you?" I asked.

"Yes of course. He was a very persuasive man." He turned to Marti. "Why is Onalee asking all of these questions?"

"Robin Stone died right in front of me. We want to find out who did it. Especially since it happened in your store. We want to set the record straight," Marti answered.

His voice rose. "So you two are going around to people and asking them dangerous questions?"

"We're careful, but we want to find out the truth."

"It seems to me you are being very foolish, Martina." He shot to his feet.

"Come on, Ed. The longer it takes to solve this murder, the worse it's going to be for you and your business."

"Both of you, back off before you get hurt. I have nothing more to say to either of you." He strode away. Marti and I looked at each other, got up and left.

Snowflakes spiraled gently down when we reached the sidewalk. To me, Ed's behavior raised a lot of red flags but before I said anything, I wanted to hear how Marti felt.

We walked for over a block before she said anything. "When we started this, the main reason I wanted to do it was to clear Ed's good name," she said idly kicking a clump of ice along like a hockey puck. I'd have to remember to ask her if she'd played the game, skating on a neighborhood rink full of kids somewhere in Detroit.

She gave the ice a solid kick and continued. "Now I'm not so sure. I mean he probably is the number one suspect. I'm not crazy about sending a friend to prison."

"No, but you don't know that he did it."

"Right now, I'd say it doesn't look good for him."

"Marti, I can tell he really likes you. He could just be worried about you getting involved when it's so risky. Ed doesn't realize he's dealing with Gutsy Gonzalez and her trusty sidekick, Onalee."

A small smile played on Marti's lips. "At least you finally admit you're the side-kick. But Onalee, there's a small detail I never mentioned to you."

I was getting a bad feeling. "Oh yeah?"

"Remember when I told you that Stone came in to the shop that day and wanted the peanut butter fudge?"

"Yes."

"There was only one slice of peanut butter fudge. I'd even mentioned it to Ed and he told me it was the slow time of year and that he'd make more in the morning."

"That doesn't mean he killed Stone."

"No, but it was kind of weird and afterwards I've wondered. Was it because Ed did it and wanted to be sure no one but Stone got the bad candy?"

"He didn't usually have just one slice of a flavor in the display case?"

"No. I don't remember ever seeing that. On, he might be the killer after all."

Ooh boy. Poor Marti. "You've never spent any time up here in the winter. Small businesses barely make enough money to survive until summer. Ed had probably just come up with a new way to cut back a little."

"You don't think it's significant?"

"I guess I don't know for sure, but I hope not."

We walked in silence until we were in front of her apartment. Marti turned to me, "Do you have time to try to track down Stone's partner, what's his name?"

"Charlie Kemp. I have time but no idea how to find him."

"That's why you're still a sidekick. Think about it. Where would a guy nicknamed 'The Muscle' hang out?"

"Hmmmm. A gym?"

"Exactly. As a matter of fact, I've heard he goes to my gym."

"Wait a minute. You have a gym? Since when?"

"My dear friend. We've known each other a long time, it's true. But you don't know everything about me."

"Oh, I pretty much do. Me thinks this is a very, very recent development. A good one, but recent."

"Come on up. We're about the same size. We'll get dressed and hit the gym. I think I can bring a guest for five bucks or something like that."

A few minutes later, I was running on a treadmill and Marti was working a rowing machine. The owner and two other brawny men were using the circuit. Mr. Kemp was nowhere in sight.

"Ixna on the ubjectsa," I called over to Marti in our top-secret code.

"On'tda orrywa."

Easy for Sleep-in Gonzalez to say. I'd already cross-country skied for ninety minutes, I'm not sure how long I can last on the treadmill. Then again, I guess if I slow to a walk maybe I'll be able to hold on until Muscles shows up.

All of a sudden, there he was, at the back of the room. He must have just come up the basement stairs. Looking over, I saw that Marti had noticed his appearance, stopped rowing and was toweling off her machine.

Hot Fudge

I did the same and nonchalantly walked over to where we'd put our jackets, boots, mittens, and hats.

Amazingly, we got there at almost the exact same time as our ubjectsa, Charlie Kemp.

"Hi. I think I've seen you here before," Marti said to him.

"Could be. I'm here just about every day," he said smiling.

"It's a great way to stay in shape. You usually go into the basement and lift weights, don't you?"

He nodded. "I do. What do you like to do?" He asked while he laced up his boots.

"Lately, I've been using the treadmill and the rowing machine, but I used to go to a women's weight lifting class and I really liked it. The trouble is, that was a couple of years ago, and I'm not sure I can remember all of the do's and don'ts."

"If you want, next time you come, I'll show you some lifts."

The dimpled one gave him her dazzling grin. "Thanks. Actually, I'll be here tomorrow."

He smiled. "I was planning to come about the same time tomorrow, myself. See you then?"

"Perfect." Marti stuck out her hand and introduced herself and her trusty sidekick.

"Nice to meet you both," he said and left.

We were also buttoned, zipped and laced up so we, too, slid out the door.

"You know, I think he will expect you to know at least a few basics since you've, I used my mittened hands to make air quotes, 'taken women's weight lifting classes.'"

"And you say you know me so well. What do you think I did to amuse myself when you went gallivanting off to Petoskey?"

We had been walking, but I stopped and stared at her. "Seriously? Women's weight lifting?"

"Yes. I took the class on Saturday mornings at the Y for about three years. It was fun."

"All I can say is, I hope you don't have bombshell revelations like this for Fiancé Frank."

Hot Fudge

Chapter Sixteen

After Marti and I went back to her apartment, showered and changed, we sat in her two small chairs and discussed the case over peanut butter and apple butter sandwiches. The sandwiches, Marti's culinary specialty, were wonderful. Our conversation was not.

"We're not getting anywhere," Marti said.

"I know. It just doesn't seem like we're shaking anything loose. Unless of course, it turns out to be Ed. Also, the killer might be back in New York City, right now."

"I think if it is someone from New York, they'd have killed him there, not here."

"That makes sense to me."

Marti nodded. "It doesn't seem to me that Maureen or Robbie Stone would have done it now. Maybe five or six years ago, before the divorce, but not at this point. I think you'd better come with me tomorrow to meet up with Charlie at the gym. We may need to spend a little time with him before he opens up to us, and as you know, I'll be gone."

I sighed. "I suppose I can reschedule my inspection."

Marti chuckled. "That flexibility is just one of the reasons why I chose you to be my sidekick."

"Aghghgh!" I checked my watch. "Okay. Here's a thought. I'll go back to my office and call my client. You come with me and we'll do some more Googling of Stone and Kemp. There must be more that we can uncover."

As soon as my car turned up the driveway, I heard a deep bark from inside the house. Poodle Boy. He was at the door ready to do his figure eights around Marti and me. After fondling his ears and murmuring sweet nothings to him, I made my phone call with as good an excuse as I could come up with. I then made a solemn oath to myself to be a more diligent appraiser starting next week and joined Marti at the computer. This time we searched back further and come up with Stone's name linked with various women, both before and after his divorce from Maureen, details about the trial, and some interesting business dealings.

Hot Fudge

In the severe recession following the 2008 financial services collapse, a lot of people were in very bad financial straits. Houses were no longer being built and lots and lots of people in the construction trades were out of work. This included builders, plumbers, electricians, painters and developers. They represented a big part of the workforce in Northern Michigan. People were living on their life savings and those were running out. I remembered reading and feeling depressed about all the foreclosure notices in the local newspaper.

Into these troubled waters knifed Robin Stone with a newly formed company called RealCashNow. They bought up foreclosed houses at bargain prices and leased them out, sometimes to the original owners who didn't want to leave their homes. They didn't have to go, but paid a very high price to stay. Resilient Robin had figured out a way to profit out of the financial upheaval he and his ilk had helped to create.

We ran a search of county records in Emmet, Charlevoix, Cheboygan, Antrim, and Otsego Counties which revealed that Stone's company had purchased thirty-seven foreclosed houses from 2009 to 2011. To Marti and I it seemed possible that one of the owners of the foreclosed properties could have sought revenge, but wouldn't their lender be the target, rather than Stone's company? Also, these foreclosures would have wrapped up years ago. This was probably another dead end, but we painstakingly got the names of all of the pre-foreclosure owners, just in case.

***

Friday morning, a couple of hours after skiing with the Dash Dog, I met Marti at the gym. I paid for a month-long membership and the two of us traipsed off to the weight room in the basement. I was studying the weights wondering if I could work with the five-pounders when we heard Kemp clambering down the stairs.

He smiled. "You both came."

"Yup, Onalee didn't want to be left out."

"Great." He launched into our tutorial. "One thing I've always heard is, if you want long, lean muscles, use lighter weights and lots of reps." He looked over at me. I guess I must've looked puzzled. "Um, repetitions."

I reached for the five-pound weights and he handed Marti another set of them. "You probably remember from your class that they told you soft knees. Don't lock them up, and keep good posture."

Hot Fudge

"Yup. It's coming back a little," she said.

"Watch yourself in the mirror just to make sure you're maintaining the proper form. Now here, I'll show you one of my favorite lifts," he said and raised his arms one at a time, each with a ten pound weight, straight out in front of him.

Marti and I copied him while he encouraged us. He showed us six or seven other lifts each time paying meticulous attention to our form. "Okay, If I do the circuit now, are you two okay on your own?"

"Sure, but can we buy you a cup of coffee for all your help?" Marti asked.

He smiled. "I enjoy teaching people about weight lifting, you don't owe me a thing."

"Well, we like having coffee with friends. Can we talk you into it?" I asked.

"Absolutely. Meet you at the front door in about thirty minutes?"

"See you then." Marti said.

"That was surprisingly pleasant," I said after he left.

"Yeah, I didn't get any bad feelings about him, did you?"

"I was talking about the weight lifting, but no he seemed pretty nice."

"Maybe we'll get a better picture of him over coffee."

Forty minutes later we were sipping coffee and sitting in a booth across from Mr. Kemp. *He really is a massive guy*, I thought. *Not fat but all muscle.* I watched his meaty hand close around his coffee mug. We each had a decadent muffin in front of us and I broke off a piece of mine.

He grinned. "This is one of the reasons I work out so much. I love these things."

"Me too," Marti and I both said, almost in unison.

He laughed. "How long have you two been friends?"

We looked at each other. "Wasn't it in that first appraising class that we met?" Marti asked.

I nodded. "Yup. I never had so much fun in a class in my life."

Marti laughed. "Me either."

"You two are appraisers? What do you appraise?"

"Real estate," I said.

"Residential or commercial?"

"Basically commercial."

Kemp nodded and took a sip of coffee. "Interesting field."

"It is. There's something new every day. What do you do?" I asked.

He hesitated. "Lately, I've been kind of overseeing some properties. We . . . I mean I might have a need for some good appraisers. Do you have cards?"

We both shook our heads. "On, you can give him my card next week." She looked at Kemp and smiled. "Actually I'm getting married in two days and will be gone for about two weeks."

Kemp's eyebrows rose. "Oh, how wonderful. If you find the right person, marriage is great."

"She did," I said. "They're getting married in a cedar swamp then moving into his log cabin on top of a hill overlooking a beautiful valley."

Kemp laughed. "Sounds like you've got it nailed."

"Thanks. Frank really is super." She paused. "What about you? Is there a Mrs. Kemp?"

Kemp looked away for a moment. He shook his head. "No, I'm afraid not. My wife died of cancer seven years ago. Actually, seven years last week. But while we were together . . . there was so much happiness." He looked into Marti's eyes. "I envy you, just starting out."

I remembered hearing about Robin Stone and all his womanizing. No one had ever said that about Charlie Kemp. I think we'd just found out why.

We talked some more and I asked him what kinds of properties he oversaw.

"The company I work for owns some businesses on Mackinac Island."

"What a terrific place to own real estate. Well, maybe not in the winter," I said smiling.

"It's pretty quiet up there these days. I like the island, but I always feel like an outsider up there."

"It's a small community this time of year," I said.

"On and I cross-country skied there this winter. It was beautiful."

He raised his eyebrows. "I'll bet it would be."

We finished our muffins and left, Marti to her apartment and me to the grocery store to secure a few ingredients for the bachelorette party. It was going to be a semi- potluck with Susan bringing an appetizer and Lacey bringing a cake. Lacey was a beginner cook and I wondered how she'd do. I had tried to talk her into an easier dish, but she was determined. I was planning to make chili, corn bread and a second appetizer. I made the chili and the appetizer that afternoon.

The following morning after Dash and I finished our sojourn, I baked the corn bread. As I slid it in the oven, the phone rang.

"Onalee! I'm trying to get this cake made but there's some stuff here that I, like, don't understand."

I pictured twenty-something, cute as a button Lacey and grinned. "Read the recipe to me."

"Okay, so it says, 'mix the dry ingredients and make a well?'"

"I don't know for sure, Lacey, but I've always suspected that they're just showing off when they say that."

"But, like, what does it even mean?"

"You just kind of make a hole in the center, like it's the crater of a volcano."

"Oh, okay. It also says to, 'fold in the whipped egg whites.' I know how to, like, fold a shirt, but how do I fold egg whites? Is that more show-offy stuff?"

I laughed. "No. That's probably important. You want to try to keep the volume of the whipped eggs so you carefully spoon the other ingredients over them."

"Okay. I'll, like, try my best."

The doorbell rang. Looking through the peephole I saw Frank and opened the door. "No you can't come to Marti's bachelorette party, Fiancé Frank."

He grinned. "I don't think I'd even want to. Aren't there usually male strippers?"

"Sometimes, but not at any I've ever been too. This one will be pretty mild, as these things go. Come on in."

"No, I know you've got places to go, but I wanted to drop these off. They're Marti's favorite cookies."

"They smell wonderful. You baked them?"

He looked a little sheepish. "Yeah."

Hot Fudge

I threw my arms around him. "You are the sweetest guy. Marti will be thrilled. Thank you."

I did a few last minute cleaning chores and was off to Petoskey. We were supposed to meet up in front of the warming house at the Petoskey Winter Sports Park. Surprisingly, I was the first to arrive on the scene, and I watched the skaters gliding around the biggest outdoor rink in Michigan. It was twenty degrees out and snow was drifting down in fat lazy flakes. It was a perfect winter day. Mrs. Willowby had opted out of this part of the festivities and I planned to pick her up on the way back to my house. Soon Lacey, Susan, and eventually Marti came along. We went over to the sliding hill to watch the North American Bump Jumping contest.

"What are those things, On?" Marti was intrigued.

"They were invented in Northern Michigan or so the local lore goes. You sit on them and keep your feet up in the air. You hold onto the sides and can steer them pretty well by pulling up one side or the other. You can also slide your feet in the snow to steer but that slows you way down and will probably cost you the race."

"Some of them are just a seat attached about a foot above a ski?"

"Yup, they make them that way now at times. They always used to make them like that one over there." I pointed to the more traditional model with a runner carved out of wood that was about two feet long.

Lacey spoke up. "Have you ever, like, ridden one?"

"Sure. We spent our winters in this park, skiing, skating, riding bump jumpers and sliding. You probably did too, didn't you, Susan?"

"No, not so much."

Really? "You grew up here didn't you?"

"Yeah, but I guess I was into other things."

Marti was studying a jumper parked nearby. "They look like they'd be hard to ride."

"Not when you're a kid. They're a lot of fun. I think they have a few that people can borrow. Want to try it?"

"No way. Not right before my wedding. When I get back, though, I'll try it."

They were starting the race, with kids going first. We saw some excellent bump jumper-manship, if I do say so myself.

Hot Fudge

One young boy sailed down the hill, clearly faster than all of the others. "Did you see that kid's form?" I asked. We all cheered as he swooped across the finish line, his body cantilevered back and his feet held high.

I looked at the spectators standing across from us. "Marti. Isn't that Robbie over there?"

She studied the winter-garbed group. "Yeah, let's go say hello," she said and loped away.

"Rob. Hi. Are you racing?" Marti called out.

He smiled. "Yeah, it looks like fun."

"Hi, Ms. Double Peppermint Non-Fat Latte." Marti grinned at the dark-haired girl standing next to Robbie.

She laughed and waved.

"I think we need to get to the top of the hill. Nice seeing you," Robbie said and he and his girlfriend ambled off, his bump jumper in hand.

In the next group we noticed a little girl, her face radiating pure joy as she raced along. Unfortunately, one of her boots dug into the snow too much and she took a tumble. Scrambling to her feet, she plopped back on her jumper and crossed the finish line to more applause. We also cheered

Rob on, even though he wasn't a contender. But for someone who didn't grow up astride the mighty bump jumper, his performance was commendable.

After his run we watched a figure skating show and part of a hockey game. It was almost three o'clock when we decided it was time to move our operation to downtown Petoskey to see the ice sculptures. When we arrived we noticed a group gathered at one end of Pennsylvania Park.

With no particular plan in mind, I said, "Let's go find out what's going on over there."

When we got closer, we could see people drinking from plastic cups. Marti pushed past us. "Oh cool. It's an ice bar."

"I can't believe it. This is supposed to be a family friendly event. Do we have to have alcohol everywhere?"

Surprised, I looked over at Susan's angry face. *What was going on with her?* It was Marti's day and this wasn't good. "Why don't we walk around and look at the sculptures?"

A couple of the works were still in progress and we watched as they took shape. A nice passerby took a picture of the four of us grinning in front of a stately ice horse. At the end of our tour we each hopped in our cars. Susan and Lacey needed to fetch their food and I had to pick up Mrs. Willowby. Marti, Mrs. W. and I made it to the house first. I went in the door to corral Dash. There would be no poodle-senior citizen accidents on my watch. After our de-coat, de-boot and de-mitten-athon, Marti and Mrs. W. sat on the couch becoming fast friends as I busied myself in the kitchen.

The doorbell rang and Marti got up to let Lacey in. She was beaming. Apparently all was more than well with her first foray into frosted cakes. Marti made the introductions and everyone migrated to the kitchen. I think it was the tomatoey tang of the chili that drew them. In the twilight of a cold winter day, nothing beats it. Marti got plates, bowls and silverware out and began setting the table as Lacey and Mrs. W. discussed cakes and the art of baking. It seemed that the fresh air had sparked everyone's appetite.

Once again, the doorbell summoned Mr. Dash with me right behind him. Susan bounded in, handing me her dip and crackers. I left her to talk to the excited Dash, and remove her cold weather gear.

Suddenly a loud voice rang out. "What are you doing here?"

Our heads all swiveled at the brash exclamation. Susan, fists at her hips was glaring at Mrs. Willowby. *What the heck? They know each other?*

"Hi sweetie," Mrs. W. said softly. "I'm sorry. I didn't know you were all friends." She turned to me, a devastated look on her face. "Onalee, If I could impose on you again, I think you'd better take me home now."

We all stood around awkwardly. Susan looked from me to Marti, and back to Mrs. Willowby. She spoke grudgingly. "No, you can stay. I sure didn't expect this, but I don't want to spoil Marti's party."

Now Mrs. W. looked at both Marti and I. "I don't know . . ."

Marti took charge. "It's my party and I really want both of you to be here. Okay?"

Both Susan and Mrs. W. agreed. It was time for action. I got out a bottle of wine and some glasses. "Who's ready for some vino?" I asked.

"I hope you've got a couple of gallons of that. You'll need it," Susan snarled.

"Thank you, Onalee, but I'd be beholden to you if I could just have a glass of ice water." She glanced at Susan. "I'm a recovering alcoholic, and as my daughter Susan insinuated, I had more than my fair share of wine back in my drinking days."

Susan is Mrs. W's daughter?

Marti jumped in. "On, put the wine away. A cup of coffee sounds much better to me on a cold day."

"Yeah, like, way better to me, too," Lacey said.

Good. I turned to put the wine back in the cupboard.

"Onalee, there's no need for that. It won't bother me one iota to be around alcohol. You girls have a lot to celebrate and I don't want to throw cold water on the festivities." She saw me hesitate. "Believe me. I could buy as much alcohol as I want any time I get to the store, but have you ever seen me do it?"

"No."

"We walk right by it at Foodrights, don't we?"

I nodded. "But are you sure it won't bother you? We're all fine with an alcohol-free night."

"In that case, I would ask again that you take me home and not allow me to be a wet blanket."

I held her gaze for a moment. She seemed resolute. I lifted the corkscrew up and began turning. Marti got Mrs. W. her water and I poured glasses of wine for the rest of us. We each held our glass up. "To Marti and Frank," I said and we all clinked glasses. Over Susan's delicious artichoke dip and my smoky bean dip and crackers, it seemed as though everyone relaxed though we weren't able to return to the jovial mood we'd enjoyed at the Winter Carnival. The chili turned out to be a better than usual batch for which I was thankful. We all had dollops of seconds and then it was time for Lacey's cake. When she lifted the top off the cake stand we all stared.

"Lacey, a three-layer cake? Wow."

She grinned. "I know. It's, like, awesome, isn't it? I already, like, have a picture of it on Instagram. Of course, I don't know yet if it tastes okay."

"Slide it over here. I get to cut it don't I, as the bride-to-be?"

It was a lemon cake and for my money, it reached the perfect balance between tart and sweet. "Lacey, maybe you should become a pastry chef," I said.

"I know. That's, like, what I was thinking," she bubbled.

Hot Fudge

We all laughed, even Susan and Mrs. W, who we were now supposed to call Dot, short for Dorothy.

Then I unveiled the cherry oatmeal cookies Frank had brought and told them he'd baked them for Marti. I don't think there was a dry eye or an empty belly in the group.

We sat around the wood stove for a while, mostly talking about old times around Petoskey. Marti and Lacey mostly listened, occasionally chiming in with some of their own experiences growing up in different areas. Susan was the first to call it a night saying she needed to get home to Riley.

Before an awkward silence could set in, Marti said, "I can drive you home, Dot. It's on my way."

"Thank you, dear. That would be lovely, " Mrs. W. said in a quiet voice as Susan looked away.

After they all left, Dash and I walked along the snowy street. It was only nine o'clock, but it had been a very long day. And tomorrow, my friend Marti would be starting on a whole new chapter of her life.

Connie Doherty

Chapter Seventeen

Marti's wedding day. How exciting. The days were growing noticeably longer now that we were inching closer to springtime. The wedding was to be at 6:30 so that it would be twilight, both Marti's and Frank's favorite time of the day. They were going to have a short ceremony and we would all leave the swamp before dark. There were only going to be a handful of people attending the wedding, but many more would be at the party at Frank's house.

Marti came over that morning and joined Dash and me cross-country skiing through several inches of new fallen snow. It was another mild 20-degree day and our skis flew over the snow. We discussed the strange turn of events with Susan and Mrs. Willowby.

"They're both such good people. It's a shame that they're on the outs with each other," I said.

"I know. It's terrible. And Mrs. Willowby, I mean Dot, is no spring chicken. If they don't get over this tiff soon, Susan may well have huge regrets after her mom is gone."

"Exactly. That would be really sad."

"Okay, On, while I'm gone, I want you to work on those two. Make each see how nice the other one is."

"You're unable to carry out this dictate yourself, Ms. G?"

"No. I can't be in two places at once. As a married woman I'll need to accompany my husband to see to his safety and well-being."

"Hmmmmph." We skied for a while in silence, each of us soaking in the beauty of a winter day while Dash scampered along ahead of us. Suddenly two deer bolted across the trail right in front of him. "Oh no. I don't want him chasing those poor animals." I pushed off hard to get some speed. Dash was on their trail as the deer leaped through the underbrush. Soon, they all went over the crest of a small hill and out of sight. "Dash. Dash, come!" I yelled over and over. I clambered off the trail and through the underbrush, Marti right on my heels. Soon I spotted the boy trotting back to us. *Whew.*

"I guess those guys are just too fast even for the world's fastest poodle, eh Dash?" I asked him as I fondled his ears. Soon we were at our turn-around spot. Our ski back was enjoyable but uneventful. Marti came in for coffee and some pumpkin scones I'd made last week and pulled out of the freezer this morning.

"You don't seem to be having any pre-marriage jitters."

She smiled. "Nah, but this is an easy wedding. It's small and it'll be fun." She stretched like a cat and broke out in another smile, "Afterward, I'll be with the guy I love."

We clinked coffee mugs.

"When I get back . . ."

"You'll go to work at Lupita's."

She laughed. "I wouldn't count on that. I think I probably burned that bridge. No, what I was going to say is, when I get back, we'll make a concerted effort to find the man of your dreams." She grinned. "Or maybe help you realize you've already found him."

Hot Fudge

For the second time that day, I snorted. I had been a little sad thinking I'd miss Ms. G., but now I was beginning to believe her absence might just turn out to be a vacation for me, too.

The rest of the day sped away in a blur and it was time to take Dash out for a last minute walk, give him his kibbles and fresh water, put my cross-country skis in the car, and follow the map Frank had drawn of their special spot in the cedar swamp.

Marti and Frank were just parking Frank's SUV when I arrived. Several other people were already there and sitting in their cars, motors running, waiting. We all got out and clamped on our skis. Frank and Marti greeted everyone before gliding off along a wooded path.

We skied for only about five minutes before entering a lacy paradise. It had been snowing softly all day and snow clung to the branches of the cedars and evergreens, creating a natural bower. Large flakes filled the air and our world was a snow globe. Frank and Marti, in a beautiful new white down parka stood in the center and a local minister skied up with a bible in hand. He recited the service and soon pronounced them husband and wife. As short as it was, I still shed a couple of tears. Marti, pink cheeked and radiant, skied over to me and we hugged. There was plenty of back slapping and hand shaking amongst the men. As the sky darkened we all skied back out, got in our cars, and drove to Frank's, oops, Frank's and Marti's house.

We were the first guests to arrive, but the caterers Frank and Marti had hired were already there. Marti and Frank quickly went in, shrugged off their coats and cross-country ski boots and got ready to greet their guests. No one needed any help so I made myself at home in an easy chair by the fire. I had corralled Frank's beautiful dog, Caesar and was doing my best to keep him from greeting every guest with love and enthusiasm.

Eventually Lacey and her friend Pete showed up, followed quickly by Susan. Other than them and Frank's brother, I didn't know anybody. It was a friendly crowd though and I met lots of Frank's family and friends. Lacey, Susan and I were in the midst of a very interesting discussion about dog rescues when a familiar voice cut across the other voices in the room. *No. She would not have done that. Not my best friend, bosom buddy, Marti.* Oh, but she had. I looked up and right into the cerulean blue eyes of Detective Costas.

Hot Fudge

I glanced quickly at Marti and caught her staring at me. I've never been one to consult Emily Post, but I knew for certain she'd caution against the use of any lewd gestures towards a bride at her wedding reception. Besides, I wasn't that kind of person. But as sure as I was sitting there on Frank's gray leather couch, Marti would someday, somewhere, realize the full sting of Onalee O'Conner's revenge rain down on her.

Meanwhile, I could also feel Lacey's and Susan's eyes on me. I cleared my throat. "Um, I missed that last thing you said." I addressed this comment to Susan.

"I was actually the one talking," Lacey said.

"Oh."

She looked at Susan who shrugged a little. "I asked if that was Detective Costas standing over there. It is isn't it?"

"Yup. Afraid so," I said.

"I haven't seen him since he hauled me in for questioning last fall." Lacey said and shivered. "Why does he, like, keep looking over here?"

Suddenly, Frank yelled above the turmoil. "Hi everyone. On behalf of Marti and myself, I want to say that we're glad you're here. There is a ton of food in the kitchen, thanks to Sun and Snow Catering. There's also beer, wine, a couple of kinds of pop and water. Please help yourself."

As always, I was hungry. We all looked at each other. "Wanna go to the kitchen?" I asked.

"Sure, I'm starved," Susan said.

"I'm going to go find Pete, first," Lacey said and scrambled to her feet.

Frank's compact kitchen was bustling with activity as Susan and I found the end of the line. "Onalee. About yesterday . . . that was the first time I'd seen Dot in a couple of years. I was just surprised she was there, but I'm sorry it happened at Marti's party."

"I apologize to you, too. I had no idea the two of you were related. Marti and I thought it would be fun to have her, and it would be something she'd enjoy."

Susan nodded. "How do you know her? You don't hang out at Ben's Den, do you?"

I laughed. "Um, no. That's quite the local dive though."

Susan sighed. "I wish I had a dollar for every glass of wine my mother drank in that hole."

"Susan, I am so sorry," I said and hugged her.

"I guess now you know why I didn't hang out at the Winter Sports Park. I was too busy taking care of my younger brother and sister when I was a kid."

"Your dad . . ."

"Took off. I guess he couldn't deal with a drunk and three little kids. I haven't seen him since I was eight."

"That's terrible."

She shrugged her shoulders. "We survived. My sister and I actually turned out okay. My brother, on the other hand, is as big a drunk as she is."

"She was," I said.

"Yeah, okay, as big a drunk as she was."

We had been steadily moving up and now were at the food table. What a spread. Four types of salad, a huge platter of fruit, jumbo shrimp and cocktail sauce, Indian samosas, and both a vegetarian and a meat-laced lasagne. Susan and I made our way through the line, and with plates piled high, went to snag some chairs. A few minutes later, Costas came over to our table. "Mind if I join you two?"

"Of course not." *What could I say?* I started to introduce Susan, but she stopped me. "I met you when you were investigating the murder of my neighbor, Gerald Pembower."

"That's right. Is that how you two know each other?" To me, Costas' grin looked slightly disagreeable.

"No. Our dogs are friends."

"That's nice. You meet lots of people when you have a pooch." Now Costas looked wistful.

"You should get a pup," I said. I'd thought on another occasion that the Detective seemed a little lonely.

"I work too much. I don't want to do that to an animal."

"I have two words for you."

"Yes?"

"Doggie daycare."

"I'll think about it, but right now, I'm going to get a beer. Can I get you two ladies anything?"

Hot Fudge

We both opted for glasses of red wine.

Susan turned to me. "So you never told me, how do you know Dot?"

"She's a good friend of my neighbor, Maybelle Stirnaman. Mrs. Stirnaman always takes your mom shopping, but she was going to be out of town and asked me if I could fill in for a couple of weeks."

"She doesn't drive?"

I shrugged. "I guess not. I don't really know her that well, but honestly, it's been a hoot shopping with her. She knows all of the people who work at Foodrights and they really like her."

She nodded and plastered on a fake smile. "That's nice. Ah, here comes your friend, Mr. Costas with our wine."

I noticed that Pete and Lacey started towards our table, but stopped when they noticed who our illustrious tablemate was. The dinner was very good, and surprisingly, the conversation never lagged. I was just finishing my last morsel of salad when Frank called out again. "The desserts are now on the table. Marti and I hope you love cheesecake as much as we do. This evening you have your choice of frozen peppermint cheesecake, peanut butter cup cheesecake, and very berry cheesecake. But, if you don't care for one of those, we also have homemade chocolate chunk cookies, peanut butter cookies and pecan pie bars. Please, try them all. We're going to."

I laughed. Marti's sweet tooth had met its match in Frank. We all got up and sauntered over to the dessert table.

I was torn between my love of peanut butter cookies and the somewhat rare opportunity to savor good cheesecake. *What to do?* After careful deliberation, I took two peanut butter cookies, okay, three, but that's only because they're always supposed to be eaten in threes, and a small slice of the frozen peppermint cheesecake. I noticed Costas helped himself to a slice of each kind of cheesecake not, of coarse, that I judged him and his food choices. Susan put us both to shame with her one slice of the berry cheesecake.

We all cleaned our plates and got up and mingled. Soon tables were pushed to the sides of the room and a small dance floor was created. A favorite local band, The Latitude Forty-Five Five started playing. I was talking with Pete and Lacey when Frank's brother Mike came over and asked me to dance. He was a tall, rugged looking man, several years older than me. He was the fellow that Maureen Stone had hung around with in high school.

We danced to the music of Maroon 5 and then a few songs by Stevie Ray Vaughan. I had started out strong, really hopping around, but the day caught up with me. At the end of the fourth song, I gasped, "Thanks, Mike. I need a break." We left the dance floor and both went over to where Susan sat with Marti.

"Did Marti tell you we met up with your high school buddy, Maureen Stone?" I yelled to Mike across the noise of the band.

He leaned towards me and cupped his ear so I also leaned forward and repeated it.

He raised his eyebrows. "No."

"She seems really nice. You know. I think she might love to see you."

He shook his head. "Nah, I'm fairly sure she's seeing someone, pretty seriously."

Now I was the one with the shooting up eyebrows. *Who knew?*

After another couple of songs, Mike leaned over and said something to Susan and soon they were hot-footing it across the floor. I moved down one chair, closer to Marti. "This is some party you've got going, here."

She was dressed in pale pink jeans and a shirt with shimmery pinks and light blues. Her eyes sparkled. "You're having fun?"

"Oh yeah. It's been great."

She turned serious. "On, you know we leave tomorrow for Costa Rica."

My guard went up. "Yes?"

"I've been thinking. We just got started investigating Charlie Kemp. I think it's a promising lead, but I won't be here to do anything with it." She paused then and her eyes bored into mine. *Uh oh. I'm going to get stuck doing something I don't want to do.* I let the silence deepen. Finally she sighed. "On, I think we need to surveil Kemp."

"We? Surveil? I liked it better when you were the sidekick."

She looked down, demurely. "Onalee, I'll always be the sidekick, but I won't be here to do the grunt work. It's . . . it's my wedding night, and I only ask this one small favor of you."

Hot Fudge

Again with the Emily Post. I also think she'd advise against glaring at a bride at her wedding reception, but sometimes nothing but a good old fashioned high voltage squinty-eyed stare will do. Afterwards, I snarled, "Fine. Don't worry about me when you're cavorting in the tropical sun in Costa Rica."

She gave me another sweet smile as Mike came up from behind and pulled on my arm for another dance. I got to my feet, spun on my heel and no, of course it wasn't Mike. I was now in the clutches of Mr. Costas. Frank was leaning over Marti and they were laughing. *If I find out that those chortles are at my expense, some newlywed heads are going to roll.*

I've always heard about a ski run out west called Tourist Trap. It is said to start off nice and easy, but close to the end unsuspecting skiers are funneled into steep, difficult terrain. The song the band was playing, one I'd never heard, turned out to be the musical equivalent of that run. The beat was fast and I was at a comfortable arm's length from Costas. An added bonus was that the band was too loud to talk over.

Suddenly there was a pause and the Latitude Forty-Five Fivers downshifted into slow-ro. Costas stepped in, his arms darted out, and I found myself in a lovers' embrace slowly swaying across the floor. Out of the corner of my eye I saw Marti and Frank in further paroxysms of laughter. My blood boiled. Costas lifted my chin to look into my eyes. He was smiling and I found myself smiling back. The song ended and he gave me a hug. *Hmmm, that was kind of nice.* Another song began with a fast beat and we sprung apart. We stayed on the floor for a few more rounds before taking a breather.

All too soon, the party wound down. I hugged both Marti and Frank and wished them a lovely time on their honeymoon. Costas and I got our coats and boots and walked out the door together. I bade Mr. C. a cheery goodbye and looked up at the starry Northern Michigan sky. It looked as though the newlyweds would have good weather to fly out of Traverse City in the afternoon.

Hot Fudge

Chapter Eighteen

The following morning, Dash and I overslept. It didn't seem like a Monday. This was the week I was supposed to turn back into Diligent Appraiser O'Conner. At direct odds with that was the Gonzales Edict to begin keeping a close eye on Charlie Kemp. I was going to be wearing a lot of hats this week, but I started off with my warm Turtle Fur skiing cap to accompany Dash on his rounds.

After our ski, we both had our breakfasts and I worked on the computer for a couple of hours. By then it was late morning and I figured it was about time to run into Kemp at the gym. Not knowing when I'd be back, I gave Dash an early lunch and then sped into town. Kemp was already in the basement lifting when I arrived. We said our hellos and I picked up the five-pound weights and began some reps, while he grunted under some heavy barbells. We continued on awhile in silence. I was trying to think of something to talk about between lifts when he started doing some stretches.

"Did you go to Marti's wedding?"

"Yup. It was yesterday."

"And you made it to the gym this morning. I'm impressed."

I laughed. "I did sleep in a little. I'm not used to going out on a Sunday night." *Or any night for that matter,* I thought.

With arms over his head, he stretched to one side and then the other. "You know, I thought of another lift you might like to try." He picked up two ten-pound weights and did some curls along the side of his body.

I followed his lead. "Yeah, that's a good one. Thanks."

He seemed to be about done with his routine, so I finished up as well. We walked up the stairs together. "I'd ask you to join me for another cup of coffee, but I've got an appointment," he said and smiled.

"Yeah, I have to run, too. I've got to get some work done today."

When we stepped outside, he turned left. My car was to the right. *What to do.*

Hot Fudge

I stopped to retie my boot lace (after quickly untying it), then I surreptitiously tailed Mr. Kemp as we walked down the street. Eventually, he climbed into a black Land Rover SUV and drove right by me, waving. I sighed. After all this time, I still wasn't an A-Grade amateur sleuth. But at least in the future I would know what vehicle to look for. I walked back to my car and went home. That afternoon I attended my Hapkido class and then got a good amount of work done.

The following day, I decided to play my cards differently and drove around until I found his car outside the gym. I parked four cars down the road, waited until he came out, and followed him. He drove to a restaurant north of Petoskey in a town called Alanson. As he went through the front door, I parked my car. All of a sudden I spotted a man who I could swear was Bill Reneveere the taco restaurant owner Stone had forced out of business. *Were he and Kemp meeting? I definitely need to check into this.* I slipped out of my car and walked into the cafe. My, my, my. There they were, sitting at a table together, big as life. I hightailed it out of there before I got spotted and sprinted back to my car.

Again, I had a productive afternoon, at least when I wasn't thinking about what scheme Kemp and Reneveere could possibly be hatching. The following day, I again parked near Kemp's Land Rover and waited for him to finish his workout. Eventually, I spotted him leaving the gym. He walked over to his car. *No, he's passing his car. He's walking towards me. Uh oh. It's too late to slink down or run. What is he doing?* He came over and rapped on the passenger side window. I pushed the automatic window button and waved cheerily.

"Oh hi. I thought that was you. I didn't make it to the gym this morning, but it seems as though you never miss. I—" He yanked open the door and slid into the seat. *Double uh oh! Why hadn't we ever learned any seated self defense moves in my Hapkido class? It was a serious flaw.*

"I saw you yesterday in Alanson. What were you doing there?"

I smiled, but it wasn't returned. What I wouldn't give to see good ole Costas strolling by right now. His eyes pinned me in my seat. "Um. . . ." Wait a minute. *What was he doing there with Suspect Number Two, Bill Reneveere?* Kemp was now Suspect One on my improvised list. *Time to go on the attack.*

Hot Fudge

I returned his glare. "I was minding my own business. What were you doing sitting across from the man who more than likely murdered your partner, Robin Stone?"

His eyes widened. I'd probably scared him. "What?"

"Hey. This is a small car. You don't need to yell."

He shook his head. "Look. You and that other woman need to back off before you get hurt," he said as he opened the car door then marched away.

Hmmpphh, we were getting the old, "Back off" talk at a rate of once a week lately. Now I wasn't sure if Kemp, Reneveere or Eduardo topped the suspect list. What I was sure of was that it was time to get back to the office and get some work done because the following day I would be in a continuing education class in Gaylord.

On Thursday, I went to the gym at the Kemp hour and there he was with his weights. He nodded briefly when I walked in. I picked up a couple of five-pounders and started my reps. When Kemp finished his lift he came over. Oh my. *We're all alone down here. How effective of a weapon is a five pound dumbbell against a two hundred fifty pound man? He's smiling?*

"Onalee. I'm sorry I snapped at you yesterday. I shouldn't have. Can I possibly make it up to you with a cup of coffee and muffin, my treat?"

I felt my eyes narrow. *What game was he playing?* He was waiting for an answer and seemed to have noticed my narrowing eyes. "I can't. I have an appointment at one o'clock, and I just got here."

He nodded. Lifting one eyebrow, he asked, "Tomorrow?"

Hmmm. Stone was poisoned. Kemp is either number one or number two on my revised list of suspects. Do I really want to break bread, or chocolate chip mocha muffins, with this man? Then again, I could possibly learn something more from him and my sight would never have to leave my muffin and coffee. I smiled. "Sure, I can go tomorrow."

I finished my workout, sped home, and got ready to pick up Mrs. Dot Willowby for shopping. We hadn't had any snow for a few days and her sidewalk was bone dry. She was climbing down the steps as I pulled up to her curb. I jumped out of the car and hurried to her side.

Hot Fudge

She smiled. "Hello dear. Prompt as always," she said placing her hand on my arm. *That's me, Prompt-As-Always O'Conner.* "Onalee. There's never any need for you to leave your warm vehicle to escort me and especially on a day like this with no ice in sight."

"Hi Dot. Thanks for shifting our grocery day to Thursday this week."

"Of course, I'm not the one working. Was your class interesting?"

"It was very good. Thank you for asking."

"You young people are a marvel. What was it about?"

"This one was all about condemnation appraising when the government takes private land for projects like roads or airports."

"I believe I would have liked your job when I was your age." She sighed. "Of course at that age I had three children and a voracious appetite for wine. Onalee, I am so sorry for what happened at your party."

I shook my head. "Everyone had a good time. It was nothing."

She squeezed my arm. "Susan is a good girl and she had every right to cut me out of her life. I'm so glad you two are friends."

We were at the car. I opened her door and went around to my side. As I turned the key I asked, "Where to, first?"

211

"I only need to go to Foodrights dear, but go wherever you need to."

"Foodrights is perfect."

We made our way around the store and were on our way home. On this day, Mrs. Willowby hadn't been her usual, ebullient self and I missed that. Finally she broke a long silence. "Sometime, if you're talking with Susan and my name comes up, would you tell her how sorry I am to have been such a bad mother?"

"Oh, Mrs. Willowby—"

"No, I was. When I didn't have a glass in my hand, all I could think about was my next drink. It ruined my life and took a terrible toll on my family. But . . . I've been sober for eleven and a half years."

"That's fantastic, Dot. Have you tried to talk to her since you quit drinking?"

"Yes, but now I don't even know how to find her. She's not in the phone book and she's moved several times. I saw her in the distance once, but the other night was the first time I'd been in the same room with her for probably twenty years. Tell me, dear, is she happy?"

I nodded. "She seems very happy. She has a cute dog named Riley, a Tibetan Terrier who is a lot of fun for her. Did you know she's a registered nurse?"

Mrs. Willowby had been looking devastated but suddenly a grin erupted between her apple cheeks. "She always was a smart girl."

"She is. She owns a house and is totally self-sufficient."

"That's wonderful."

After getting Mrs. Willowby and her groceries in her home, I unloaded my own purchases and went for an afternoon outing with the dashing Dash. It was about 3:30 and snow clouds were moving in pushed by a cold winter wind. I was glad I'd gotten Mrs. Willowby home before bad weather set in. Dash was frolicking about thirty feet ahead of me on the bike-path when he suddenly froze. *What did he sense?* I looked around as the creeps took over my body and mind. "Dash, let's go home." We turned around and walked back quickly beneath the gathering storm clouds.

The following morning as Dash and I skied through the quiet of a softly falling snow, I again had the feeling of being watched. *Where are all of the other dog walkers when you don't want to be in the woods alone? If ever there was a day for an abbreviated outing, this was it.* Dash wasn't happy about it, but he willingly trotted back to the house with me. All the way along, I mulled over the case as my eyes roved the scenery to my right and left, looking for any untoward movement. Was I imagining that someone was following us? If anyone was, who could it be? And, how much danger were Dash and I in?

Hot Fudge

Chapter Nineteen

About eleven o'clock I walked into the gym nodding and calling out hellos to some of the other gym rats on my way to the basement. Kemp wasn't there. I started the routine I'd been doing the last few days with reps followed by stretches. After a few minutes, I looked up as someone clambered down the stairs.

"Hi Onalee." He smiled. "You beat me, here."

I smiled back. "Yeah. What happened to you?"

He waved his hands dismissively. "I just got held up. Nothing important."

We both worked through our routines. I stole a few glances at him as he hoisted massive amounts of weights. *How would I fend this brute off if it was he following me?*

"That about does it for me. I'll wait for you upstairs," he said.

Whew. I was ready to quit ten minutes ago.

We decided to leave our cars parked where they were and hoofed it over to the coffee shop.

Once again, we each ordered the two ton chocolate chip monster muffins and coffee. While we chatted about everyday matters, I tried to find a way to broach the subject of his partner, Robin Stone. We sure hadn't gotten down to any nitty or gritty last time Marti and I had coffee with him.

"I'll bet you miss having your pal Marti around."

"I sure do, but I'm pretty sure a change of locale will do her a world of good."

"Wedding stress or work?"

I leaned in towards him. "She'd been taking a break from appraising and working at Lupita's."

Kemp's eyebrows rose as he too leaned in. I pulled my muffin closer to me. "When did she work there? It's been closed ever since . . ." he swallowed. "Ever since my partner was killed there."

I nodded. "She was there."

A look of pain flooded Kemp's eyes. "I really miss that guy." His voice was hoarse.

He was either a really good actor or I was looking at an innocent man. On the other hand, somebody killed Stone. And, I was, or at least it felt like I was, followed the last couple of days.

"It was terrible. It's ironic, she's from Detroit, but she'd never witnessed a murder before."

"Did she see who did it?"

"No, but she was there when he died. It was horrible for her."

He shook his head. "I can imagine." Neither of us had touched our muffins during this conversation. I finally took a sip of coffee, and Kemp leaned back and did the same. Then he bent close to me again and I kept my muffin under close surveillance.

"I know Rob was having some trouble with Marti's boss."

"Yes, over that Mackinac Island property they both wanted."

Kemp eyed me. "So, you know about that."

I nodded. "Marti told me about it." I decided to keep pushing for information. "She told me that when Robin came into Lupita's, her boss Eduardo became very uncomfortable."

"Robin could be a little intimidating sometimes when he really wanted something."

"You mean like when he drove Bill Reneveere out of business just because he wanted to garner his location?"

Kemp just nodded.

"So . . . why were you meeting with Reneveere the other day?"

"Because I need to find someone to run our restaurant, Paco's Tacos, up there. Our head chef quit. Who better than Reneveere?" He flashed me a smile.

"Is he considering it?"

"I don't know, but I think so. I told him I'd make it worth his while."

"But aren't you concerned that he might be Robin's killer?"

He shrugged. "Do you think he is? Remember, Robin dropped dead after eating fudge in Lupita's."

I cocked me head. "You think Ed did it?"

Hot Fudge

Again with the shrug. "Search me. I want to know what you think. Marti must know something. What has she told you?"

Hmmm. What was Kemp after?

"Marti just moved up here, right?" Kemp asked.

"Yup, but how did you know that?"

"I don't know. I hear things. Anyway, why did she go to work at Lupita's? How long has she known Ed?"

"I believe she answered an ad and it sounded like a fun place to work until after her wedding." I thought for a minute. "I'm pretty sure she just met Ed."

"They're both Hispanics. I heard they were friends from way back."

I sighed. "Yes they are both Hispanics. Marti's family was originally from Mexico, Ed's from Puerto Rico. They're not up here to recruit gang members or to engage in human trafficking as I heard your partner, Robin, was telling everyone about Ed. I hate that kind of racist talk and you and Robin should both be ashamed to be slandering good American citizens." I was getting to my feet.

Kemp grabbed my arm. "Whoa, slow down. You're right. I hate it too, but how do you know it's not true?"

"What proof do you have?" I noticed people at other tables looking at us.

"None, but I have heard that Michigan is a prime area for sex trafficking. Anyway, let's drop that subject." He paused. "Does Marti think Ed did it?"

No, we both think you did. "She really likes Ed," I said, truthfully.

"And?"

"And honestly? She didn't like Robin."

Kemp looked away for a moment and took a sip of coffee. "Not many did. Sometimes I don't know why I did, but we were like brothers from day one."

"How did you meet?"

Kemp smiled. "At college. We became fast friends and eventually roommates. After grad school, we both got jobs at the same firm and I guess the rest is history."

"What kind of work did you do?" I asked pretending he and Robin hadn't been Googled by us.

"We were in investment banking."

"Hedge funds?"

"Yes."

"What did you two do after the meltdown in '08?"

He studied me for a moment before speaking. "We diversified into other fields."

"Residential real estate?"

"Sounds like you've got all the answers already."

"I just know that a lot of hedge fund operators started buying foreclosed homes since there were so many great deals on the market if you had the cash to do it." He was still looking at me skeptically. "As appraisers, Marti and I were caught up in the whole mess as well. We watched real estate prices take a nose dive and people who had scrimped and saved all their lives lose their jobs and then their homes. It was awful."

"Yeah, it was bad." He shook his head. "Honestly, greed drove the whole thing and Robin and I weren't immune. I look back now at some of the stuff we did and just shake my head."

"But nobody went to jail—"

"No," he said in a quiet voice.

"Some of those people who lost their homes had tragic stories to tell. It seems to me that your partner made a whole lot of enemies during his life. Maybe one of them poisoned him."

He drained his coffee, then looked at me. "Yup, one of them could have, but as I said, he died in Lupita's."

Ignoring him and casting a wider fishing net, I said, "And there's also his ex-wife and his current wife. They both may have had good reasons to kill him."

He glared at me. "Leave them alone. Anyway, I've got to run," he said, his voice cold, as he got to his feet. He put on an elegant tan cashmere coat with a blue and tan plaid scarf. *Fine clothes are nice but a clear conscience is always better*, I thought.

Hot Fudge

I hadn't touched my muffin even though I'd kept a close eye on it. It had been an upsetting conversation. The truth was as Kemp said, Stone had died in Lupita's. What do they say? Motive and means? Ed had both. I sure got the feeling that Kemp believed Ed was the killer, or at least he was trying to convince me of that.

There was still so much we didn't know. Was it the fudge that had killed Stone or something else he ate? Where had he been during that day before he stopped into Lupita's? I needed more information.

It was possible, in a no chance in Hell, Michigan kind of way, that Ed might be thrilled to see me and continue our conversation. I would be a paying customer. Didn't he have a duty to serve the general public? Lupita's was only a short walk from the coffee shop. Based on my last experience with Ed, I figured I didn't need to invest additional hard-earned money in the Petoskey parking meter in front of my Honda. Instead I would take a calculated risk that I'd be back in less than the nine minutes the meter still allotted me.

It was after the busy lunch hour and there were only a few customers in Lupita's. Ed was alone behind the counter. He looked up as I opened the door and I watched his face darken as he recognized his visitor. "Hi Ed. I came to buy some fudge for a friend of mine."

"Hello."

My greeting had been warm and cheery. His? Not so much. I looked at the display case with four kinds of fudge. Since the Stone-slaughter, I'd lost some of my enthusiasm for the stuff. Nonetheless, I bought all but one slice of the white chocolate cherry. Ed was boxing it up for me when he quickly glanced out the window. I turned to see what had captured his attention and caught a glimpse of a tan coat and blue and tan scarf. *Was Kemp the one who had been tailing me the last few days?* I turned back to the counter. Ed was staring at me.

I cleared my throat. "How much do I owe you?"

He mentioned a sum that clearly didn't include any friends and family discount. I paid and hotfooted it out of there. The street was empty at least of any tan coats and plaid scarves.

I drove back to my house, took Dashiell for his midafternoon stroll, and worked on my appraisal. At about four o'clock, I went back to Lupita's. Ed didn't even answer when I greeted him. I strode over to the display case.

Hot Fudge

Aha. There on the shelf lay a big new slab of white chocolate cherry fudge. Did I want more of the creamy concoction? No. Was it smoking gun-ish? Yes.

"Ed, you made more of the white chocolate cherry fudge."

"Yup."

"It's February. Aren't we still in the slow season?"

"Now you're an expert on my business?"

"No. I was just curious. You like to keep well stocked up on all of your assortment of fudge, I guess."

"Of course."

"Huh."

"What are you driving at, Onalee? Do you want to purchase additional fudge or not?"

"Nooo. It just makes me wonder why you didn't replenish your supply of peanut butter fudge on the day Robin Stone was poisoned. There was only one slice, Ed. One slice of peanut butter fudge. His favorite as you well knew. You also were aware that he was coming to see you and that he would want that slice of fudge."

Connie Doherty

Ed's eyebrows formed a black, angry vee above flashing eyes. He was leaning on his fists on the counter and towering above me. "All lies. I've told you before I don't want you in here. Get out and never come back!" He screamed as I sprinted to the door. As I slammed it shut I spotted a black Land Rover SUV parked down the street.

Hot Fudge

Chapter Twenty

I stepped into a "mom and pop" drugstore that had been around since I was a kid. I said a quick hello to the owner, Mr. Barney, and ducked out the back door. I slunk back to my Honda and slid behind the wheel. *There are too many enraged suspects in this case. It's like a hornet's nest. What is Kemp up to and how long will he wait for me to emerge from Barney's?*

I drove around the block and came up on him from behind. I parked three cars away. My doors were locked and if he got out of his car, I could simply drive off, pretty as a picture. He waited about ten minutes then exited his car and went into Barney's. Now it was my turn to wait. I switched on the ignition for some heat. Not intending to be involved in a surveillance op I hadn't dressed in the layers necessary for winter work. After a few minutes he came back out and I believe spotted the O'Conner-mobile. He strode back to his car, got in, wheeled it around, and zipped by me. I couldn't tell for sure, but I thought I observed a grim expression plastered on his puss.

Following his lead I too flipped a uie and sped down the street, but his evasive tactics were sound and I lost him. I turned around again, this time legally and drove home.

The following morning I was working on my report in between bidding out other jobs when the phone rang. It was a local number, but one I didn't recognize. I answered in case it was a business call.

"Is this Onalee O'Conner?"

"Yes it is."

"Thank heavens. Onalee, it's Maureen Stone. I need your help. Robbie is missing and your friend knew his girlfriend. I hope he's with her."

"He's missing?" The last time I'd seen him was at the bump jumper contest last weekend."

"Yes. Please get the name of that girl from your friend."

"Marti got married to Frank last weekend. They're in Costa Rica."

"What? Oh no. Do you know who she is?"

"No, and I don't think Marti does either." I heard her expel some air. "How long has he been gone? Have you called the police?"

"He left last night. We had an argument and he walked out, slamming the door behind him. I knew he was angry, but I figured he'd come home when he cooled off. I waited up all night for him."

"And the police?"

"I've always heard that they don't do anything until someone is missing for forty-eight hours."

"I'm not sure that's true in all cases. I think you should call them."

It sounded like she was crying. "He's probably . . . okay, and if I do something like that it'll just drive a wedge between us."

Thoughts were racing through my mind. "What's your plan of action if you're not calling in the police?"

She was crying harder now and didn't answer. Finally she said. "I don't know. I'd pinned my hopes on you and Marti. I guess I'll drive around and try to spot him."

I sighed *My appraisal was due today, though technically I could probably email it over the weekend.* "Want some help?"

"Oh, could you?"

"Sure. Give me a couple of minutes." I closed down the computer and scurried around setting out kibbles for Dash and getting my boots and other outdoor gear on.

A few minutes later I was on Maureen's front porch. She opened the door almost immediately and I stepped in and gave her a hug.

"Thank you so much for coming." She swiped at her teary eyes and led me into the living room.

Holy eye-widener! There on Maureen's couch, looking very much at home, sat Charlie Kemp.

He gave me a crooked smile. "Hi, Onalee. I guess we're both skipping the gym today, eh?"

My eyes skittered back and forth between them. Maureen walked over, sunk down on her luxurious sofa and snuggled next to him. "Charlie's been such a comfort," she told me. And to be honest, it did look as though he was providing solace to her.

Hot Fudge

I was stunned, but a conversation replayed in my head. Mike, at Marti's wedding was telling me that Maureen was tight with someone. Who knew it was ole Charlie-Follow-Onalee-Everywhere Kemp?

I pulled myself together. "What have you done so far?"

"We've called the college and his step mother."

"To no avail?"

"Right," Kemp said.

"The step mom didn't know his girlfriend's name, either?"

"No, she was as in the dark as I am."

"Well, I think I'll hit the streets. Hopefully I won't be tailed," I said pointedly to Kemp.

Now Maureen looked bewildered. Maybe they weren't in cahoots. Then again, they might be, and I felt uncomfortable in Maureen's uber cozy home.

In my Honda, I sped away to, once again, stake out Lupita's where hopefully Miss DoublePeppermint Non-Fat Latte would appear between college classes. I had left my house quickly upon Maureen's cry for help, and like yesterday, I wasn't dressed warmly enough to sit around in a cold car. Always conscious of my carbon footprint (as well as the high price of gas), I kept the car off as long as I could. Finally turning it on, I held my cold hands up to the heat vents when the warm air finally came.

I also hadn't brought a book or any snacks and I was becoming uncharacteristically bored and testy. I listened to the radio, but still. I needed a book and food. The time dragged on. I checked my watch again. Had it stopped? No, the second hand was still making its steady path around the numbers. *Oh goody.* A great interview was starting and just like that I saw: *a mirage? A vision brought about through fasting? No it was definitely Miss Double Peppermint herself.* She must have appeared because of the eleventh law of physics. The one that states that if your favorite song or something else you're dying to hear comes on the car radio you'll either lose reception or some other phenomenon will prevent you from catching most if not all of it.

In this case, I did get to listen to some of the program because I waited until Ms. Latte reappeared. When she did, she carried a bag and two drinks. I slipped out of my car and walked forty feet or so behind her. Not accustomed to being followed, she didn't look back. I, on the other hand, kept turning my head expecting to see Blood Hound Charlie. I never did, and after two blocks we left the commercial district and started up the steep Lake Street hill. Soon, Ms. Latte walked up on a porch, set her drinks down, rang the doorbell and slipped through the door.

Could my surveillance have paid off? It would be the first time ever. I hotfooted it up to the front door. No one answered my doorbell rings, but I was not going to let this chance of surveillance-success slip through my fingers. I laid my finger on that buzzer and kept it there until Ms. Latte finally threw the door open. A normally pretty girl, her scowling face did not do her justice. I quickly stuck my foot out effectively jamming the door open.

"Hi. I'm a friend of Rob's," I said smiling.

"Yeah. I remember you," she said blocking the entrance.

"Can I talk to him?"

"When I see him, I'll let him know you asked about him."

"Look, Miss Double Peppermint Non-Fat Latte, I just want to make sure he's okay. If I talk to him and it seems reasonable for him to stay with you, I won't tell anyone where he is. I promise."

Rob himself came to the door beside her. "Hi Onalee." They both moved and let me in the house.

I looked around at the honey colored wood floors and ten-foot ceilings. "Nice place you've got here."

"Some family friends own it, but they're only here on weekends this time of the year," Ms. Latte said.

"Handy," I said. I turned to Rob. "Can we talk alone?"

He shook his head. "Naw. Sam knows everything. Come on." They led me into the kitchen where their coffee drinks sat on a table by a take out bag.

"You guys go ahead and eat," I said, hoping my stomach wouldn't growl at the sight of a sandwich.

"I don't want to eat in front of you. Would you like half of my ham and cheese?" Rob asked.

The boy had good manners for a fugitive. "No thanks, I'm fine," I said, but it's hard to lie on an empty stomach.

Ignoring my reply, Rob handed me half of a thick sandwich.

"I'm vegetarian, but thanks."

Rob looked at Sam.

"Um, I'm vegetarian, too. Take half of mine. It's a wrap with hummus and veggies."

I felt my mouth water. Besides, isn't breaking bread together an age-old icebreaker? "Are you sure?"

Sam gave me a dazzling smile. "Of course." She found a knife, sliced that lovely sandwich, and I was saved.

We chatted about the Winter Festival, fun in the snow and other safe topics while we ate. Samantha and I bonded over our love of hummus. After we all had chewed and swallowed for the final time, I got down to business.

"So Rob, your mom is really worried. Don't you think it's time to go back home?"

He and Sam exchanged a look. "I can't."

"Your mom told me you argued, but whatever it is, I'll bet you can work it out."

Rob just looked at the floor.

"Rob?"

Rob shook his head, his eyes still downcast.

"Rob, you can probably tell me what's going on a whole lot easier than you can your mom. Come on, you can trust me."

"I think you should talk to her," my new veggie-buddy said.

Rob looked up, searching her eyes and I began to wonder what I was getting myself into.

"Okay, but you can't let anyone know what I'm going to tell you. Promise?"

Somebody needs to write a parenting manual for non-moms thrust into sticky situations. This was a scary promise to make. Should I? Did I have any choice? "I promise."

"My mom and my dad's partner have hooked up." I nodded. "I overheard some stuff. . . I'm pretty sure they killed my dad." He looked at me with anguished eyes.

"Wow. I don't know what to say." I thought for a minute. "What did they mention to make you believe that?"

"It's just stuff I've heard over the last couple of months that finally added up. Then yesterday I heard them toast to their future together now that their 'stony problem was gone.' They laughed and I just lost it. I said some things I guess I shouldn't have, grabbed my jacket, and ran out the door."

"How about going to the police with this?"

Sam nodded. "Please listen to her Rob."

"And accuse my mother of killing my father?"

"If she's guilty, you've got to," I said.

"But what if I'm wrong? She's been a great mom, but my dad was a mean guy. In some ways, I couldn't blame her for doing it but—"

He didn't finish. There was an uncomfortable silence. "Rob, if you talk to the police they'll just take your statement and then check into it. They're not going to divulge where they got their information. And if your mom is innocent, everything will be fine. I have a friend who is a detective. If you want, I can take you down to see him."

Rob and Sam looked at each other again. I thought I saw an almost imperceptible nod from Sam. "Okay, I guess," he said.

"Great. First of all, can we call your mom and tell her you're okay?"

"I can't go back there, not knowing what they . . . did." His face crumpled up and he was close to tears. Sam and I looked away. I found my cell phone and handed it to Rob.

He punched in the number. "Hi mom." He waited. "Look, I'm okay, but I'm not going to come home right now." Again there was a pause. "No, I can't tell you where I am, but I'm fine. Bye. . . . No, goodbye."

I took the two kids to the station and we waited until Costas came out of his office. After filling him in on the situation I offered to take Sam back home, but she elected to wait for Rob. I gave her my phone number and asked her to call after the interview. Mission accomplished, I headed home. I pulled in my driveway and just as I got out of the car, Charlie Kemp pulled in behind me and screeched to a halt. For a brawny guy he was a fast mover and grabbed my car door before I had a chance to jump back in and lock it.

Hot Fudge

Chapter Twenty-One

Rummaging through my purse, I tried to find my cell phone. All this time I could hear Dash barking frantically from inside the house. *At least he's safe,* I thought.

"Onalee. We need to talk."

My hand still hunting through purse detritus, I looked up at him. "How about if I meet you for a cup of coffee in ten minutes or so? You go ahead and I'll catch up after I run into the house and check on my dog."

"No. right here is fine." *Ah ha! I found it.* I heard sirens on the road, they might create a diversion for me. "Charlie, I called the cops. I think that's them."

He swung his head to look. I stood up and punched him hard in the chest. He fell back and I hit 9-1-1 on my phone.

They answered as he regained his footing. "Why'd you hit me?" He roared, blotting out the dispatcher's voice asking me questions.

I didn't have time for backing and forthing. "Help! I need the police. Charlie Kemp is threatening me."

Kemp had a stunned look on his face, but at least he wasn't attacking me.

. "Now I really did call for help and you'd better hightail it out of here while you have the chance."

"Are you crazy? I never threatened you."

"Not in so many words, but you grabbed my car door and even now you're standing there menacing me."

He stepped back, but still blocked the path to my house. "I'm sorry. I didn't mean to scare you."

"Listen, I really do need to get to my dog. You can hear the poor thing for yourself."

"First call 9-1-1 back and tell them it was a mistake."

"I don't think so."

"I'm not going to hurt you, but you do have to answer some questions."

I could hear sirens again and they were definitely closing in. Kemp shook his head. "What were you thinking?" All of a sudden his face changed and he starred at me open-mouthed. It was like looking into the face of a bass out of water. "Noooo," he said. "You think I killed Robin, don't you?"

He made a strangled noise and bent over from the waist. I jumped out of the car to lend assistance. *What kind of attack was this?* He exploded into laughter.

A county sheriff's car followed closely by the Costas-mobile screeched to a halt behind Kemp's vehicle. A deputy and Costas jumped out and rushed over to us. Kemp looked up, but then burst into more guffaws.

The policemen looked at him and then at me, puzzled expressions on their faces. "What's going on, Onalee?" Costas asked.

"I'm not sure. I know I called you guys—"

"And we know from past experience to come running when you're in trouble."

I pointed my thumb at Kemp. "This man has been following me for days, and just now I was afraid he was going to attack me." Kemp was now wiping tears from his eyes, and if anything, my accusations made him laugh even harder. His behavior was downright weird. *Could he have suffered from some bizarre barbell injury to his bean?*

"Mr. Kemp? What do you have to say?"

At the official tone of Costas' voice, Kemp swiped at his eyes again and straightened up. "Sir, I'm not sure, but I think I do know what's going on. It just occurred to me that Ms. O'Conner here has the mistaken impression that I had a hand in killing my partner Robin Stone." I noticed he was fighting back the urge to giggle.

"Have you been harassing her?"

"Um, if by 'harassing' you mean following her, then yes."

"Why did you do that?"

"Because I thought she and her friend Marti were involved with their partner Eduardo in Robin's death."

Costas quickly looked away and I had the irritating sensation that he might be laughing as well.

"It looks like this is all a merry mix-up but all's well that ends well, right? I'm really sorry to have troubled you, officers."

Hot Fudge

"That's our job, ma'am," Costas said. *Is he channeling Sergeant Friday, these days?*

"Mr. Kemp, you're free to go. You too John. I'm just going to have a word with Ms. O'Conner."

"But Officer, I have a complaint as well. This woman," he pointed at me, "has been tailing me, or as you called it 'harassing' me."

Costas turned towards me. "Is that true?"

The jig was up. "Yes, but ask him what he was doing meeting with Bill Reneveere, you know, the taco shop owner that Stone put out of business."

Costas scowled at me. "I know who Bill Reneveere is." His head swiveled back towards Kemp. "You met with Reneveere?"

Kemp laughed. "I did and she knows that because she followed me into Leroy's Grille in Alanson. I'm handling our company's portfolio on the island now and I want Mr. Reneveere to run the restaurant for us."

"Yeah, he spun me the same yarn. Haven't there been other witnesses who have come forward implicating this man, Detective?"

"Huh. So you two have had each other under surveillance. At least that's kept you both out of my hair. I acknowledge both of your complaints and I'll take them both under advisement. I see no reason to detain you, Mr. Kemp, any longer."

"Officer, Ms. O'Conner knows the whereabouts of the son of a friend of mine. The boy's been missing and his mom's worried sick. Can you persuade her to tell us where he is?"

"That would be Robbie Stone, Detective. I don't think he wants Mr. Kemp or his mother, Maureen Stone, to know his location. It's enough for them to know that he's safe."

Kemp gave me a hard look, but I met his gaze, so he turned to Costas. The Detective shrugged his shoulders. "I can vouch that the boy is safe and he'll come back when he's ready to, Mr. Kemp."

Kemp let out an exasperated sigh, pivoted and strode to his vehicle.

"Better move your car, John," Costas said to the other officer.

After the two of them left I turned towards my house. Dash was still barking non-stop. "Do you want to come in? My dog is going crazy."

"Sure," he said following me up the porch steps.

Hot Fudge

As soon as I stepped inside the door, Dash jumped up pawing me. "Hey boy, steady. Everything is okay, now." I rubbed his head and kept talking to him until he calmed down. Costas was petting him, too.

"Why did you decide Kemp was Stone's killer?" Costas asked.

"First of all, it was Marti's idea to keep a watch on him."

"Sure, blame her when she's not here to defend herself."

It was irritating how he always accused me of being the ringleader when Marti and I ran afoul of the law. "It's true. Those were some of the last instructions she gave me before she left. Secondly, we hadn't 'decided' he was the killer, but he seemed like a pretty strong suspect. Why do you say he's not?"

"I didn't."

"Oh, here we go again. You always want me to spill my guts and there's never. Never. Any reciprocity."

Dash's eyes were closed as Costas rubbed behind his ears, but I wasn't so easily taken in.

"So, go ahead, spill your guts," he said, taunting me.

"I brought Rob in to tell you what he knows."

"Which is meaningless." He held his hand up, I guess to stave off my retort. "Nice kid, but I think his imagination has run wild." He shook his head. "He put two and two together and came up with six hundred forty-seven thousand and nine. What I'm saying is, don't put too much stock into what he told you."

"He didn't tell me much, just his suspicions. He's not going home."

"I don't think so. I couldn't convince him that his ideas were not much more than wild guesses."

"Do you think Kemp and Maureen Stone are innocent?"

"At this point, we're not ruling out any suspects. Well, except possibly you and Marti. Ed's another story."

Hot Fudge

Chapter Twenty-Two

The following day I decided I'd go to the gym. It would be a bit uncomfortable seeing Kemp there, but I'd paid for a month and he wasn't going to stop me from getting my money's worth. And of course, he was there.

Standing under an enormous barbell, he grunted a greeting when I walked in. I gave him a bright, if mostly phony smile and cheery hello as I picked up my weights. We worked out in silence for a while. He finished and put his equipment away. "Hey, how about a cup of coffee for old time's sake?" He asked, grinning. "Seriously. We'll both have a whole lot more time if we're not spending hours spying on each other."

"Umm, I don't know—"

"Oh come on, Onalee. You must see the humor in the situation."

I wiped off my set of weights, put them back on the rack and turned to him. "You've got an advantage over me. You know now that Marti and I aren't killers but I'm still not at all sure about you."

"That's what I want to talk to you about." He seemed earnest. "Look. You're not still scared I'm going to attack you or something, are you? We'll be surrounded by people."

Come to think of it, I would be safer than where I am now, in this basement with no one else around but Kemp. "Yeah, okay."

At the coffee shop, Kemp said he planned to order just coffee, no gooey muffin.

"I heard on the radio that yesterday was national glazed doughnut day."

He was ahead of me in line and turned around at this news. "I did not know that. Did you observe the holiday?"

"Nope."

"I would have if I'd known. Do you think it would be within the rules to celebrate a day late and with a muffin in lieu of a glazed doughnut?"

"I do. I understand that the regulations for that day are fairly lax."

Hot Fudge

He was at the display case now, an array of baked goods before him. "What's your sweetest muffin, ma'am?" He asked, smiling at the barista. Her green hair nearly glowed under the artificial lights.

"That would be the triple chocolate chunk orange."

He turned to me. "Want one? I'm buying."

"Sure. Thanks."

We poured our coffees and found a table. Kemp took a bite of his muffin. "Ooh, yeah this definitely is as good as a glazed doughnut. Delicious."

I tried mine. "It is yummy." We took a few more bites, savoring the contrast of the sweet fudgey bits with our bitter coffee.

"So, any word yet on Rob?" He asked after a sip.

"Haven't seen him. And, in case you plan on following me again, I won't be seeing him today."

"I say we call a truce, okay?"

"Like I said, I still don't know that you're innocent."

He sighed. "Do you have any sliver of evidence for this cockamamie theory of yours?"

"They always say that most people are murdered by those close to them. You were his business partner, lifelong friend, and now you're involved with his ex, who may or may not be in cahoots with you in a murder."

He shook his head. "I told you we were like brothers. I had no motive. Maureen? She was swimming in motives years ago, but as you can see she's moved on. Anyway, I'd like to declare a cease fire, okay? And then propose a partnership."

I was just about to take another nibble of my muffin, but my hand halted just in front of my lips. "What? Like Currier and Ives? Simon and Garfunkel? Bonnie and Clyde?"

"More like Holmes and Watson."

"What do you mean exactly?" I said narrowing my eyes as I completed the paused muffin-to-mouth gesture.

"You've got some chocolate on your lip."

What a time for that to happen. Of course, is there ever a good time?
"Thanks." I did a quick lip swipe with my napkin.

Kemp leaned in and lowered his voice. "Look, I loved Robin, but he was a complicated guy, especially the last few years. I'll give you a condensed version of our history. Years ago, we, like a lot of guys in the hedge fund game made more money than we knew what to do with. Then along came the big collapse and we had to scramble. So we decided to diversify and started buying up foreclosed homes." He saw me nod.

"All of this you knew, but what you don't know is that those real estate ventures sparked something in Robin. Real estate got in his blood in a way that investment banking never had. Me? I didn't like the business at all. Robin could see that, and we talked it over. The upshot was that he joined forces with another guy and formed a commercial real estate group. Robin was the silent partner in that deal. They were involved in big real estate deals all around the Midwest."

Kemp paused and stared past me out the window. Finally he gave his head a little shake and started talking again. "I. . . always thought there might be something crooked going on, but Robin seemed fine with it. Now I wonder if there was and that's what led to his death." He looked at me under raised eyebrows. For a brute of a guy, he sure had an expressive face.

"Hmmm, that's an angle we haven't pursued."

"Of course not. You wouldn't be aware of it."

"Do the cops know?"

"I mentioned my suspicions to your Detective Costas—"

"Whoa. Wait just a minute here. There is no 'my' Detective Costas."

Another eyebrow arch. "Oh. Sorry. I just assumed. Anyway, I got the impression Costas was underwhelmed by my suggestion."

"That may have just been his way of playing his cards close to his vest." *What is Kemp trying to convince me of?* "Sooo, you think his new partner may be the killer?"

Kemp sighed. "I honestly don't know. It very well could have been him. Or maybe it was Ed Reneveere—"

"Whom you offered a job to."

Kemp gave me a crooked smile. "Yeah. That's one way of keeping tabs on him now, isn't it? But, seriously, my buddy Rob stole a lot of hearts and left a lot of jealous husbands and boyfriends in his wake. It might have been one of them. Then there's my number one suspect, your buddy Eduardo."

I ignored that last comment and went on the attack again. "What about some of the people whose houses you and Robin snapped up for pennies on the dollar after the '08 collapse? It seems like there might be a few disgruntled types there with strong motives."

Kemp pursed his lips. "That's a big part of what I dislike about the real estate business. That was awful."

Huh. Maybe the big guy does have a heart. "Did you ever hear if anyone who lost his or her home vowed revenge?"

"No, but I'm not sure I would have. In those days, Robin was in Northern Michigan quite a bit of the time, but I was still mostly in New York."

"We've got a lot of their names."

Kemp smiled. "See? That's why I think we need to become partners. I love your initiative. Do you plan to contact all of them?"

"I figure that we may get in touch with some of them if more promising leads don't show up, but that was over a decade ago. What's the name of Robin's partner in the new company?"

"John Mischlik. You're an appraiser, ever hear of him?"

"Doesn't ring a bell. Did they do deals up here?"

"I don't really know. It was totally Rob's thing."

"So, if you suspect him, he must've been in the area at the time of Robin's death."

"I think so, they have an office in Harbor Springs. Robin called me a couple of days before he was killed. Something was wrong, I could tell by his voice. He wanted to meet with me for lunch. Problem was, I was in New York and trying to put this deal together." He paused. "Honestly? I was sick to death of cleaning up his messes. The upshot was that it was a couple of days before I got to Petoskey."

I chewed the last of my muffin, swallowed and asked, "Were you in town the day he died?"

Kemp narrowed his eyes. "Short truce, eh?"

Hot Fudge

"I told you, you're still on my list. Fairly close to the top, I might add. So, were you in town that day?"

"Yes, I was."

"Did you meet with him?"

"No. He asked if we could make it the following day. That was after I'd flown in from New York at his request."

"You were upset?"

"To put it mildly." He stopped and stared out the window again. I sipped my coffee and waited. I could tell that the chocolaty, orangey muffin delight had loosened his tongue. It would have anybody's.

He turned back, facing me again. "The thing with Maureen. It was driving a wedge between Rob and me. He didn't know about us."

"You never told him?"

He shook his head slowly. "No, it never seemed like the right time. Of course I knew the way Rob had treated her and that made me spitting mad. Anyway, I was on edge because of all of that and I said some things I regret now."

"Like what?" I asked employing my best empathetic tones. *A partnership with this fellow is questionable, but that won't stop me from pushing him further in his gut-spill-apolooza.*

He heaved a sigh. "Basically, what I just told you, about being at his beck and call, interspersed with some words my mother wouldn't have approved of. So, of course, when I heard he died, I was racked with guilt. Still am I guess."

"Would Robin have minded you being together with Maureen?"

"Oh yeah."

"But they'd been divorced for a long time. You didn't have anything to do with their break up, did you?"

"No. I was still happily married when that happened. No, Rob drove her away all on his own. It's called having an agglomeration of other women and engaging in spousal abuse."

"A great combination. Let me see if I've got this right. You believed Robin would be really mad if he knew about you and Maureen, but you were becoming more involved with her every day. If Robin were to, say, suddenly be out of the picture—"

"Come on. That's not a motive for murder. If he had found out it would just have been unpleasant for a while."

"What would he have done?"

"Lots of snide comments. He would've tried to lecture me on the reasons it was a bad idea as well as all trotted out all the negatives about Maureen. There would've been hot words but nothing that would end our friendship."

We sat in silence for a moment. Kemp raised his cup, took a sip and looked at me over the brim. "What do you think? Want a Watson to do some grunt work, Sherlock?"

Hmmm, I like his style. It's so refreshingly different from my current partner who is always trying to push me into the sidekick role. Of course it behooves me to be very wary of this fellow/possible perp. "What would this partnership look like?"

"There are a lot of leads to follow up on and I think with you and Marti and me investigating different ones, we'd be able to move much quicker and hopefully solve this before it devolves into a cold case. Also, say the inquiry into someone like John Mischlik. I wouldn't get very far with him because he knows me, but you or Marti could." He paused. "It's the same with Eduardo. I can probably investigate him better than you two could."

"Before I'd consider such a thing, will you swear that you are not the killer of Robin Stone?" I gave him my utmost steely-eyed stare but there was no flinching of Charlie Kemp. Instead he returned a cool, level gaze. *Huh. Maybe he is innocent.*

He raised his right hand. "I swear I did not kill Robin Stone. Now it's your turn."

"What?"

"Earlier you claimed I now knew that you and Marti were innocent. I know nothing of the sort, though I do tend to believe that to be the case. I want a sworn statement from you as well."

"Oh, all right," I said, raised my hand, and going out on a limb swore to the innocence of both myself and Marti (she did sell Stone the peanut butter fudge).

When I'd finished, Kemp smiled and reached out his hand for me to shake.

Hot Fudge

"I'll get you some information on Mischlik Properties. I can bring it to the gym. What do you think is the best approach for me to use to research Ed?"

"I don't know much about him, either. I thought for a moment. "I guess you could just start going to Lupita's as a customer. Get some conversation flowing and see what you can learn. You might be able to find out something online too, of course."

"Sounds like a plan."

We partners got up, bussed our table, and made our exit.

Connie Doherty

Chapter Twenty-Three

It was Saturday and it seemed as if my Number One partner had been gone forever. I hoped she was having a good time frolicking in the warm Costa Rican sunshine as her poor colleague schlepped along sidestepping danger whenever possible as she attempted to perform the spadework of two. I was on my way to the gym to meet with my other partner. My cell phone rang as I was driving and I let it go to voice mail. After I'd parked I saw it was Robbie and called him. My call also went to voicemail. "Hi Rob, I saw that you'd called. I'll be out of pocket awhile *(I love that term)* because I'm at the gym. I'll call you later."

I had the basement to myself for about ten minutes before Kemp made his appearance.

"I brought the dossier. It's upstairs in my bag."

Hot Fudge

Dossier? "Great. I'll look it over and come up with a plan. Mischlik's still in town?"

"Yeah. Unhh." He was struggling under his barbell. I waited while he finished. He set the weights down and turned to me. "He's staying at the Magnus Manor," he said mentioning our new boutique hotel.

"Can you tell me anything else? Got any icebreakers?"

Kemp thought a minute. "Robin used to complain about the fact that Mischlik is crazy about dogs. 'He's always wasting time stopping to pet some mangy mongrel,' he'd grouse."

"It's possible Dash will want to go for a walk by the Manor this afternoon."

He smiled. "I'd invite you to coffee, but I plan to try out a new establishment today called Lupita's. Have you heard of it?"

I nodded. "Yes. I recommend the coffee but not the fudge."

My routine finished, I left the basement. As I was putting on my winter togs, Jeff the owner of the gym came over to chat. Another storm was predicted and it was a great topic of discussion. Jeff, was a fellow cross-country skier, and we were both of the opinion that we could use a fresh snowfall, but I have to admit, quite a few Petoskey-ites were deep into the throes of their winter whines.

"We're way ahead of where we were last year at this time," Jeff said grinning. "Wait a sec. I'll show you." He walked over to his desk and came back with a newspaper in his hand. "See? Every week they give the snowfall totals for Petoskey and other towns around. We're at 140 inches so far. But we haven't had much lately."

"Wow. And another storm coming," I said, grinning along with him. Just then Kemp joined us.

"What's going on?" He asked.

Jeff showed him the snowfall data.

"Does the snow ever quit falling around here?"

That brought out some chuckles from Jeff and me. We finished garbing up and Kemp and I left the gym together. Outside he handed me the file. "Read it over and we can discuss it here on Monday."

"Sounds . . . Oh no." Rob was leaning against my car, but strode quickly away when he spotted Kemp and me together. Kemp swung his head to follow my gaze.

Hot Fudge

"Robbie . . . Robbie!" He yelled.

Rob turned a corner and was gone.

"Shoot. Maureen and I need to talk to him," he said still looking in the direction Rob had fled. He turned back to me. "Onalee, if you know how to get in touch with him, will you please tell me? Maureen is going crazy."

"I don't know. I saw him one time and that was it." I said, lying to my new compatriot. Yes, my fingers were crossed. I know that doesn't fully exonerate me, but I still harbored doubts about Mr. Charlie Kemp.

Charlie and I went our separate ways, and as soon as I was in my car I called Robbie. No big surprise, it went to voice mail. "Rob. It's me, Onalee. We need to talk. I know you saw me with Charlie Kemp, but I can explain. Please, call me. I'll be available the rest of the day."

Over lunch I read about Robin's commercial real estate company from the file Charlie had given me. They'd been in business for three years and had brokered some large deals, mostly in southern Michigan, Ohio, Indiana and Illinois. They seemed to specialize in shopping centers and occasionally, regional malls. The company was small, consisting of John,

Robin and an assistant. They had offices in Harbor Springs and Birmingham, Michigan, both prestige locations.

There was a list of the transactions that had closed during 2019. They sold the Hall of Fashion in Ferndale and The Parklands in Fraser, both large malls built in the last ten years in Metro Detroit and filled with high end retailers. There were also a number of small office buildings in Southeastern Michigan, Grand Rapids, Toledo and Chicago. Mischlik Properties was definitely a player in the big league.

I turned on my computer and their website invited me to meet with them to discuss my real estate investment goals. I thought I might just do that. Later Dash and I went for our afternoon walk and ran into Susan and Riley. It was good to see them. Susan and I bantered back and forth the whole way, but our thoughts about Susan's mom, my friend Mrs. Willowby, were left unsaid. As we yammered on, Dash and Riley wrestled and chased each other up and down the beach and got great workouts.

There were no calls from Rob the rest of that day. Finally around dinnertime, Dash and I took a drive into town to the house where he'd been staying. Even though it was dusk no lights were on, and no one came to the door. Once again, he'd vanished.

Sunday morning I bounded to the window to see if we'd gotten our promised snow. My car windshield was clear. After Dash and I cross-country skied and had our breakfasts, I started making some crusty baguettes and a big pot of vegetable soup. If we did get the storm, I'd be ready. By late afternoon, our house smelled of vegetables, rosemary, bay leaf, thyme, and baking bread. Outside, the sky wore a coat of an eerie shade of yellow, and the wind was picking up. Dash and I had our dinners, kibbles for him with a small soup chaser, and soup and bread for me.

I curled up in my chair by the wood stove with a good book, Dash asleep and dreaming by my feet. Around 8:00, I could hear the wind roaring. When the house shook after an especially large blast, the dog woke up and made eye contact with me. "Dash, it's a little early for your last walk, but I think that tonight, sooner is better than later."

We stepped out the door, and the wind lashed pellets of snow in our faces. We'd already gotten about six inches although drifts were piling up much higher. We fought our way along the road. For once Dash decided to cut the outing short and did several quick leg lifts. We turned around to head back when a jagged streak of lightning cut through the falling snow. Soon after came the rumble of thunder. Thunder snow! It was only the second time in my life I'd seen it.

Hot Fudge

Chapter Twenty-Four

I didn't wind up walking Dash near Magnus Manor after all. Instead, I'd decided it might be better to pose as a buyer— a woman of means with money to invest and not much knowledge of real estate. I could take advantage of the Mischlik Properties' advisory services.

I scooped snow for about an hour and a half that morning. It was hard to tell how much we'd gotten because there was about four inches in some spots and it was over my knees where it had drifted. Finally I finished, staggered into my house and heard the sound of an Emmet County plow truck rumbling by.

"Nooooo." I ran to the window, Dash on my heels. "Aghghghrghghr!" They had done it. The cursed plow had dumped snow about a foot deep in the end of my drive. How do they know when a homeowner has cleared his or her drive? They have an uncanny sense about it. I realize that they work through the long, dark blizzard-riddled nights and in high snow years like this one, they don't get much time off. But oh the fringe benefits they enjoy. The ability to, over and over again, inflict havoc and heart-ache on their friends and neighbors must be immeasurably gratifying to them.

I put my boots and jacket back on, all the while grumbling to myself. Let me set the record straight. I enjoy shoveling snow, I always have. But there can be too much of a good thing at times. This was one of those times. Grimly, I set about my task. The snow left by my friendly plow-man was as always, much heavier than that in the rest of the drive.

***

Kemp was already in the weight room when I got to the gym that morning. He may not have engaged in a pre-gym workout in his driveway. Indeed, it was entirely possible that as a billionaire, he didn't even own a snow shovel. After exchanging pleasantries we went through our routines and got down to sleuthing business.

"I did go to Lupita's Saturday, like I said I would and started worming my way into Ed's confidence."

"Are you also planning on tailing him like you did me?"

Hot Fudge

Kemp glared at me from between arms held high with a barbell. "I was doing . . . a great job." He paused again, grunting as he slowly lowered the weight. "How could I factor in that my prey was simultaneously stalking me?" He grunted again, starting another lift. "If it hadn't been for that . . . and that it does seem like . . . you're innocent . . . you'd be in the clinker now."

"Because of your superior bloodhound skills?"

He grinned. "Yup."

"Then I'm glad you're putting those talents to work on my team. Speaking of team, I have a plan that may help uncover any skullduggery that might be going on at Mischlik Properties. Want to hear about it?"

"Sure."

I outlined my idea of contacting the firm to invest some money for me as a wealthy woman named, Donna Mendleson, who needed portfolio diversification, in investment lingo (or so I hoped).

"Onalee, I think Mischlik will catch on pretty quickly that you don't, at least I assume you don't, have lots of spare cash floating around."

I looked pointedly at him. He raised his head slowly as the fullness of my plan hit him.

"This is where the partner-thing comes in I imagine."

I was swinging my weights out to my sides. "Uh huh." I smiled at him. "Would you consider transferring a rather large sum of money to my bank account?"

He gave me a narrow look. "No matter how clever I think I'm being, you constantly outplay me."

At this point, I was raising myself from a bench, stretched out like a plank. It's impossible to smile demurely with a clenched jaw. I was the one now grunting and gasping. "I need . . . money so that he'll . . . take me . . . seriously, but we could put something . . . in writing that it . . . reverts to you." I finished my ten body lifts and panted for a moment. "I'm not trying to scam you."

His gaze softened. "No, I know you're not, although if I agree to do it there will be written backup."

"Soitanly."

Hot Fudge

We finished our workouts. Kemp said he needed a little time to think about my scheme and would let me know. He left to spend more time at Lupita's, schmoozing with Ed. I had lunch and rushed off to my Hapkido class.

Dash and I had just finished our afternoon walk when I got a call. It was Kemp.

"All right. I'll do it. My lawyer is drawing up an agreement for you to sign. He thinks I'm nuts by the way."

"He's right," I said chuckling.

Kemp started laughing too and affected a thug-accent. "You mess wit me Girlie and my boy Eddy will be delighted to fix you up a nice plate of peanut buttah fudge. Ya git my drift?"

"I hear ya. When do I get my wad?"

"How about you come to my office in thirty?"

"Minutes?"

"Of course minutes, you idiot! You probably already know it, Ms. Snoops-A Lot, but my office is at 230 and a half Belle Drive."

Great. That would give me twenty minutes or so to shovel up another surprise package from the plow-jockeys.

In thirty-eight minutes I was sitting across from Kemp and his lawyer in a small room situated above a tee shirt shop. Kemp handed me papers to read. They seemed pretty straightforward. He would loan me three million dollars to start with and more on an as needed basis. The money would be returned to him as soon as our charade was over. He saw I finished my perusal.

"Any questions?"

"Can I have it in an attaché case in stacks of twenties?"

"Um no. It will be wired to your bank account." He smiled. His lawyer sat in stony silence.

"So what should I do if Mischlik wants me to buy a property from him?"

The lawyer studied Kemp as Kemp's eyes bored into mine. "Onalee if Mischlik killed my friend, I'll do whatever it takes to nail him. I can afford to take a flier on a piece of real estate if I have to. Go ahead and buy it, and we'll figure out the mechanics of it afterwards. I don't think that's exactly spelled out in those papers. Give them back to me and I'll add some verbiage to that effect."

  He took a couple of minutes and wrote a few lines. His lawyer looked them over and nodded. They were passed over to me. There was an authorization to buy property from Mischlik Properties on his behalf. It looked good to me and I said I was ready to sign.

  His lawyer stood up. "I'll get Estelle to come over and act as a notary."

  While he was gone Kemp asked, "Any word on Robbie?"

  "Nope. I'm certain he's okay, but I don't know where he is."

  "Yeah, I'm sure he is, too. It's just that Maureen is at her wits' end over this." He thought a moment. "I would be too, if it were my son missing."

  "Do you have kids?"

  "No, sadly it never worked out."

  Estelle and the Legal Eagle came in. Kemp and I both signed in triplicate, and our signatures were witnessed and notarized. I left with a copy tucked under my arm knowing that my bank account would be slightly larger by morning.

Connie Doherty

Even though I was now, or soon to be a millionaire, I decided I wouldn't make any radical changes to my life. I would still perform my duties to the best of my abilities as an appraiser in Northern Michigan. This is why after leaving Kemp's office, I went straight home and bid on several jobs. Afterwards, Dash and I ate our dinners in companionable silence.

That evening I purchased a cheap track phone to use to call and set up my appointment with Mischlik. As I waited in the checkout line to pay for my phone, I decided I'd crossed over from amateur sleuthdom to caper-world. I didn't know much about my new role having never read any novels in that genre. I would simply have to rely on my wits backed up by a rather large bankroll.

It was still early when I called Mrs. Willowby to confirm our weekly shopping trip for the following afternoon. "Hi Dot. What time should I pick you up tomorrow?"

"Hello Onalee. As I always say, you're the working lady. It's up to you."

Hot Fudge

"What about 3:30?" I said as my lead gambit. I was pretty sure she enjoyed this game as much as I did.

"That would be fine, dear. I can probably pick up one of those TV dinners for a quick meal when we get home."

"Which ones do you like?"

"They all seem to be nutritious."

Nutritious not delicious. "Maybe we should go earlier so we both have time to cook our dinners."

"That would be lovely. Pork chops are on sale this week."

"Terrific. See you at one o'clock?"

"Wonderful."

I was smiling as I hung up the phone. She was so cute. I just wished she and Susan would mend their differences.

***

After Dash and I had exercised and eaten our breakfasts I placed a call to Mischlik Properties. I spoke with a lady who told me Mr. Mischlik was in a meeting but promised to let him know I called. *Drat. I want to discuss my million dollar bank account with somebody and I can't very well go*

Connie Doherty

telling his assistant or whatever she is. I know it's not real but it's fun to pretend. If I really had a million dollars that was mine to keep? I probably wouldn't change much. It would be put into a nice high interest account so I'd have it to fall back on if I ever needed it. Of course there is that sweet little row boat I've had my eye on for a couple of years.

I checked my email to see if I'd gotten any of the jobs I'd bid on. I definitely didn't get two of them and there was no word on the third. A little before one o'clock I moseyed on over to Mrs. Willowby's house. Mrs. Stirnaman was coming home soon, and I was going to miss these jaunts with Dot. I parked the car at the curb and looked at her striped house to check for the flicker of her curtain. *Hmm, she's not at the window.* I climbed out of the car, went up to her porch, and rang the doorbell. I waited. No answer. *Uh oh. this is not good.*

Hot Fudge

Chapter Twenty-Five

I got my cell phone out and called her number. Again no answer. I tried the door. It was locked. I called 9-1-1 and waited in my car for the ambulance. When the first responders came they asked me a couple of questions regarding why I thought Mrs. W. was in trouble.

"We were going to go grocery shopping at 1:00 today. We confirmed it last evening and she always has her coat and boots on and is ready to go."

Using a tool, they broke into her house. Mrs. W. was in trouble. They found her in the bathtub. She told the EMTs that she'd gone in to take a shower at about ten a.m. and fell as she was trying to climb out. As they wheeled her past me, bundled up in blankets, she made eye contact. "Oh Onalee. I'm so sorry about this. Thank you for calling the ambulance for me."

"I just wish I could have gotten here sooner. Is there anything I can do?"

"No, dear, but thank you."

They left. I called Costas to find out how to go about securing the broken front door for her. After that was taken care of I went on a solo expedition to Foodrights. I saw the sale pork chops and picked up a package. If I knew the intrepid Dot W., she'd soon be back at her house. Everyone at the store wondered where she was. I had a feeling Mrs. Willowby wouldn't lack for company if she was admitted to the hospital. After walking my favorite poodle, I called Susan. She wasn't there so I just left a message to call me. Then I hopped aboard the Honda and drove over to the hospital.

Mrs. Willowby was still in the emergency room. They'd taken her for x-rays and she was waiting for the results. About an hour later a doctor came into the room. She nodded at me then said to Mrs. Willowby, "Dot, I'm afraid it's just as you feared, you have a broken hip. The standard treatment is surgery and the doctor would put pins in to stabilize it."

Hot Fudge

Mrs. Willowby nodded. "Yes, many of my friends have been in the same boat the past few years." She managed a weak smile.

What a trooper. I stayed with her for a couple of more hours until they took her to the room. Surgery was scheduled for the following morning.

When I got back home there was a call on the burner phone. I had forgotten to take it with me. It was from John Mischlik, himself, and he was apparently looking forward to meeting me. It was after five o'clock so I figured I'd call him in the morning. I checked my other phone, but Susan hadn't called back. Dash and I had our dinners, leftover soup for me and fresh kibbles for him.

Rather than clean up the kitchen, I rushed out the door and got to the bookstore before it closed. I knew Mrs. W. was a reader and unless she was on powerful sedatives would be yearning for reading material. I found a Sleuth Sisters book by Maggie Pill. It was a mystery but would be lighthearted enough for a person facing surgery. Mrs. Willowby was dozing when I reached her room. I jotted a quick note and left the book on her table.

***

The early morning sun pushed back the clouds and flowed through my office window, finding me ensconced in front of my computer. I was accepting my next appraisal, a proposed industrial building that would be constructed in Gaylord, a town about forty miles away. The phone rang, and it was Susan.

"Hi Onalee. I saw that you phoned, but I didn't get off work until too late to call. What's up?"

"Hi Susan. It's your mom. She fell and broke her hip. She's probably in surgery right now." There was silence. "Susan?"

"Had she been drinking?" She said in a flat voice.

"No. She fell when she was taking a shower. I told you she's been sober for many years." *Maybe Susan has a right to be angry with her mom, but Mrs. W. is my friend too, and I'm getting tired of her snarky remarks.*

"Okay. Well thanks for letting me know," she said and hung up.

I'd hoped that this crisis would bring Susan and her mom back together, but that didn't seem very likely.

Hot Fudge

I called Mr. Mischlik back and was thrown into his voicemail. About an hour later, just before I left for the gym, he called and we agreed to meet at 2:00 at his office.

Kemp was at the gym when I arrived and we strategized about how I should present myself to Mischlik. He also said that he and Ed were becoming buddies. Ed had even told him about the building he was buying on Mackinac Island. He said that there had been a lot of holdups, but the sale should close in about a week.

"Do you still think he's running a human trafficking ring?"

"I haven't seen any evidence of it, but that doesn't mean he isn't. I am going to do some surveillance on him today."

"Is it because he's Hispanic that you think he's involved with that or do you have a valid reason for being suspicious?"

He smiled, but not in a friendly way. "I know you don't know me very well, but if you did you wouldn't ask that question. I think about the only prejudice I have is against people who are prejudiced. It really bugs me. And no, I don't have any evidence against Ed. I just remember hearing Robin talking about it."

"Okay. I'm sorry I implied you might be racist." I paused to pick up one of my weights. "What exactly did Robin say about it?"

"That's all right. I guess you were just looking out for your friend. Let's see, what did he tell me?" He thought a minute. "Just that Ed didn't seem like he was on the up and up. He'd heard that the Island was a known place for trafficking and he thought maybe that was why Ed wanted that building so badly."

"It's also known for it's tremendous volume of fudge sales."

"That's true. I haven't ruled out the fact that my old partner may have been waging a smear campaign. Then again, if that's the case, that gives Ed another motive to kill him."

"Yup, you're right. Keep up the good work." We finished our workouts and I dashed off to get ready for my appointment.

Kemp and I had agreed that I'd go over to Maureen Stone's house and borrow some of her clothes. I always feel as though I'm dressed fairly well, but my wardrobe was partly garnered from our wonderful thrift stores, augmented by sale items and a few splurges. You won't find any designer names in my closet unless they're second hand.

Hot Fudge

Maureen is about my size and she loaned me luxurious coats, sweaters, silk shirts, and slacks so that I could look the part of a big bucks lady. I loved her taste and it was going to be fun to wear the garments.

I stashed the clothes in the back of my car and zipped home. Dash and I went for our walk and afterwards I dressed in a sky blue cashmere sweater and creamy wool slacks. An elegant, high-waisted wool coat and my dress boots completed the ensemble. I still had a little extra time, just enough to go see Mrs. W. and find out if her surgery was successful. At the hospital I slipped into her room. She was asleep and looked good, but I couldn't find anyone to ask about her.

It was time to meet Mr. Mischlik so I hurried back to my car. At his office, an assistant had me ensconced in a comfortable waiting room and offered me coffee or bottled water. I declined and it was only a few minutes before Mischlik appeared. I took stock of him as he strode over to me and introduced himself. He was a little taller than average and had curly black hair turning to grey. Not handsome in the conventional sense, but he had a pleasant face. Leading me back to his office he chatted about the weather and how much he and his family enjoyed Northern Michigan.

His office had several overstuffed easy chairs in front of a large oak desk. He bade me sit and instead of taking the executive seat behind the desk, took the chair beside mine. In spite of myself, I had to admit the man was charming and I was enjoying my time with him. We talked a little more and then he asked, "What brings you in here today?"

I told him the story Kemp and I had fabricated about my recent inheritance and my wish to invest some of the money in something solid like real estate. "My parents were fairly well-to-do. My father rose up through the ranks of Ford and my mother was a partner in a law firm. I'm an only child and I married well. Twice actually." I grinned at my new friend John. "I've always had stocks and mutual funds and of course savings, but for some time now I've wanted to diversify. Now with this, I guess you might say windfall I received from my late aunt, I thought it was the time to do it. What do you think?"

Mischlik's eyes crinkled as he grinned. "I think you might be asking the wrong person. I'm a real estate guy, remember? I eat, drink, and breathe the stuff. I'll always encourage you, or anyone who can, to invest in it." He shook his head. "I've been lucky enough to put together some pretty good deals for people over the years. But, if you ask me about stocks, I barely know an option from a dividend." He laughed. "I guess what I'm trying to tell you is I'm one of those one-trick ponies you sometimes hear about. But if the trick you want to know about is real estate, I'll do my darndest to help you."

I nodded. "Actually, I've thought a lot about this before I called and I would like to proceed."

We discussed the money I would be able to invest and its liquidity. Shaking my head I said, "It's stupid I know, but all of that inheritance is just sitting in a bank right now, not making me any money at all."

"It may not be so stupid. I often come across deals that are absolutely terrific, but they're great because they have a short fuse. They take a person who has ready cash and is willing to act immediately. Unfortunately in the real estate game prudence isn't always rewarded." He was leveling with me, but then he flashed me a smile. "Remember though, I'm working for you. If you're not comfortable with any venture we explore, it's off the table."

"I like that. I want someone I can trust." I pretended to surreptitiously peek at my watch.

"Do you need to get going?"

"Um, I have a few more minutes." I looked over at him and grinned. "It's just that I always try to walk my dog at around the same time every day."

John became excited. "What kind of pup do you have?"

"A standard poodle."

"So he or she has brains as well as beauty."

What a nice thing to say. "Thanks. I am crazy about poodles. Do you have a dog?"

"Oh yes. Three of them, actually. All rescues."

I loved this guy. "My boy Dashiell is a rescue too." We spoke about dogs and various dog rescues for another twenty minutes.

"I could talk with you all day long, but I do need to get going."

He nodded. "Take a few days and think about what we discussed, and if you want to proceed I'll go to work for you."

Hot Fudge

I left the office and walked to my car. A soft snow was falling and big flakes filled the air. My windshield was covered but I knew the wipers could handle it. I brushed off the side windows. *Is it just my imagination or is someone watching me? Not again.* I shivered. Finishing quickly, I hopped in the Honda, and motored back home.

Chapter Twenty-Six

The following morning Dash and I skied on our usual trail It was one of those times when the snow was perfect, loosely packed down but not icy. I danced along the trail as Dash loped beside me. It was about twenty degrees and a snowy wonderland morning.

After we finished our breakfasts I sat down in front of my computer to work on my new appraisal. Dash laid down near my feet. It was a little after nine, and time to call Mischlik Properties.

"John, I thought all night about what you said and I know for sure that I want to go ahead. I'm excited."

"Excellent. I'll get back with you as soon as something comes along that I think you'll like."

Hot Fudge

Okay, Item One knocked off my to-do list. Next? Download plans and specs for the proposed building in Gaylord. I worked for a couple of hours before getting ready to hit the gym.

***

Kemp listened intently as I detailed my meeting with John Mischlik.

When I finished he looked over at me from beneath his barbells. "It sounds like you like the guy."

"I do, though I don't know him very well."

"Do you think he'd still be charming the socks off you if you didn't have three million dollars to invest with him?"

"Probably not, but he is an easy person to be around."

"Just be careful. I'm leery of the guy."

"How well do you know him?"

"Not well at all, but just from things Robin said I don't trust him."

"Then why did Robin keep him as a partner?"

"I don't know. At first he was all gung-ho about him, but it seemed to me he was cooling off towards the end."

"What did Robin say?"

"Nothing specific, at least that I can remember. It was mainly just a feeling I got."

I nodded. "Men's intuition."

Kemp grinned. "Something like that."

"Anything new with Ed?"

"Nah, only that he seems to lead a pretty dull life. Just work and home."

"No visits to motels or other havens for sex traffickers?"

"Not that I've seen so far."

"Are you going to keep up the surveillance?"

"Oh yeah. Absolutely. Today he goes to St. Ignace to close on that Mackinac Island building."

"Are you following him up there?"

Kemp set down his weights and lowered himself to the floor. "Eh? Probably not. If he is involved in something like trafficking this would still be his base of operations, right?" He started doing push-ups.

"Seems like it. Do you and Maureen have any plans for the weekend?"

Hot Fudge

"Eighteen . . .nineteen . . .twenty." Panting, he got to his feet. "No. Since Robbie has been missing she's been really depressed. She doesn't want to do much of anything. What about you?"

"I'm not planning on much, but they are having the viewing of the crucifix tomorrow."

Kemp nodded. "I've never done that."

Many years ago, a large statue of Christ on the cross was damaged in shipment and the people who had commissioned it no longer wanted it. A diving club bought the statue and placed it on the bottom of Little Traverse Bay as a diving attraction and also as a memorial to all who have been lost at sea. During most winters, when it's deemed safe, a group of volunteers cut a hole in the ice for divers to use and for a public viewing. The event takes place for one day. "You two should go, especially if you've never seen it."

***

After Dash and I had our lunches, I went over to the hospital. Mrs. W. was sitting up and had company. She broke into a smile when she saw me.

Connie Doherty

"Hello dear. I'd like you to meet my daughter Rhonda. Rhonda, this is Onalee O'Conner."

Rhonda's hair was much darker than Susan's but she had the same wide smile. She had driven into town the day before from Chicago and was staying with Susan. We talked awhile, but I didn't want to intrude on their family time. The two of them were chattering together like old friends as I left. I was glad Mrs. W. had the support of at least one of her daughters.

Parking at our local hospital can be challenging and I had left my car about two blocks away on a side street. It was calm and in the mid-twenties, an altogether pleasant day for a walk. That is until I got that creepy feeling again. I quickly turned but didn't see anyone behind me or across the road. *Once this case is solved, I am never going to stick my nose in a murder investigation again.* Now that Marti was a permanent fixture in the area, I could just see her dragging me into every unsolved crime north of Gaylord. I would have to put my foot down.

I managed to reach my car with nothing untoward happening, but I could swear a vehicle tailed me on my route across town. At the house I worked on my report for a couple of hours before going for a walk with

Dash. When we got back home I noticed footsteps in the snow leading to one of my windows. I don't generally go in that part of the yard in the winter and I hadn't for at least several snowfalls. Besides, my feet weren't as big as the ones who'd created the craters in my lawn. It scared me, but mostly it made me mad.

I unlocked the door and entered cautiously. Dash didn't sense anything and I couldn't see anything amiss. I did a walk-through of my main floor, then got up the gumption to check out the basement. Everything seemed copacetic. It was Friday and I wouldn't see Kemp at the gym until Monday. I wasn't about to wait until then to get to the bottom of this.

"Why do keep following me? You asked to be my partner and yet you still don't trust me? This is crazy. You—"

He broke in, "Onalee? What are you talking about?"

"You know. The last couple of days I thought someone was tailing me and today I've got proof."

"Onalee, it wasn't me. I've been in my apartment on the phone with clients all afternoon. But, what do you mean, 'you have proof'?"

"There are footsteps in the snow outside my window from someone with big feet."

"Lock your doors. I'm coming right over."

"They're—" He hung up. Shortly after that I saw Kemp's car outside my house. I went to the door, but he detoured to examine the footprints. He was on his haunches as I waded through the snow to get to him. He looked up. "I don't care for this one bit. If someone doesn't like what we're doing, I wish they'd go after me, not you."

"Yeah, well, that's not good either."

"I think you should call your friend, Mr. Costas."

"And tell him someone has been tromping through my snow?"

"Hmmm, I guess you're right. Maybe you could stay with Maureen for a few days."

"I've got a big dog and I don't know how welcome we'd be there. Plus, I would be putting her at risk."

He nodded. "Would you go to a pet friendly motel? I'll gladly pay the charges."

Hot Fudge

Wow. I'm touched. Kemp seems genuinely concerned. "No, but thanks. I'll be careful and it helps to have Dash around, even though I don't like the idea of having a dog for protection." Dash of course had been barking all this time.

"Yeah, he's got a deep voice. I wouldn't want to tangle with him."

"Charlie, can I ask you something?"

"Sure."

"It's something I've been wondering about. If Robin Stone was such a jerk and you're clearly a nice guy, why were you two such great friends?"

He looked across my yard at a big maple tree as if the answer were hidden in its tangle of branches. Turning back to me he said, "In the past few years I found myself asking that question. Quite a bit actually. But he wasn't that way in the early days. All that wealth . . . it isn't always good for people. It twisted him and made him feel like he was entitled to anything he wanted, no matter who it hurt. If he hadn't been killed I'm not sure if we'd have stayed friends that much longer." He paused. "I truly miss the guy I knew and loved twenty years ago, but I guess I've been missing him for a long time."

We talked for a few more minutes and I assured Kemp I was safe. After he left I locked the door, turned on my computer and got to work. Shortly before dinner the phone rang and it was Mr. Costas himself. Had Kemp called him?

"Hello. Onalee?" He sounded odd and I was put on guard.

"Yeah, hi. What's up?"

"I have the day off tomorrow and I . . . thought. Well, I wondered if you'd be interested in going to view the crucifix?"

Whoa. Costas is asking me out? "Um."

"I know it's last minute, so if you can't do it, I understand."

"Did Kemp call and put you up to this?"

"What? Who?"

Huh! He sounds sincere. "Sure. That would be fun. I'd love to go." *Wait until Marti hears this.*

Hot Fudge

Chapter Twenty-Seven

Saturday morning dawned with clear skies and the warmest temperature we'd had in some time. The forecasters claimed we'd see close to forty degrees by late afternoon.

Dash and I hit the trails early to jump ahead of the rising mercury and get the best snow. As it had been the day before, the skiing was excellent. Nearing the end of the wooded area, I heard a hollow knocking sound close by. I stopped to see if I could find the culprit but he had stopped his rat-a-tat-tatting. I decided he was further on though it was hard to tell because his drumming echoed through the trees. *Oh. There he is, a pileated woodpecker.* He was about eighteen inches from head to tail. As his beak banged against the tree, chips of wood dropped to the ground. All of a sudden one of his beady eyes fixed on me and he took to his wings, gangly and almost prehistoric-looking as he flew low through the trees. Getting to see him made this morning's ski extra special.

Since I'd spent so much of my week in sleuth mode, I figured I'd better put some time in on my appraisal. I worked until taking Dash out for his afternoon promenade. Costas was coming at 3:30.

***

From the highway above the waterfront I saw a ragged line of people stretched about a quarter mile across the ice.

Costas saw me looking at it. "It was even longer earlier."

"Wow, but it'll probably move fast."

We parked the car and climbed out onto the snow-covered ice. It was about a half-mile walk to get to the end of the queue. The vivid blue sky was a stark contrast to the white frozen lake. Lots of people were with their dogs and I wished I'd brought Dash. He would have enjoyed it. A couple of cross-country skiers joined up behind us. In the distance I could see a couple of kids and their parents climbing up on the breakwater. I spotted Lacey and Pete ahead of us as well as a couple of people I knew from the gym. Smiles were on everyone's faces as they chatted and joked with those around them.

"No one could ever accuse us Northern Michiganders of not having a hot social life," Costas said, laughing.

"That's for sure. I wonder if people in other parts of the world would stand in line for an hour and a half to glimpse an underwater crucifix?" We had heard that was the typical wait, but the time was going by fast as we moved along towards our destination. The sun felt warm and, if the truth be told, I think a whole lot of us were coming down with spring fever.

By the time we got up to the viewing tent, our new good friends the cross-country skiers who were visiting from Royal Oak, Michigan had filled us in on their jobs and their kids.

"Do you think Jess will sign up for another tour in Botswana?" Costas asked Marge the skier whose son was in the Peace Corps.

She and her husband Jim exchanged a look. "All we know for sure is that whatever he does next will be a surprise." They both laughed. "We think it's great he's doing these things while he's young. Oh, look, you're the next ones to go inside."

Costas and I stepped into the small tent and looked down into the hole. We'd heard they'd had to chop through over six feet of ice. The water was about twenty feet deep and we had a clear view of the statue below. We looked at it for a couple of minutes and then exited out the rear of the tent so that Marge and Jim could have their turn. After they finished we said our goodbyes and Mr. Costas and I went for pizza.

***

Sunday morning Dash and I were at the county park when we ran into Susan, her sister Rhonda, and Riley, the Tibetan Terrier. Dash rushed over to greet his good friend and the two of them began a game of catch-me-if-you-can through the trees.

"How's your mom doing?" I asked whichever of the two of them wanted to answer.

"Pretty good, actually, but she's got a long road ahead of her. Lots of rehab," Rhonda said. "She's going to be transferred in a couple of days to whichever nursing home has a bed for her."

Hot Fudge

"Do you think she'll ever be able to get back to her house?"

"Oh yeah. If she had her way, she'd be there now," Susan said laughing.

Huh! Have she and Susan reconciled? It sure sounds like it. I smiled. "I'd much rather see her at home."

Rhonda looked at Susan. "So would we."

Instead of skiing, they were walking and just starting out so Dash and I left them and skied on our way.

When we returned to the house there was a call from Lacey and I remembered seeing her at the crucifix viewing. Gee, I wonder what that busybody wants I thought sarcastically, but I called her anyway.

"Yes it's the first time we've done anything together. Yes we had a good time. No I didn't find out anything about the murder. . . I don't know if he'll call again. Yessss, I would go if he does call again." Geeshshsh. I wished we hadn't picked such a public venue for a date.

I had decided to cook a curry for dinner and after breakfast began cleaning and chopping vegetables. I placed a legal pad (yellow dogs one of my old bosses called them) and a pen on the counter. That way, I could sort through ideas about the case as I cooked. I picked up two onions and began dicing. As I chopped, I decided to list the suspects in chronological order, so the first one was Eduardo. As I thought about it I could see that he had all the ingredients for a stellar suspect stew.

Start with one highly desirable chunk of real estate on Mackinac Island. Throw in a batch of motives including cut-throat competition for the building, probable slander by Stone about Ed's alleged involvement in human trafficking, pressure by Stone to let him have the building, and maybe other vexations we didn't know about. Bring to a boil and let simmer for several weeks. Stir up trouble frequently with Stone's visits to Lupita's. Add a pinch of poison and? Voila. Death is served.

I finished the two onions and started on my six cloves of garlic. Let's see, I guess Charlie Kemp possibly aided by Maureen Stone would be next on my list, I thought. Robbie's continued disappearance was like an underlying thrum of wasps in a blackberry patch— a constant reminder of trouble, although it might never be dangerous. Robbie must still believe that his father was killed by his mother, Maureen and Kemp. To this humble observer it didn't seem as though Maureen would still have enough motive to kill her long-divorced ex. Kemp might have a motive related to one of their businesses, but he truly did seem as intent as Marti and I were to find the killer of his good friend.

I wrote down all my thoughts before turning to my spice cabinet and large container of special Indian spices. I gathered all the greats including mustard, coriander, fenugreek, and cumin seeds, and turmeric. A couple of dollops of oil went into my cast iron skillet. When it was hot, I added the seeds and stood back as they popped and sputtered. A lovely aroma engulfed me as I added onions and garlic cloves. After a few minutes it was time to add a quart of tomatoes, pressed tofu and peas. I let the pan simmer for a while as I started preparing potatoes.

Spicy Indian potatoes are a wonderful addition to any meal. Speaking of additions, I couldn't leave Bill Reneveere off any self-respecting list of possible perps. He had to be angry that Stone had ruthlessly undercut his beloved taco restaurant and driven him out of his life's work. Also, he was in Petoskey the day Stone was poisoned, so he may have had opportunity. Everybody on the island had gone on and on about what a nice guy he was. Wasn't it usually the nice guys who turned up with blood on their hands in the last chapters of most of the amateur detective novels I'd read?

Yup, Mr. Kind and Good Reneveere definitely needed further study by our team, and another trip to the island might be in my future.

My current research subject, John Mischlik, former Stone real estate brokerage partner, should also be listed though so far I hadn't found any reason to be suspicious of him. There were also several avenues we hadn't pursued yet, such as the current Mrs. Stone and the people whose houses Stone and Kemp had purchased out of foreclosure. I made a note for either Marti or me to start contacting some of them.

I finished the potatoes, pea and tofu curry, and stirred up a small amount of raita. By the time I'd finished cooking dinner for that night and the next few days, it was time to take Dash for a walk. As we strolled along, I kept mulling over the case. Oddly, while walking with Dash in my neighborhood and even through the woods at the county park, I didn't get the feeling I was being followed. I watched very carefully around me and never saw anything or anyone acting suspiciously. My stalker seemed to zero in only when I was active on the case.

Hot Fudge

It was another day of sunshine, but today the forget-me-not blue sky to the east was dappled with small puffy white clouds. Meanwhile, across the bay, Harbor Springs was cloaked in a curtain of snow.

Upon returning to my house, I called Kemp to see if he knew how to get in touch with Mrs. Stone.

"Hi Onalee. Everything okay?"

"Yes, but I was wondering if you know how to reach the current Mrs. Stone."

He paused a moment. "Ummm, you know she lives in Bay Harbor, right?"

"I'd heard that." Bay Harbor was a large development built in the mid-1990s with expensive, mostly second homes.

"She lives on the Peninsula, and as you probably know, it's a gated community. You or I can't just walk up to her house."

"Wouldn't she allow you access?"

"I tried to talk with her right after Rob was killed and didn't get anywhere."

"Do you think she might have done it?"

"Murdered Rob? It's possible, but I've got to believe there was a prenup. I'm guessing he was worth way more to her alive than dead."

"But if he had been mean to her like he was to Maureen, maybe she couldn't take it anymore."

"Yeah, maybe." He sounded doubtful.

"Even if it's a long shot, I'd still like to talk with her. If nothing else, she would probably know his whereabouts that day."

"True. I'll call her if you want. I could tell her there's some business I want to go over with her. She'll probably agree to come."

"Perfect. Maybe I could be present, acting as your assistant or something."

"Sure. I'll give her a call in the morning. It might look odd if I call her on Sunday afternoon, and I actually do have a couple of items I should discuss with her. What's your schedule look like for Monday and Tuesday?"

"I'm available anytime except between one and two on Monday. Other than that I'll be working at home both days."

"Do you actually get any appraisals done?"

Hot Fudge

I could hear the smile in his voice. "Yes." I might have come off sounding a little defensive. My billings had been down the past couple of years as I probably spent more time than was prudent in my sleuthing endeavors.

Connie Doherty

Chapter Twenty-Eight

Midway through a bowl of porridge my phone rang. It was Kemp and we had a meeting with Lisa Stone at 2:30 that afternoon at his office. He told me to think of questions I wanted to ask her and we could brainstorm in our usual sanctum of strategy, the gym. Later, as I was typing a description of the proposed industrial building my cell phone dinged and it was a text from Mischlik, also wanting to meet this afternoon. Things were heating up. We agreed on 4:00. It looked like I'd be able to fit in a solid two hours of work today around the appointments, the gym, Hapkido, taking care of Dash and my meals. It was a good thing this client wasn't in the normal rush for his appraisal.

***

Lisa Stone strode into Kemp's office a few minutes before 2:30. She looked to be in her mid-thirties and was gorgeous. She greeted Kemp with a smile and nodded at me. Kemp introduced us, offered her a chair, and they got right down to business. As Kemp had said, there were several matters to discuss with her. In assistant mode, I jotted down notes as I took stock of Mrs. Stone. She struck me as more than just a trophy wife. Lisa seemed intelligent and asked several pertinent questions. When their business was concluded, Kemp leaned forward a little and clasped his hands on top of the desk.

"Lisa, how are you doing, really?"

She looked away for a moment. "Life is crazy, isn't it? As I'm sure you knew, we'd had problems. His stupid womanizing. I told him I would divorce him if he kept that up, but he agreed to go to counseling and we worked through it. We were finally in a really good place . . . and then. . ." she shook her head and bit back tears. After a moment she said, "I'm sorry. Usually I keep it together pretty well, but every once in a while like now, because I know how close you two were—"

Kemp reached out his hand and covered hers. "I know. I miss him like hell."

Lisa still on the verge of crying, nodded.

"Have they made any progress toward finding whomever was responsible?"

"I don't know. Of course as the spouse I was questioned. I might still be a suspect for all I know, but I haven't heard from the police in a long time."

"Did Rob say anything to you about any problems he was having?"

"I have racked my brain trying to think of something he might have said that would be a clue as to why this happened. I haven't come up anything." She paused and thought. "The only thing that has struck me is that he seemed preoccupied. Something definitely was on his mind."

"By 'preoccupied', do you mean worried?"

"Yes, absolutely."

"Did he tell you about the building he was trying to buy on the island?"

"Sure. He was kind of obsessed with it."

"And he mentioned Eduardo and that he was bidding against him?"

She nodded. "Yes. He was frustrated that Eduardo was standing his ground."

"Did he say anything about any suspicions he might have had about Ed?"

"You mean the human trafficking?"

Kemp nodded.

"He did, but I had a feeling that it was kind of conjecture on his part. Do you think it's true?"

Kemp shrugged. "He mentioned it to me. So did a few other people, but I've also heard that Rob could have cooked up the story in order to get that building out from under Ed."

"He might have. I loved the guy, but he was no angel," Lisa said and heaved a sigh.

"I've tried to get to the bottom of the truth about Ed."

Lisa shot Kemp a puzzled look. "Really? How?"

Kemp turned to me and grinned. "I think we can tell her, don't you?"

I nodded.

"Onalee and I are a crime solving duo. I've been cozying up to Ed, while she investigates John Mischlik."

Lisa's eyes flicked back and forth between Kemp and I. "So . . . that's really why you asked me to meet with you today?"

"Partially."

"Why didn't you level with me?" She pulled her hand out from under his and started to get to her feet.

Kemp eyed her for a moment. "Lisa. I am truly sorry if I've hurt you by this, but as you said, I cared deeply for Rob. I'll move heaven and earth if I have to, to find his killer."

"And her?" She said pointing at me.

"Onalee's best friend Marti was there when Rob died, so they also have an interest in seeing his killer brought to justice. Please help us."

I wasn't sure what would happen if I jumped in, but it might be the only chance I had to talk with Lisa. "One thing that would really help us is if you know what his schedule was that day."

Lisa swung her head to face me. She sat in silence for a few minutes. Finally she seemed to come to a decision and spoke, "The last time I saw him he told me he was going to the office." She looked at Kemp,

"Mischlik Properties, not Amerirock. They were working on some real estate deals around Detroit."

"And where was he going after that?" I asked.

"He didn't say. We both kind of did our own thing during the day."

"Did he usually come home for lunch?" I asked.

"No. He was used to going to lunch with clients or people from the office so he usually ate lunch out."

"You didn't usually see him until?"

"He'd get home anywhere from five until nine or ten, sometimes even later. But over the last six months or so, since counseling, he was trying to get home at least by six or seven."

"Would you know of any old girlfriends that might be upset that he changed his life around?" I asked.

"There probably are some, but he kept that part of his life pretty separate from me. I wouldn't have any idea who they were. Charlie, you'd know way more about that then I would, I suspect."

All eyes turned on Kemp who was pinking up. Even the tips of his ears had a rosy tinge. I felt sorry for the guy and jumped in, "Actually, I had heard that Charlie was with Rob when there were women, but it sounded like it was mainly just drinks in the bar. I'll bet Charlie never even knew more than their first names."

Kemp gave me a grateful look. "That's about the size of it."

Lisa smiled at him. "Rob always said that Charlie is such a boy scout."

We all chatted a few minutes. Lisa agreed to help if there was anything else we needed. She left and I said to Kemp, "Robin had good taste in women."

"Yeah, at least the ones he married."

***

Before going to Mischlik's office, I stopped at the house and gave Dash a short walk. I also changed into my heiress attire. A few minutes later I was driving down the hill into the picturesque town of Harbor Springs. I found a parking space on the street and parallel parked. An older model light blue car passed me. That was definitely not the first time I'd seen that vehicle. *I wonder what size boots the driver of that car has?* I thought and shivered. I ducked into the building where Mischlik Properties is located.

Hot Fudge

As I opened the hefty wood door I was again struck by the heavy ambiance of luxury.

The assistant looked up from her keypad. "Hello Mrs. Mendleson," she said using my alias.

"Hi Laurie. Is John Mischlik available?"

"No, but he should be back any minute." As before, she offered me beverages and I declined.

A few minutes later John rushed through the front door, greeted both Laurie and me, and ushered me into his office. He shucked off his jacket and again took the chair beside mine rather than on the other side of his desk. "How's Dash?" He asked, smiling.

I returned his smile. "You remembered his name. I'm impressed."

"You know how it is with dog lovers, we can remember pooch names but usually not their owners'. You should have brought him with you."

"I thought about it, but you have such a lovely office, I wasn't sure if I should."

"He's always welcome." He got to his feet. "Now let me grab the information on this property. It just came from our Birmingham office."

He sorted through a couple of files on a credenza behind his desk, sat back down beside me, and punched some keys on his laptop. "How much of our lives is spent idly waiting for these things to boot up?" He chuckled. "Okay, here it is." He turned the screen so I could see it. "It's a small neighborhood shopping center in Metro Detroit. It's got nine tenants and a great rental history. There's almost never a vacancy and the rents are pretty decent. I've printed some of the financials out for you, just the basics." He pushed the computer out of the way and opened the file. "If you decide you're interested, I can give you more specifics, but look at the bottom line. Their net operating income, that is the income before interest payments, income taxes and capital expenditures, like a new roof. You know, the stuff that doesn't come up very often. Anyway that net income is just under a mil. This building is located in Troy. Are you at all familiar with the Detroit area?"

"A little. Troy is a pretty nice area, isn't it?" *He doesn't need to know that I lived there for ten years.*

He nodded. "Yup. It's very solid. If it's priced right, and this one is, you can't go wrong with an investment in Troy."

Hot Fudge

"What is the price?"

"This is one of those cases where the buyer is overextended and needs to divest quickly. He's willing to let it go for $800,000. That would give you a helluva good return. What do you think?"

"I wasn't expecting to buy something so fast. How soon would I need to act?"

John looked me straight in the eye. "Honestly, I don't know. It'll be first come, first served. I promised the seller that I wouldn't sit on it, so I need to get it in front of as many eyeballs as possible. You're the first one I've told, but I am meeting with three other clients yet this evening. Look, I told you before that I'd never pressure you and I won't. You have to take the time you think you need." He paused, lifted his eyebrows and smiled. "That being said, I'm afraid if you ponder too long, this property along with its beautiful return will be gone."

"Could I have until tomorrow?"

He tilted his head. "I actually think my five o'clock is going to pounce on it if it's still on the market."

I rubbed my eyes. "Oh no. I—"

"Look, Donna. There will be other deals. I can't guarantee they'll be this attractive, but they might be. You need to be comfortable when you proceed."

He was smiling at me and I returned the smile. "I hope you're not disappointed in me, but I just have to think about it a little."

"Of course."

"If I decide to go ahead with it, assuming it's still available of course, what would I need to do?"

"You would have your bank wire me the money in the amount of the purchase price."

"I wouldn't get a mortgage?"

"On the regular, run-of-the-mill deals with average returns, sure. Taking the time to get a mortgage, and waiting for an appraisal is doable. But on these great deals? No. I call them my hot potatoes. I can't hang onto them for very long, but anyone able to act fast can win big."

I nodded and got up to leave. "I'll let you know tomorrow."

He reached out and laid a hand on my arm, briefly. "That's perfect."

Hot Fudge

Chapter Twenty-Nine

Dash and I had exercised and eaten our breakfasts when I called Mischlik. "John, I've gone over and over that file you gave me yesterday. I think I'd like to go ahead with that deal. If it's still available I mean."

"Oh boy. I was afraid this was going to happen. The gentleman I met with at five o'clock snapped it up."

I sighed. "I should have jumped on it. It was a great deal."

"Donna? It was your first time. There will be others."

"Thanks for not giving up on me." I hoped I wasn't laying on the helpless female thing too thick.

"Never. Take care and I'll be calling you about another deal soon. You'll see."

Later at the gym, I related the details about the shopping center to Kemp.

"There will be other deals. I think it might have looked suspicious if you'd acted on the first one."

"Thanks. That's what I kind of thought."

***

The rest of the afternoon I worked on my appraisal. During the evening I called Susan to ask about her mom.

"She's been transferred to Birch Lake Rehab Center. She's doing really good."

"Great. Is your sister still here?"

"No, Rhonda had to get back to work. Onalee . . . all that stuff I said about my mom. . . I was so mad at her, but when all this happened and I saw she had finally quit drinking. . . oh my gosh. Its like we have another shot at being a family."

I felt tears flooding my eyes and I was glad we weren't face to face. "That is fantastic, Susan. I'm so happy for both of you."

The next couple of days were fairly uneventful. Dash and I got our exercise. Kemp and I hashed and rehashed theories and suspicions. He was becoming frustrated with his efforts regarding Ed, and couldn't understand why he wasn't finding evidence of the trafficking or making any headway on him as the killer of Rob Stone. The more he dug into it and fussed with his lack of progress the more I believed in Ed's innocence. I kind of thought that Kemp was coming to the same conclusion. He was going to set up another appointment with Bill Reneveere, but this time it would be on the island, ostensibly to further discussions about Reneveere managing the taco restaurant. I was afraid that Kemp was going to try confronting him about his dispute with Stone. Kemp was a strong guy, but who knew if Reneveere packed heat?

As for me? I was counting the days until Marti and Frank got back this coming weekend. It seemed like they'd been gone forever. Mischlik wasn't calling me so I was dead in the water on that investigation. I pulled out the list of names of people who'd lost their homes in the financial crisis that were then purchased by Kemp and Stone. This might be like finding a needle in a haystack or more aptly for Petoskey, a contact lens in a snow bank. But I found an old newspaper story about one hard-luck homeowner.

Connie Doherty

The name of the family was Delray, Rick and Lynne Delray and their two kids. Both Rick and Lynne worked because the family needed two incomes to pay their bills. Lynne got breast cancer and their insurance company dropped her. She couldn't get insurance anywhere else and her medical bills were astronomical. They got behind on their mortgage and their house was foreclosed on.

Mr. Delray went to the local bank where he'd gotten the mortgage but was told that it had been sold. There was nothing the bank could do. Delray's efforts to contact the financial group that bought the mortgage proved fruitless. The giant company wanted immediate restitution of all of the missed payments plus interest. They weren't interested in restructuring the loan so that the Delrays could handle it.

When his house came up for auction, Mr. Delray was on hand to plead with any possible purchasers to let his family stay in their home. Surprisingly Stone himself had shown up to bid on the house. According to the reporter, Stone turned a deaf ear on Mr. Delray. He bought the house that had cost the Delrays over $100,000 for $69,000. Later one of Stone's staff contacted the Delrays and offered to allow them to rent their home for $1,000 a month. The monthly mortgage payment that they couldn't afford had been roughly $750.

The reporter continued to check in on the Delrays from time to time. They were living in their van when Mrs. Delray died of the cancer. It seemed possible that Mr. Delray might be someone who would have reason to hold a grudge against Rob Stone.

I Googled Rick Delray. There were hundreds of them, but only three lived in Northern Michigan. I checked the phone book and got phone numbers and addresses for two of them. One lived in Alanson and the other lived in the country between Petoskey and Charlevoix. It took me two tries to catch the Alanson Delrays at home. When I did talk with them I found out they had recently moved to the area from Metro Detroit. The country Delrays turned out to be a young couple in their twenties. The good people at Google told me a third Delray was living in Wolverine, but I couldn't find a phone number for him. *What the hay. It's a fine day for a drive.*

I motored out Mitchell Road going east toward Wolverine. This drive is beautiful in the fall as you glide between hills splashed with crimson, gold, orange and green. In the summer there are rolling hills, a lovely farm market, and vistas of far lakes of vivid blue. In late winter I drove through towering cliffs of snow that had been pushed to the roadside throughout this season of heavy snowfall and wind.

I followed the county road all the way to Wolverine. In the summer people flock to this town to canoe and kayak down the swift moving Sturgeon River. On this day in early March I didn't see much action on the streets of the nice Northern Michigan community. With not much of a plan, I stopped in the market on Clibourne Street. As I was paying for my package of gum I asked the man behind the counter if he knew Rick Delray.

"Yeah, I know him. Why you askin'?"

I knew Marti had told me to always tell the truth, but somehow I didn't think it would work here. "His deceased wife was a dear friend of mine. I'm in the area and thought I'd drop in and see how he is doing. Is he okay?"

"Yeah, I'd say so. You should go see him for yourself."

"I know he's in Wolverine, but I don't know exactly where he lives."

Hot Fudge

"He's just up the way on Cantrell Street in a green and white trailer. You can't miss it."

I thanked the shopkeeper, picked up my gum, and drove to Delray's street. As I made my way down the road I watched on both sides for a green and white mobile home. After about a mile, I found one. There was a car in the drive so I hoped someone was home. I rang the bell and heard footsteps moving towards the door. It opened and I saw a well-lined face under a mop of gray and black curly hair.

"You're a friend of Lynne's? I'm sorry, I honestly don't remember you."

"Hi Mr. Delray. The store owner called you, eh?"

"He did. This is a small town. We watch out for each other."

"That's a great thing. My name is Onalee O'Conner. My friend Marti was on the scene when a man named Robin Stone dropped dead possibly because of some fudge she'd sold him. She and I got kind of involved in—"

"I guess I don't follow you. What does this have to do with my wife and me?" He seemed genuinely confused.

"Robin Stone? You don't remember him?"

He rubbed his chin. "Should I? The name kind of rings a bell."

"He's the person who bought your house out of foreclosure."

He nodded. "Okay. I vaguely remember." He scowled. "Then they wanted to rent it back to us for way more than our monthly payment. Man, I'm glad those days are in the rear view mirror. Anyway, what can I do for you?" He stepped back. "Here, why don't you come in? It's freezing out there today."

I liked this fellow and felt no fear, but he was on our list of suspects. *Should I?* It didn't strike me as a dangerous situation. I moved inside and was immediately in his small kitchen. Everything was orderly and clean. We sat at his kitchen table.

"So you were saying you got 'kind of involved' in something with this Stone fella."

"Someone murdered him and we're trying to delve into his past a bit—"

"You're walking into strangers' houses to see if they're killers? Boy howdy! If one of my daughters was doing that, I would be out of my mind with worry for her. Do you really think you should be doing this?" He gave me an earnest look.

Hot Fudge

"Probably not, although we're pretty careful—"

"You're sitting inside a trailer with someone you suspect may have killed a person. You call that being careful?"

"Um, you don't seem like a murderer. Besides, it was very likely a crime of revenge and other people wouldn't be on the killer's hit list."

"But you do, indeed, think I may have killed this man because he bought my house and then my family was suddenly homeless. Is that correct?"

"I thought it was a possibility."

"I will tell you that those were dark days for my family." He studied the checked vinyl tablecloth. "Of course you probably know that my poor wife died as we made our home in my Dodge Caravan. But I made sure my kids got to school every day and I took the best care I could have of my wife. After she died and I filed for bankruptcy, with no house payments, I was eventually able to save up a little money and we settled down here in Wolverine, where real estate prices aren't so outrageous.

Connie Doherty

"My kids are smart and they worked hard in school. They both got scholarships and went to college. One is at the University of Michigan and the other graduated and is working as a nurse at the hospital in Petoskey.

"I kept my job at Northern Robotics through the whole recession thanks to an understanding boss. I commute to work near Petoskey everyday no matter what the roads are like. Last year I met another lady as wonderful as my wife and we're planning to get married in the not too distant future. But was I intent on revenge for the wrongs that were done to my family twelve years ago? Honestly? I was so busy taking care of my wife and kids and working that I didn't have time to think about anything or anyone else. Of course this is just my word on it, and you may still think I'm a murderer. But I'm not. You'll have to keep on looking. That is if you insist on continuing this dangerous pasttime of yours." He stood up. I was pretty sure that was my cue.

"Thanks for talking with me, Mr. Delray and I'm glad things are working out for you now."

Hot Fudge

He walked me to the door. "Say, you wouldn't happen to know of anyone else who was bent on revenge after losing their house, would you?"

He closed his eyes then shook his head. "I can't believe you. No. But it's not like we formed a house-losers-club or something. I don't even know the names of the other people. All I know is that there were a lot of us. Now go and stay safe."

The good news was that I'd found the right Delray. The bad news was that it looked like, once again, I hadn't uncovered the killer.

Chapter Thirty

On Friday morning when I met up with Kemp at the gym, I told him about my Delray searches in Alanson, the countryside towards Charlevoix, and my trek to Wolverine.

"You should've taken me with you to those places. We are looking for a murderer you know, not a sweepstakes winner."

"I decided to go on the spur of the moment. Have you found anything else out about Ed?"

"You're changing the subject, but no I haven't. So far, he seems to be a genuinely nice guy. I hate to say it, but I'm beginning to think that against all odds he truly is a genuinely nice guy."

"Then if Ed's peanut butter fudge didn't do Stone in, who and what did?"

Hot Fudge

"Remember, Lisa, the current Mrs. Stone, said he was going to meet up with John Mischlik that morning. Maybe he's our man."

"He definitely could be."

"Has he called you lately?"

"No. That's why I started looking into those foreclosure people, so at least I was doing something. There are lots more of them we can track down."

"You mean search for them one by one online and go interview them?"

"Yup."

"That sure seems like a ton of work."

"As I have to remind Marti from time to time, being an amateur sleuth isn't all glitz and glamour."

He grunted though whether it was from the weight he was lifting or his distaste for the work ahead of us, I guess I will never know.

Kemp and I walked out of the gym together, discussing our plan to wade through the group of foreclosure people. We parted company. I walked to my car and started it up. A mile or so from my house I began to think I was being followed again. I turned down a sparsely populated street and the car behind me also turned. I pulled into an alley and stopped. The tailing car slowed down, saw my car sitting there and drove on. It was the old blue sedan I'd been seeing for the past week or so. Unfortunately, I couldn't identify the driver. I backed out of the alley and looked, but the blue car was nowhere in sight. I drove the rest of the way home with no further sign of my surveiller.

At the house I locked and bolted my door before petting Dash. Then I scanned part of the list of the people who had lost their homes and emailed it to Kemp. I hoped Marti would want to jump right in and help out with this tedious task when she returned from her two weeks of marital bliss.

I spent the rest of the afternoon working on my appraisal. The next step would be to drive to Gaylord and inspect the site of the proposed building and also look at the comparables I'd found.

After Dash Boy's afternoon outing I looked for more of the people who had lost their homes. Some of the names didn't show up anywhere in Northern Michigan. They must have moved on or were no longer with us. After a couple of hours, I did have a list of four couples who were still around. In each case both the names of the husband and wife matched the names on the foreclosed house, so I assumed it was a match. I was also able to get their current addresses from phone books or the internet.

By this time my stomach was rumbling and I fired off my computer and fired on a delectable pot of popcorn. Very soon Dash and I were eating a lovely dinner.

***

It was Saturday and Doggie-cakes and I were up bright and early. We had a lot to do, and with warm temperatures predicted we needed to get to the good snow before the sun made it sticky. The skiing was delightful, but we were at the time of year when our days of skiing were numbered.

After we each had our breakfasts, I packed lunches and water for us both, along with my appraisal gear, and we set out for Gaylord. There wasn't much traffic on the roads which was why I liked to do these inspections on weekends whenever possible. With Dash riding shotgun we drove around industrial parks, snapped pictures and took notes. At noon we stopped at a park and ate our lunches. In the bright sun it was warm enough to sit outside on a bench. I'd also packed snowshoes, and after eating Dash and I hiked a trail alongside a cross-country ski track. Later we went back to the industrial area and finished up.

We pulled into our driveway at about three o'clock. There was still time to go to the address of the foreclosed people who lived in Oden, just north of Petoskey. I dropped Dash off at the house and hopped back on the road.

***

After knocking at a bungalow on Northwest Way, a stout woman who looked to be in her fifties opened the door. I could hear a television in the background.

"Are you Katie's mother?" She asked.

"Um, no I—"

"You're not delivering Girl Scout cookies?"

I smiled. "No, but I'd love to have a package of their peanut butter sandwich cookies right about now."

"That's exactly what we ordered," she said smiling back.

"Actually, I'd like to speak with Mrs. and Mr. Sandacre."

"I'm Sara Sandacre."

Hot Fudge

I introduced myself. "I'm looking into some of the foreclosures that happened during the financial crisis of '07 and '08."

"Yes we did lose our house back then."

"Do you remember Robin Stone and his company RealCashNow that bought your house?"

She looked over her shoulder. "Terry? Do you remember a man named Robin Stone and his company RealCashNow?"

The volume on the television was lowered. A fellow a few inches taller than Sara and just as sturdy came up behind her. "Why, wasn't that the group that wanted to rent our house back to us after they stole it?"

"Now Terry."

"They did and you know it, Sara." He looked at me from beneath bushy eyebrows.

I introduced myself again.

"What can we do for you?" Terry asked.

"I wanted to ask you both a couple of questions about Robin Stone if I could."

Sara and Terry looked at each other. Terry shrugged. "There's no law against asking, but I've never heard of him, have you Sara?"

"No. As I recall it was a kid, probably in his twenties that we dealt with. I guess his name could have been Stone."

"That would've been an employee I guess. Did you rent from them?"

"No, ma'am. We had to move in with my dad until we could get back on our feet, but we did it." Terry said.

"I imagine it was tough."

"The hardest part was leaving our home, but we had no choice. We'd both been laid off because of the recession and nobody was hiring."

"That's terrible that the bank wouldn't work with you."

"We talked with them but there was nothing they could do. Why was that, Terry?"

"They'd sold the loan to a big national conglomeration. Anyway we got jobs finally and caught back up, thanks to my dad of course."

It didn't look to me like they had revenge in their hearts, but I tried again. "Did you hear that Robin Stone was killed a couple of months ago in Petoskey?" I watched them closely. They both looked surprised.

Hot Fudge

"He was the man who dropped dead in that fudge shop?"

We didn't have many murders in Petoskey and when we did they were the talk of the north. "Yup."

"My goodness," Sara said.

"Why did you want to ask us about him?" Terry asked as a car pulled into the drive. We all watched as the passenger door opened and a girl climbed out with a big grin on her face.

"Hi Katie," Sara called.

The cookies had come. I was tempted to see if Katie had any extras in the car, but instead I made my getaway. I was pretty convinced there was no murderer here.

When I got back to the house, I listened to two messages, one on my landline the other on my burner phone. The first one was from Costas calling to see if I'd like to go to a spring festival in Boyne City that evening. The highlight was going to be an appearance by the Petoskey Steel Drum Band. I'd read about it in the Petoskey paper but it had completely slipped my mind. *I can't believe I forgot about this. My on and off involvement with the crime scene in Northern Michigan is becoming too time consuming*, I thought as I waited for the message on my other phone to start. This message was from Mischlik.

"Hi Donna. It's John Mischlik. I didn't forget you and I have an opportunity for you. I know it's Saturday but if you're interested, give me a call at your earliest convenience."

I called John back right away and he answered. "It's another one of those deals with a great return but a short fuse. Are you interested?"

"Yes."

"Good. Can you meet me at my office tomorrow so that I can show you what we have?"

"Sure."

"How about one o'clock? That gives you time to take good care of Dash, first."

I laughed. "See you then."

It was time to phone Costas back. I wanted to see the steel drum band, but two weekends in a row with Mr. C? I called him, we talked and he picked me up at 6:30 that evening. He said I could bring Dash, but despite

Hot Fudge

all of his wonderful traits, being in a crowd of people and dogs wasn't the big dog's strong suit.

We wandered around the downtown for a while until the band started. Many of the stores offered food and glasses of wine or cups of hot cocoa. We also stopped in a few galleries and saw wonderful artwork by some of our talented local artists. At a little before eight o'clock we spotted the double-decker trailer roll by with the kids from Petoskey High School. It was time to stake out our spot near the band.

They started with a couple of Jimmy Buffet's tunes. As usual the talented group sounded great. A steel drum is a wonderful thing and when you get about thirty of them plus big kettle and base drums it makes for happy ears and tapping toes. I looked over at Costas and he had a big smile on his face as they played the Irish music from River Dance. Snowflakes were spiraling slowly down and the streets were filled on this starless March night. At that moment, there was nowhere else I'd rather be. Costas caught my eye and grinned. *Uh oh! Looks like I have some decisions to make.*

Chapter Thirty-One

It had been a fun evening in Boyne City with Camille Costas, but I had the feeling he was more serious than I was. We had to have the talk. I figured I should probably do it soon before Marti attempted any interventionist matchmaking maneuvers. But first things first. Right then I was driving over to Harbor Springs to meet with John Mischlik. I parked the car, opened the heavy wood door and stepped inside.

"Come on into my office, Donna. Unfortunately, my assistant has a life and likes to have a day or two off." John called out, chuckling.

Mischlik was sitting in his chair on the other side of the desk, punching away at his computer. When I entered he looked up and smiled, showing the crinkly lines around his eyes.

Hot Fudge

"I hope this isn't another wild goose chase for you, especially since I dragged you out on a Sunday." He got up and pushed his laptop across the desk in front of the two chairs.

"Yeah, this better be good." I said giving him a fake scowl.

He laughed again. We both sat and he opened a new screen on the computer. "Okay. This is the property. Nothing glamorous, I'm afraid." This time he smiled with raised eyebrows. The screen showed a nondescript office building. "The property is in Shelby Township a suburb of Detroit, an upper middle class one. Are you familiar with that area?"

"No. You say it's by Detroit?" I plastered a puzzled look on my face.

"Yup. In the northeast suburbs."

"Oh. I've been though Detroit many times but never really spent time there," I said mendaciously.

"Shelby Township is a nice area and very solid."

He turned to his computer monitor and showed me a video of the exterior and interior of the building and some of the surrounding properties. "Not sexy but sound. And the return is excellent. Here, I'll show you." He leaned over, opened up a file, and pulled out a couple of papers. "There are nine tenants and all but one of them have been there for more than five years. They are all signed to triple net leases which means that you don't have to worry about paying real estate taxes and insurance or short-tem maintenance.

"The owner has never had a problem with vacancies. The net income last year was roughly $138,000. I just listed it for $1,300,000 which works out to $100.00 per square foot. But before I even started to market it, the owner called me. He's in a real bind and is willing to let the building go for $1,000,000 cash if he can sell in the next couple of days. The rate of return on the original price was a respectable 10.6%, but you or whoever buys it, can achieve a return of 13.8% if the price point is a mil. Try to get that rate consistently in the market or anywhere else."

"My goodness." I sat and pretended to be thinking it over. "I guess I know just enough to be dangerous. It is a good rate, but . . . I hate to put you on the spot here—" I looked over at him. "What questions should I be asking you?"

He smiled. "That's a great question right there. Whether you're buying real estate through me or anyone else there are certain things you should ask. Such as?" He looked through his marketing package. "Such as how's the roof? I can tell you that the roof is a shingled gabled roof. It was replaced three years ago and should be good for probably twenty more years. Another thing to find out is the durability of the income stream. Look. The net is a little higher than last year's income and it has been consistent for the last five years according to this. Actually the owner told us that even during the recession he was able to keep most of his tenants."

Mischlik continued in this questions I should ask along with the answers format.

When he was finished he sat back and looked at me. "Do I have any time to think it over?" I asked.

There was an eyebrow raise and a head shake.

"Your five o'clock is going to latch onto this one too?"

"I'm giving you first crack at it, but this time there's a four o'clock. Sorry, but the seller truly needs to act fast. Then again, you can skip this one and maybe another will happen by. We were lucky to get two of these hot deals so quickly."

I perked up. "You don't usually get two so close together?"

"No. This completely caught me by surprise. I usually sit and wait a good long time before being able to offer one of my clients a return of over twelve percent. At least in this economy and for such a sound building in a strong location. But again. You've got to be comfortable with the deal, Donna."

"What do you think the property is worth?"

"It's a solid buy at its listed price of $1,300,000 and a bargain at a mil."

"Ooh boy." I paused and closed my eyes for a moment. "Okay. I'll do it."

John beamed at me. "Atta girl. I have a purchase agreement all filled out. I knew that at this price it would sell by the end of the day." He rifled through the file again, found the buy-sell agreement, and handed it to me. "Here we go. Read through it before you sign and let me know if you have any questions."

The document was several pages. I was breaking out in a cold sweat. It wasn't my money I was committing, but it was still a $1,000,000. Was I excited? More like panicked, but I knew Kemp would happily kiss this money goodbye if it meant zeroing in on his friend's killer. Most of the document was written in legalize but had been issued by a title insurance company. "Is this a standard contract?"

"Yes. It's the form the Lucretz Title Insurance Company relies on. They're a local company and very highly regarded in the industry. Nearly all of the form is boilerplate and includes protections for both the buyer and the seller."

I nodded and kept reading. "Okay. It looks fine, I guess."

"You saw the stipulation we added that the money has to be in my escrow account by close of business tomorrow?"

"Yes. I can have my bank wire it, right?"

"Absolutely. All set?" His eyes searched mine.

"Yes."

"Good. Then we need a signature right here along with today's date." Mischlik handed me a pen. It was weighty and definitely not one he'd picked up on the counter of the local tire store. I signed it and handed it back to him. He tore off the back page and handed it to me as my copy.

"You'll need to notify your bank tomorrow morning first thing."

"Okay."

Mischlik held out his hand. "Congratulations, Donna. You're going to do very well with this property. On Tuesday I'll have the rest of the paperwork for you."

We talked about dogs for a few minutes and I left to go relax with some much needed poodle therapy.

Hot Fudge

Chapter Thirty-Two

Yesterday had been another sunny day with temperatures reaching into the low forties, but the thermometer had dipped below freezing last night and everything was icy. It was a good day to skip cross-country skiing. Instead Dash and I walked through the neighborhood. As dog walking outings go, it was a four on a scale of one to ten. But if my cross-country skiing days were numbered and it certainly looked like they were, we'd had a great run this winter.

As soon as nine o'clock rolled around I notified the bank that I needed to send the $1,000,000 (gulp!) to the bank account of Mischlik Properties.

I'd called Kemp Sunday night to tell him about my use of his money.

"I don't like all these deals made at warp speed. I told you I'm not a real estate guy, but I have bought and sold the stuff, both personally and with Robin, for many years. I've never been involved in anything like this."

"I know what you mean. As an appraiser I'm not at the heart of the action but I do look into every sale I use as a comp, and I've never heard of it either. As soon as I get the money sent off tomorrow, I'm going to drive down to Shelby Township and check this building out."

"Good idea. Think I'd better come with you?"

"Nah. I should be fine. I'll be careful."

Marti had gotten back and called after I'd hung up with Kemp. She'd had a terrific time in Costa Rica and both she and Frank were planning to buy new toys.

"On, you've got to try boogie boarding. It was so much fun. I just couldn't quit laughing." She talked for quite a while about what they'd seen and done. "Frank did most of the driving and it was kind of scary. Lots of switchbacks on narrow mountain roads."

Gradually we got around to the case. Marti admitted she hadn't given it a great deal of thought while she was on her honeymoon. What nerve. I started telling her that Kemp was palling around with Eduardo and keeping him under surveillance in order to determine whether he was our perp.

Hot Fudge

"Whoa. Hold up just a minute here. Who is 'our' as in 'our perp?'"

"Geez Louise, you've been gone a long time." I thought back for a minute. "I guess it was just after you left that Kemp and I realized we were on the same side and became a crime-fighting duo with the understanding that we'd expand to a trio when you got back."

"Really."

"Yes and there are other developments." I filled her in on everything I could think of. If I omitted anything, it was of a personal nature and nothing that should be of any interest to Meddlesome Marti. When I finished I asked her if she was available for assignments.

"What do you have in mind?"

Up until this point she had been an active, friendly listener. There was a tinge of churlishness to her question in my opinion. "We have that list of people whose houses were foreclosed on and purchased by one of Stone's companies."

"And they were all good solid leads right?"

I had just told her in detail about the encounters I'd had with the people who'd lost homes and that they had amounted to nothing. "Um. I know it's a long shot, but we don't have many other avenues to pursue right now."

"And they lost their homes when?"

She must have a bad case of jetlag was all I could think. "We looked them up together. It was from 2008 to 2012, during and after the housing collapse and recession. There are still a large number of people we haven't talked with and one of them could have harbored a grudge all that time."

"And what are you doing the next few days?"

I sighed. We'd just gone over this, too. "I'm going to continue my investigation of Robin Stone's real estate partner, John Mischlik."

"It sounds like I'm getting all the grunt work again. You know, Onalee, just because you're a body ahead of me it doesn't mean you can boss me around."

So that was what was eating her. We were back to the old question of whether she or me (I know it should be "I" but I can't resist the rhyme) was the sidekick. Appraisers usually aren't known for their superior social skills and smooth-talking. I had to think a moment.

"Did we get cut off?"

Maybe two moments. "No, I'm here. Marti, I was forced to head up operations while you were gone. Both Charlie Kemp and I had to forge ahead the best we could. We both really missed you and your expertise, but though we mentioned it numerous times, we could not in good conscience call you back prematurely from your honeymoon. I know that talking with those long ago foreclosure people is way beneath your skill level, but I'm afraid it's all I can think of for you to do right now."

"Really? You two wanted me to come back early from Costa Rica?"

I could hear the smile in her voice. Oh my gosh. My schmoozing had worked. "Heck yes, but it wouldn't have been fair to you. We muddled on without you."

"Okay then. But I also think I'm going to do some research on poisons. We still don't know what killed Stone. That is unless Detective Costas told you anything."

"He didn't and it would be great if you looked into that."

***

Connie Doherty

In the morning I got everything squared away at the bank, called Mischlik and told him the money was on its way, and hopped into my car for a four to five-hour drive down to Shelby Township. Marti was going to take care of Dash while I was gone. It was a mild March morning and mostly sunny. The roads were clear and I would be able to make good time down I-75.

Rolling into the parking lot of my newly acquired property, I noticed it was just before two o'clock. I sat in my car for a while looking the building over. Mischlik had told the truth. It looked in very good shape physically. I got out and entered the building. The hallway finishes were adequate but not upgraded. The doorway to the second suite on my right was open so I decided to start there. When I entered, a gray haired lady looked up and smiled.

"Hello. Who are you here to see?"

"Hi, I'm Donna Mendleson and I might buy this building. Is it all right if I look around a little?"

"Certainly. I'll tell Mr. Richards you're here. He doesn't have any clients right now so I'm sure he won't mind if you poke your head in his office."

Hot Fudge

She introduced me to her boss and we talked for a couple of minutes. "You're the second possible buyer in the last week," he told me.

Say what? Mischlik told me it was just been listed and he had told no one else about it yet. "Really?"

"I hope I didn't let the cat out of the bag," Jim Richards said when he saw my surprise.

"No, no." A thought occurred to me. "Did you happen to get the other interested person's name?"

"As a matter of fact, we got to talking, just as you and I are, and he gave me his card. Just a sec and I'll get it for you."

I looked at the card he handed me. The address of his business was in Canton Township, another suburb of Metro Detroit. It wasn't anyone I knew or had heard of. "Can I keep this card?"

"Sure, but let me make a copy of it first." He snapped a picture of it with his phone and again gave me the card.

"Have you been happy leasing space in this building?"

He smiled. "Yes. it's been great."

"No maintenance issues?"

"We haven't had any problems and we've been here for going on six years."

We talked a little longer before I left to inspect other units. The next two offices were closed up, but there were names on the doors so I assumed they were inhabited. Further down the hallway, I stopped at a non-profit entity. The receptionist was very friendly and also made positive comments about the building. She too remembered the other man who had toured the building. I talked with all of the tenants who were available and established that they were relatively long-term lessees just as Mischlik had said. I popped back in the office with the open door policy and thanked Mr. Richards again for his help.

It was about two forty-five. I could take another couple of hours and go to the other end of Metro Detroit to the prospective buyer's address in Canton Township, or get back on the road and call him when I returned to Petoskey. Four and one half hours later I pulled into my drive. When I was greeted by the Dash dog, I knew I'd made the right decision.

I quickly called Marti to let her know I was back and would give Dash his nightly sojourn. She told me she had contacted four of the foreclosure families and crossed them off our list of suspects. She'd also started delving into the dark art of poisons.

"On, it's downright scary how easy it is to get hold of some very lethal substances. It's all around us. Depending on the poison used and the dosage, Stone could've been poisoned ten or twelve hours before his death or within minutes."

"How will we be able to tell what the poison was?"

"We won't, but in a murder investigation like this they would have done a toxicology test. Your Costas would very likely know."

"He's not 'my' Costas."

"Whatever. I wonder how we can get our hands on that information?"

"We're sure not going to get it from Mr. Costas, as you well know."

"Nah, probably not. We need a mole in the PD."

Connie Doherty

Chapter Thirty-Three

For the first time in a very long time, I was meeting Marti at the gym. When I finally got to see her, she glowed with happiness.

In the basement we met up with Kemp, and our weight lifting session was crammed with catching up. It was all sleuthing news, and we heard almost nothing about Costa Rica.

I could tell that Marti enjoyed the Kemp turnabout from prime suspect to crime-solving partner. We listened as he told us of his time spent talking with Ed over coffee at Lupita's and then surveilling him. "I've got to admit, I really like and admire the guy. After all this time, I haven't uncovered one shred of evidence that he is anything but a nice man and hard worker."

"I always thought he was great too, but—" Marti and I exchanged a look, both of us remembering when Ed had gotten angry at us.

Hot Fudge

"Maybe we misinterpreted his reasons for getting so mad," I said.

Marti nodded. "It sounds like we did. I sure hope so. I do not want to believe that Ed is capable of poisoning someone even if they did have their differences."

"It sounds like you're also saying there is no evidence of Ed engaging in human trafficking either. Right?" I asked Kemp.

"I haven't seen any sign of it."

"Hmmm, maybe he'll lift the ban on us and welcome us into Lupita's again," I said.

"Yeah, I could use a piece of fudge right about now."

When I mentioned my detecting efforts at the Shelby Township office building, both Kemp and Marti thought that my hearing about a second buyer was odd. I wrapped it up by saying I'd tried calling the man earlier that morning but was sent to voice mail and his box was full.

"Do you think you were followed when you went downstate?" Kemp asked.

"I'm pretty sure I wasn't." Marti gazed at me, concern flooding her eyes. I summarized the little old blue car sightings to fill her in.

"Don't forget that someone was messing around your house, too, Onalee."

"What?" Marti gasped.

I shot Kemp a dirty look. "I've thought about it and that could've been a meter reader for all I know," I said.

"No. They do not work on weekends," Kemp said.

"I haven't seen that car lately and if our perp turns out to be Mischlik, well all I can say is that old beater does not look to me to be a Mischlik-mobile."

"Onalee, don't make light of this situation. I'm worried and both of you should be too," Kemp said.

***

Marti and I went to our favorite coffee shop and both ordered homemade vegetable soup. I got to hear more about Frank's and her adventures in Central America, and I told her about Mrs. Willowby and Susan.

"The two of them are reconciled?"

"Yes, so some good came out of it. I'm going to see Dot later this afternoon. Want to come?"

"Probably not since I'm still catching up from being away for so long. I will see her soon, though."

Marti told me more about her poison research. According to her, it is easy for poisoners to obtain the weapon they choose. They would have to do some research to figure out doses and timing but that was also fairly easy to obtain.

"I wrote down what I remembered about Stone's final minutes. Just a sec while I find it." She opened her purse and pulled out a small notebook. "Ed said he'd started clutching his stomach and throwing up when they were in his office. Then he kind of lurched out of the back of the restaurant and made for the door. After he collapsed and I went over to him I remember seeing sweat on his forehead and that he was panting. Then he started breathing slower and slower. . . and slower until he was gone."

Marti's voice changed as she read this to me. I could tell that she was reliving it and it still bothered her more than she let on. "I'm going to look up the likeliest poisons again and try to match up those symptoms with the substance."

"That sounds like a great idea. If Ed didn't spike that fudge, do you think it was someone targeting Lupita's as well as Stone?"

"Maybe. If that is the case, it seems like it would really shrink our suspect list."

"Right. The only other piece of the puzzle we have is that, according to the current Mrs. Stone, her husband was going to meet up with Mischlik that day. And speaking of Mischlik, I've got to go to the closing for my new office building at two o'clock so I'd better get going."

After I got back home I took Dash out for his walk, changed into one of Maureen Stone's elegant outfits, and with Dash by my side, drove over to the offices of Mischlik Properties. We arrived about five minutes early which was in keeping with my role as a rich heiress. John's assistant was working and welcomed us in with an offer of bottled water and a milk bone. *I guess this place is dog friendly.*

Soon John bounded out of his office and beelined for Dash. He'd been sitting by me and stood to greet John. They seemed to hit it right off. Eventually the three of us went into John's office. As we chatted, I realized

Hot Fudge

I felt no compunction to tell him about my jaunt to Shelby Township. After a few more minutes, we got down to business.

He grinned at me. "The seller called and told me that the money you wired to my escrow account yesterday has been deposited in his account. Thank you. Now to get the paperwork sorted out. If you've ever closed on real estate with a mortgage, you'll appreciate how much more streamlined this process is." He pushed a paper in front of me. "But before we get started, do you have any questions or concerns?"

"I was wondering, did you tell other buyers about this deal?"

He studied me for a moment. "Not exactly because of the time constraints, but I did mention it in passing to another person who buys and sells a lot of property through me. If you hadn't wanted it, I would have explored a sale more fully with him. Why do you ask?"

I felt some heat invading my cheeks and tried to will it back. "It's just idle curiosity. I guess when you're buying something you like to think you snatched it up ahead of a bunch of other people who would love to get their hands on it." I grinned.

He laughed. "I can guarantee that it would have happened that way if I'd given some of my other clients a chance at it."

"Why did you let me in on it?"

"I guess by all rights I shouldn't have. I hear from a couple of guys on a weekly basis and they're almost foaming at the mouth for high-yield properties like you've got here. I'm not bragging, but I've reached the point in my career, after a lot of hard work, that I can do things the way I want to. What keeps me coming to work every day is being able to present great deals to good people." He chuckled. "Last night my wife got sick of hearing me talk about you, your dog and this building you're buying. Those other guys are already sitting on millions of dollars of marvelous real estate and they don't need to have every fabulous deal that crosses my desk."

"Thank you." We smiled at each other as Dash looked back and forth between us. I fondled his velvety ears.

"Okay. We'll get to it. The paper in front of you is the buyer's settlement statement." He went through all of the credits and debits that brought us to the bottom line of $998,042.00. There was a check made out to me for the balance of $1,958.00. "We need your signature here." He pointed at the line and I signed it. Pushing that paper aside, he put another in front of me. "This is the deed and as you can see, it's been signed by the seller. It needs to be recorded in Macomb County and I will take care of that as soon as we finish here. Okay, that's it. You're now the proud owner of a beautiful and lucrative property in Shelby Township. How do you feel?"

"Poorer but great. Oh, I had a couple of questions. When will I get copies of the leases?"

"Remember, I mentioned there is an off-site management company that handles everything. They collect the rent, deduct any expenses that accrue including their management fee of seven percent, and remit the net to you. In fact, if you give me a bank account number it can be direct deposited. No muss no fuss."

"But sometime in the future I could contact the management company and see the leases?"

"Of course. It's your building and your tenants, but I can't see why you'd want to bother. You're paying those guys seven percent, let them have all the headaches."

"What about title insurance?"

"No need since there's no mortgage and take it from me, a complete waste of money. Of course the title insurance people would just love to sell you a nice, pricey policy."

We talked for a few more minutes. "By the way, what kind of car do you drive?" I asked. "I thought I passed you the other day."

"Cadillac Escalade. It's good in the snow and great for hauling dogs."

"Then it wasn't you. I guess that's why the guy didn't wave back," I laughed.

We shook hands, Mischlik promised he'd be in touch with other deals, and we left. It was 2:30 and hopefully a good time for Dashiell and me to go visit Mrs. W. When we arrived at the rehab facility the receptionist was happy to let Dash accompany me to Dot's room. It was slow going because so many of the residents wanted to pet the big poodle. When we finally got to the right room, Mrs. W. was sitting in a chair reading.

Hot Fudge

She looked up from her book and a big smile creased her face. "Onalee. It's so nice to see you, and you brought your dog. How wonderful." They remembered each other from the night of Marti's bachelorette party and Dash went right over to her.

We talked for awhile and Dot told me how happy she was to have Susan back in her life. "They tell me I'll be here for another week at the most and then I'll go to Susan's house for a week or two. Isn't that marvelous?" Her button eyes were dancing.

"It sure is. Dash and I can come visit you there too because Riley and Poodle Boy are good friends. Maybe I'll even try to drag Marti away from her new hubby for an hour or so."

Mrs. W. giggled. We stayed until Dot's dinnertime and accompanied her as she moved behind a walker to the dining room. Dash and I motored home anticipating our own dinners. I have to confess I was careless. It had been a long day and I wasn't on my toes. We pulled into the driveway and a little old blue sedan pulled right up behind us.

Chapter Thirty-Four

Uh oh. I hit the door locks and scrambled to retrieve my cell phone from my purse. A shadow loomed outside my window. I looked up and into the eyes of Robbie Stone.

I opened my window a couple of inches. "Robbie. What's going on? You've been tailing me for days now. Why?"

"What have you been doing hanging with my father's old partner? I told you he and my mom probably killed dad."

"No, they didn't. I tried a bunch of times to call you and talk. Charlie Kemp is just as interested in finding out who killed your dad as the rest of us. They were best friends for a lot of years."

"Yeah, but he and my mom—"

I nodded. "I know they're together now, but your mom and dad have been divorced for what? Four years isn't it?"

"Something like that."

Hot Fudge

"Charlie's wife died a number of years ago. They didn't need to kill anyone to be able to see each other. Look, Robbie. Marti and I had suspicions about Kemp too. As it turned out, he suspected us. All I can tell you is, he didn't do it."

"If he didn't, who did?"

"I don't know." I didn't want to tell him about any of our detecting efforts. He was just hotheaded enough to go confront someone and possibly get himself killed.

"Why have you been following me? You scared the heck out of me."

"Because you're trying to find my dad's killer. I wanted to be there when you did in case you needed help."

"But you didn't worry about giving me cardiac arrest when I saw that someone with big feet was pussyfooting around my house?"

He gave me a sheepish smile. He really was an adorable kid. "I'm sorry."

"Robbie will you please go back home? Your mom is so worried about you she can barely see straight."

"But—"

"They did not hurt your dad. Come on, you know your mom could never do anything like that. And Kemp is a big teddy bear who loved your father."

"Yeah, I guess you're right."

"How's Miss Double Peppermint Non-Fat Latte these days?"

He grinned. "She's fine. That's a great dog you have. Bye."

"Bye, Robbie," I called as he sprinted to his car.

***

The following morning at the gym Kemp saw us come in, strode over, and gave me a big sweaty hug.

"Wow. Hello," I said.

"Robbie came back last night and he said it was mostly because of you." His swiped at his eyes. "It was so good to see him and great to see Maureen happy again. I think maybe there's a chance for us to be a family now."

He let me go and he, Marti, and I started working with weights.

"I have one question. Whose little blue car was Robbie driving?"

"It's his girlfriend's."

Hot Fudge

As we exercised, Marti told us more about her internet research into poisons. From what she said, it sounded like arsenic and cyanide were the poisons of yesteryear. One article she read said that poisoners were generally cold-blooded, methodical people who planned, sometimes for a very long time, to kill their quarry. She was able to eliminate a few of the possible substances because of the symptoms. As she said, an arched back was characteristic of strychnine poisoning and Marti hadn't seen that. She was still unable to identify the toxin that was used or when it was administered.

I launched into a recap of yesterday's closing.

"Tell me exactly what the closing documents were," Kemp said with laser focus.

"There was a buyer's settlement statement which I signed."

"And you have a copy of that?"

"Yes. The other paper was a deed."

He looked at me with lifted eye brows. "Copy?"

"No. He's emailing the deed to Macomb County to have it recorded."

"Title insurance?"

"According to Mr. Mischlik, I don't need it, but of course I disagree. I called a title company in Macomb County that was recommended to me by a friend who lives down there. They told me they could have a policy for me in seven to ten days."

"Good. I assume there were also no appraisal or loan docs because it was a cash transaction."

"Right."

"It's fishy business isn't it? Did you bring the buyer's settlement?"

"It's in my car."

"I definitely want to see that."

"So I guess you've bought yourself an office building in Metro Detroit. At least after I transfer the title. I hope this all works out for you." I was concerned about his huge outlay of cash. "What do you think?"

"If it turns out that Mischlik is the killer, then it was a worthwhile use of my money." He shrugged his shoulders. "If not, then I have an income producing property in Shelby Township that supposedly generates a good return." He paused for a moment. "It sure seems like he's pulling something, doesn't it? If he is and Robin got wind of it and tried to stop him, Misclik might have been desperate enough to want to silence him."

I nodded. "If that is what happened, he's been able to get away with it so far."

We finished up. Kemp and I traipsed to my car. I handed the document to him, and we went our separate ways. It was a clear day and very warm in the sun. The thermometer in my car already registered nearly fifty degrees, and it was only early afternoon. Our snow was melting quickly though not nearly fast enough for some people. When I arrived at my house, I tried calling George Rudolph, the other buyer. There was still no answer, but this time the voice mail allowed me to leave a message.

"Hello Mr. Rudolph. My name is Onalee O'Conner and I'd like to speak with you regarding an office building on Maplewood Drive in Shelby township."

I took Dash out, and I could tell he had a bout of spring fever. As soon as he was off leash he zoomed around and up and down the beach. Unfortunately we didn't run into any of his dog playmates who could've helped him burn off his extra energy. As the second best alternative, I threw sticks for him to chase and not retrieve.

Back at the house I got my spud out. In Northern Michigan, as winter turns into early spring those of us with layers of ice in our drives become obsessed with ridding our driveways of it. Spudding is very satisfying work. Occasionally large areas of the stubborn white stuff yielded to my efforts and a whole patch of pavement cleared. I chopped until my arms and shoulders ached from lifting and slamming the heavy instrument into the two-inch thick crust. I left the spud by my snow shovel and scoop, all lined up for ready access near my porch stairs. The rest of the afternoon was spent working on my appraisal of the proposed industrial building.

Marti called after dinner. "Have you heard from that other buyer yet?"

"No. I wish he'd call. Like Kemp says, that whole deal with Mischlik didn't seem to be on the up and up. But Marti, he seems like such a great guy. I really hope it doesn't turn out that he has a fetish for poisons."

An hour or so later it was time to take Dashiell out for his last walk of the night. A soft rain was falling and inky black storm clouds flew across the sky playing hide and seek with the stars and nearly full moon. Dash ambled along at the end of his extended leash as my mind hopscotched over details of the case. The nights were darker now that most of our bright white snow was gone. The moon broke free from the clouds and suddenly a shadow loomed up behind me. Adrenalin shot through my body down to my toes as I whipped my head around. Mischlik was a few feet away hoisting a huge pole. As it slammed down toward my head I lunged to the right. He couldn't compensate quickly enough, and his weapon, an ice pick, smashed into the road. My beginner Hapkido training came through as I landed a roundhouse kick to his midsection and a hard jab to his face. A blur of motion caught my eye and Dash was upon him. Mischlik screamed as my dog knocked him over. I grabbed the ice pick, pulled it away from him and dug my cell phone out of my pocket. As soon as I called 9-1-1, I pulled Dash off the sobbing Mischlik. He lay on the ground in a fetal position as we heard sirens approaching.

EPILOGUE

An investigation into Mischlik Properties' real estate sales over the past months revealed Mischlik's pattern of deception. The office building that I had forked over $1,000,000 of Kemp's money for was actually owned by Mischlik through a limited liability company. He never recorded the deed made out to me and consequently I never would have been the legal owner. The other potential buyer, George Rudolph, had plunked down a million smackers for the building as well and also didn't have any proof of ownership.

Mischlik had been setting up these bogus transactions for about a year and Robin Stone had become suspicious. A few of his questions tipped off Mischlik. The day Stone went in to meet with him, Mischlik slipped some poison in his coffee. It took a couple of hours before it activated and by then Stone was in Lupita's meeting Ed and eating fudge.

Hot Fudge

Mischlik hoped to make a few more million dollars and then flee the country with his family. Initially he was pleased that I was helping him toward his goal, but when he received a call from George Rudolph that, "an Onalee O'Conner called about the office building on Maplewood Drive" alarm bells rang in Mischlik's mind. Googling Onalee O'Conner he saw an online photo and realized that I was AKA Donna Mendleson. The gig was up, as they say.

Mischlik drove over to my house and as he sat in his car trying to formulate a plan of how to strangle me, Dash and I emerged for our walk. He saw my ice spud and decided that would be a faster and easier way to dispatch me to the next world. He's now in the Emmet County jail awaiting his trial for murder, attempted murder, and fraud. There are a number of lawsuits against him as well.

According to Detective Costas they strongly suspected Mischlik of the murder of Robin Stone but could not establish a motive. So with Kemp's ability to throw a million dollars at the problem and Marti's, Kemp's and my real estate knowledge we were able to crack the case when he was at a standstill. He even so much as admitted this to us when he revealed that the poison Mischlik had used was nicotine.

Connie Doherty

Now an update on all of my friends, old and new. Bill Reneveere is planning to manage the taco restaurant on Mackinac Island. Kemp hopes that Bill will eventually become a partner or the sole owner. Susan and her mom Mrs. W. are really enjoying getting to know each other again, and Dot is healing well. Kemp and Maureen Stone are engaged to be married. Robbie Stone says he will happily walk his mom down the aisle, and Ms. Double Peppermint Nonfat-Latte will be the maid of honor. Kemp's new bestie, Eduardo will be his best man. And speaking of Eduardo, Marti and I have been welcomed back to Lupita's with open arms though Marti still hasn't touched any peanut butter fudge. Ed apologized to us and admitted he was scared we were going to get hurt. Marti and Frank seem to be on a lifelong honeymoon and Marti is still meddling in my affairs.

Dash and I are happy and spending long hours in the spring woods now attempting to locate the elusive morel mushroom. Actually, I do the hunting while he runs up and down the hills and chases squirrels. Mr. Costas called earlier today but I was, as we appraisers say, "in the field."

I hadn't been on a date with Camille since the Boyne City Spring Festival but still planned to talk with him to make sure he wasn't getting

Hot Fudge

too serious. On a sunny Sunday afternoon he, Dash, and I went for a walk on the beach. The bay was still mostly locked in ice but there were large pools of brilliant blue water near shore. The sand was free of snow and walking was easy. Mounds of ice that had been pushed up onto shore by early winter waves glistened with ice crystal stalactites fastened to icy overhangs. As small waves rolled into them their tinkling filled the air. We strolled companionably while Dash ran ahead zigzagging between dunes and the bay.

Costas picked up a beautiful azure piece of beach glass and handed it to me.

"Thanks." I'd found a couple of pieces that day but none that pretty. I was about to start my spiel when he turned and looked into my eyes.

"We've gone out on a couple of dates now and I've had a good time. I hope you have too. Anyway what I'm trying to say is. . . If you want to continue to be an effective amateur sleuth, you have to be involved with a policeman such as myself. Otherwise it's going to start looking suspicious that you're nosing around so many murders. You know this, you've read the literature."

"Yes, but my goal was always to find only one body and solve just one mystery. I've surpassed that and I'm now thinking of retiring."

A horrified look crept across the Costas countenance. "You can't do that. What would you do with all your spare time?"

"You've got a point," I said smiling. As of the writing of these chronicles, we haven't had "the talk."

Hot Fudge

Acknowledgements

Thanks to Jack Campbell for sharing his knowledge of Hapkido.

I'd also like to thank Trish Martin, owner of the Bogan Lane Inn on Mackinac Island for her help and conversation. Also for providing such a lovely place to stay on Mackinac Island's cold winter nights.

Luci Zahray, AKA The Poison Lady gave me invaluable assistance with selecting the best poison to do in Mr. Stone. Thank you so much, Luci!

Karen Doherty, Jill Swartout, and Paula Vaughan gave me invaluable help as first readers of the manuscript. Thank you so much!

Thank you to Meredith Krell for her great covers! Once again I was able to talk her into leaving her preferred subjects of captivating crows, laughing horses, and little old travel trailers to work a miracle on my behalf. Meredith's and her artist-husband Steve Toornman's works are for sale in galleries and other places around Northern Michigan.

Connie Doherty

About the Author:

Connie Doherty lives in Northwestern Lower Michigan where, on some days, the air is so fresh it has never been breathed. When she's not writing or appraising she loves to walk with her dog, kayak, paddle board, rollerblade, cross-country ski, write and eat.

Dear Reader:

Fortunately for all of us, that magical place known as Mackinac Island has protections in place to guard against a developer changing it as the fictional Mr. Stone tried to do in this book. If you have not been to this historical gem, try to go. Soon!

If you enjoyed this book, please leave a review somewhere other readers will see it. Authors depend on readers passing the word on books they like.

Thank you!

Connie Doherty

Made in the USA
Monee, IL
11 September 2023

42489395R00213